Fractured Masks

D.L. Wainright

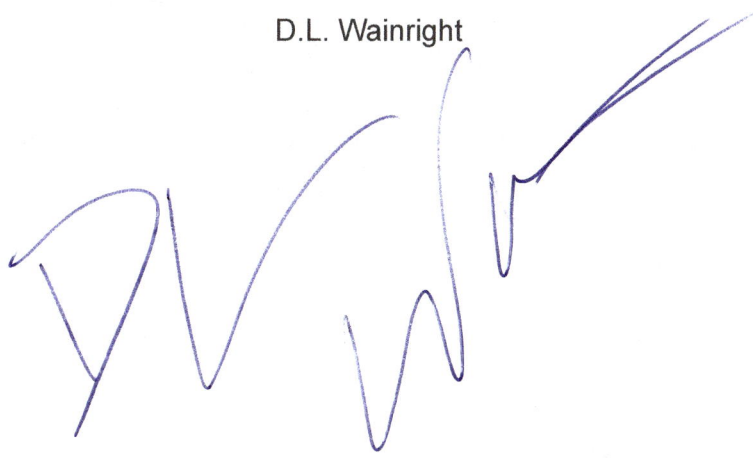

Minter Media

Copyright © 2016 by D.L. Wainright.
Produced in association with Minter Media.
No part of this book may be reproduced, stored in a retrieval system, or transmitted in any form or by any means, electronic, mechanical, photocopying, recording, or otherwise without written permission from the author. For information regarding permission, write to inquiries@thehollowsun.com.

Editor: Michelle Henson

Cover design by Minter Media.
Cover models are Dominique Alford (Jim) and Josh Brown (hands), photographed by Brooke Hanna.

For Mom

Lamia 1 by Stephanie Burgee
www.stephanieburgee.com

Lamia 2 by Stephanie Burgee
www.stephanieburgee.com

Prologue

The music was beautiful.

Billy didn't know what kind of instrument it was, didn't know the difference between violins or violas or any of that. He was only ten. What he did know was that it was the most beautiful sound he had ever heard.

He slipped out of bed and hurried to his window, standing on his tiptoes to unlock it before pushing hard to slide it open. It was easier to hear the music that way, even if the autumn air leaked in, cold and biting. The music was so pretty. Billy just had to get closer, had to hear it better until the sound could wrap around him like a comforting hug.

In the corner of the room, his little sister stirred in her crib and released a gurgling coo. *Of course,* he thought, *she wants to hear it better, too.* Billy was a big boy, and had helped his parents with little Lonnie many times before. He knew exactly how to lower the barred side of the crib, and just how to hold her so her tiny neck was supported.

They slipped out of the house easily enough, his father's snores masking any creaks the floor made beneath Billy's feet or the click-click of the doorknob. The music could be heard even better from their backyard, but Billy still pressed on, holding Lonnie tightly to him to keep them both warm. From the house it was just down a small slope, and then they were in the forest. Usually Billy was afraid of the forest, even during the day, but the music made him brave. It urged him on, told him to ignore the things watching him in the branches above, not to mind the thing that chittered like a cruel laugh.

Soon enough he came upon the river, its waters seeming to be nothing but a strip of black against the rest of the shadows of the night. Sitting upon a large rock on the opposite side of the river was a young man with strange, elegant clothes, and he smiled ever so softly as he played upon the stringed instrument tucked against his chin. He was as beautiful as the music, and for a moment Billy could only stare. Lonnie shifted in his grip, turning her head as best she could to see the man herself.

They needed to get closer, Billy decided. That was the best thing to do.

So he began to walk into the river, toes sinking into soft silt and pricking against small stones. As he walked, the cold water numbed his feet, dulling the sharp jabs of random rocks. Onward he pressed, the water rising higher and higher until he began to float and needed to swim to keep going. He couldn't really swim, though, with Lonnie in his arms.

As if understanding his conundrum, a pair of arms reached up from the water in front of him and gently cradled the the baby as they took her from his loosening grip. Too grateful for their help, he failed to look back at them after he swam past, failed to watch as they dragged Lonnie down beneath the black, lazy water.

He was halfway across the small river when something brushed his leg, the sensation dulled through the chilled numbness in his limbs. At first he ignored it, assuming it was merely his pajama pants sliding against his skin as he kicked and paddled. Maybe even a fish. But then something wrapped tight around his ankle and tugged.

The water was so dark and so cold. There was only so long he could keep it out of his mouth, out of his lungs. As the stabbing chill filled him, he thought he saw a maw of sharp teeth grin before opening impossibly wide.

    Above, sitting on the rock, the handsome man continued to play his beautiful music, smiling gently.

Chapter 1
Flee

The scent of blood was overpowering Eva's senses, even beating out the repugnant stench of scorched flesh from the recent burning of the Grin Reaper. All around her, the forest reeked, as if the trees themselves were bleeding out into the night. Then, of course, there was Lucy lying limp in her arms and dripping fresh, tainted blood from her torn hand. The strigoi's venom added a nose-crinkling astringent note to the metallic scent. Seemed even Pulchrum's saliva hadn't been able to neutralize it.

"Krysti," Eva called cautiously as soon as the car came into view. It wouldn't do to startle the already traumatized girl.

Suddenly Krysti was spilling out of the car, clutching Eva's HK USP 9mm in front of her. "Eva?" came her voice, shaking as much as her hands where they gripped the handle of the gun. "Is that you?" Then she seemed to spot Lucy in Eva's arms, because she screamed sharp and short. "What happened? Oh my god, Lucy! Is she dead? Eva!"

Making soothing, hushing sounds, Eva hurried the last few meters to the car. "She's just passed out. Help me get her into the back."

"Her hand! Eva, she's bleeding! We have to get her to a hospital!"

"No," said Eva, firm and calm, "No hospital. We have to leave." *We have to go where Pulchrum said.*

Krysti fumbled with getting the back door open while still carefully holding the gun. "But," she choked out through a new onset of panicked tears, "we have to report this. There might be someone out there who's still alive and needs help!"

There wasn't. Eva knew it by the lack of human heartbeats and the suffocating stench of gore. Somewhere in the forest, something was chewing greedily at wet flesh. Something with no scent of its own. "Come on," she urged Krysti gently. "Get in the car. We have to get out of here."

Once Lucy was carefully laid out across the back seat, Eva took the gun from Krysti. She looked up from Krysti's pale, trembling fingers to her large eyes tensed in terror. A pain jolted through Eva like an electric shock, and she swallowed back a whimper as she pulled Krysti into a tight hug.

Krysti was someone meant for warm smiles. Seeing her like that, scared and bloody and lost, was like watching someone tear the sun out of the sky. It left Eva feeling just as cold and desolate as the world would be without the sun, too.

"I'll protect you," Eva whispered into platinum blond waves before kissing Krysti on the temple. The sweat that transferred to her lips tasted of fear. "You're safe now." Slowly, she felt some of the tension leak out of Krysti. "You'll always be safe, as long as I'm with you."

***

For a long while, Krysti didn't say anything. She was curled up in the front passenger seat, fingers twisting idly at the shirt she'd borrowed from Eva, as she stared blankly out at the darkness blurring by. When nearly an hour had passed, she asked, voice so quiet that it barely carried above the sounds of the car's engine, "You aren't going to take me home, are you?" Resignation weighed heavy on the words.

Eva glanced at her as she considered her answer, trying to think of how to explain the situation without setting Krysti off again. "No," she eventually sighed, going for the truth in as gentle of terms as she could paint it. "Neither of us can ever go home."

Krysti leaned her forehead against the window and breathed on it, then made little squiggles in the condensation. "Because the thing will get us?"

It was more complicated than that, but Eva nodded. It didn't matter that the Grin Reaper was dead; others would come in his place. "It isn't safe for us at home anymore."

On the window, Krysti's fingers stilled, but she didn't lift her head. "What about our families?"

"They'll be fine," Eva assured, putting as much confidence in her tone as possible. "The bad thing only wanted to kill those at the LARP."

Krysti curled her fingers inward and let her hand fall to her lap, head still resting on the glass. "You weren't supposed to be at the LARP."

"I came to stop him," Eva confessed, voice going just as faint as Krysti's. She had failed so many people tonight. Eva would almost think it was luck that she'd managed to save Krysti, but something about Krysti's story had Eva doubting that. Why would the Reaper have stared at Krysti, laughed, and run off without killing her, too? It didn't make any sense. What would the Reaper have accomplished by sparing Krysti after she'd seen what he was?

Unfortunately, the answers to her questions likely had died with the Reaper.

"You can't stop him," whispered Krysti, voice like cracking

glass.

They had, though. The Grin Reaper was dead. Still, Eva supposed Krysti was partially right, in that Eva couldn't stop the Gehealdan. Maybe Fenris could.

***

They were almost out of North Carolina before Lucy awoke. One moment Eva was listening more to Krysti's sleep-steady breaths than to the radio, then suddenly Lucy was sitting up with a gasp. Before Eva could open her mouth to ask if Lucy was okay, smoke was coming out of the hood of the car.

"Shit," she cursed, swerving the car over onto the shoulder. Luckily she was the only one on that small back road.

Carefully as she could, Eva shook Krysti awake. When those big blue eyes blinked open, Eva tried to smile. "We have to get out of the car now," she told Krysti, keeping her voice as neutral as possible.

Krysti merely nodded and moved to comply. In the back, Lucy was breathing heavily and making sounds of distress. "Where am I?" she asked, fear coating her words. "What happened?"

Keeping one eye on the hood of the car, Eva reached for her gun under the seat. Much like the fire had earlier that night, the smoke seemed to be in sync with Lucy's breaths. "Lucy, get out of the car," Eva commanded, hoping Lucy's training would kick in and she would obey that tone. Thankfully, it seemed to work, and Lucy was soon stumbling out of the car and onto the grass on the roadside. Eva followed, urging the other girls to move even further towards the nearby treeline.

"What's going on?" Lucy asked, wide eyes going between Eva and the smoking car.

"I'm sorry," was all Eva offered as reply, before punching Lucy hard enough to knock her out cold. Krysti screamed again, skittering back and away from Eva. "I had to," Eva explained as she caught Lucy in her arms. "She's about to explode the car."

"*What?*" shrilled Krysti, her fearful gaze transferring to Lucy. "Are you *serious?*"

"Unfortunately, yes." Eva carefully laid Lucy out in the grass, then stood again to look back at the smoking hood. She wondered if she should get their things from the trunk. Probably. While she'd stopped Lucy from exploding the engine, it still seemed to be on fire. They would likely have to walk to the next town.

She looked around at herself, Lucy, and Krysti, and wondered at how she was going to explain their states to whoever they happened upon down the road. While Eva and Krysti had changed clothes, Lucy was still covered in blood. Beneath her clean shirt, Eva felt dried blood flaking on her skin. Christ, Eva really wanted a shower. She'd been lucky so far that no one really paid enough attention to notice when she stopped for gas, but she knew that luck wouldn't hold up if they went somewhere seeking help.

What would they even do after reaching a town, anyway? It wasn't like there was anyone they could call. Eva had packed some money, but not nearly enough to get them a car. Besides, Lucy was the only one of them who was over eighteen, and she was in no condition to go car shopping. Maybe they would luck out and there would be a bus station or a train station. It was doubtful, though.

"What are we going to do?" Krysti whined, looking around at the dark road with wide eyes and a crinkled brow. Not for the first time, it was almost like she could read Eva's thoughts. Again Eva felt like a failure. Some rescuer she'd turned out to be, getting the rescuee stranded in the middle of nowhere.

The sound of an approaching vehicle drew Eva's attention away from her thoughts, and she moved to look down the road. As the headlights appeared around a sharp curve, she felt a mix of hope and dread. They might be able to get a ride, though it would likely lead to a lot of questions, what with all the blood and the unconscious girl.

Also, it was just as likely to be someone from Gehealdan as it was just some random civilian. Who knew just how quickly that organization worked, and how well they could track her? She and Lucy had made sure to ditch their phones before even arriving to the LARP, and Krysti had told her that her own phone was in another LARPer's bag, so at least no one could track them using those.

When it was obvious that the driver had spotted them and was slowing down, Eva subtly reached behind herself to clutch the gun stuck into her belt. Firearms weren't her favorite weapon to wield, but she was just as accurate with a bullet as she was an arrow. There was no way that she was going to fail a third time that night. If whoever stepped out of that vehicle meant any of them harm, they'd learn the folly of going up against a tengu. Her lips twitched a little as she realized that their transportation problem would also be solved, once the driver was out of the picture.

As the vehicle pulled up behind her car, she saw that it was a dark orange SUV with only one occupant. "Stay behind me," Eva whispered to Krysti over her shoulder, eyes not once leaving the newcomer. A second later, Eva felt Krysti's fingers gripping at her shirt. She was a bit closer than Eva would have preferred, so Eva started mentally adjusting the strategies needed to protect her.

"Eva Kuntz-Tenno?" a male voice called out from the SUV before a figure stepped out of the driver's side and onto the asphalt. "I'm from Fenris. Alek Pulchrum sent you on this particular route so that our agents could watch over you." He stepped into the headlights, arms raised in peace. "Which is a good thing, by the looks of it."

The harsh light cast him in sharp relief, but Eva could make out a young Native American man with straight black hair that fell even longer than Günter's. As he moved, his shirt seemed to shift colors from green to purple. His dark denim jeans were flared just enough at the bottoms to accommodate what looked like snakeskin boots. "I'm Uktena," he offered, meeting her eyes without even a hint of fear. It sent a chill down Eva's spine to realize that he was absolutely confident that she was no match for him. Her fingers flinched on the butt of the gun.

"How do I know you aren't lying?" she called back to him. Krysti's hands twisted their grip tighter in Eva's shirt.

He started to take another step closer, but then paused and lifted his eyebrows in question. "May I approach and show you the mark?"

Eva shifted her grip on the gun and gave a short nod, even though she didn't know what mark he was talking about. He only moved a few more steps before stopping and extending his arm. Very slowly, he moved his other hand over to pull back the cuff enough to reveal his wrist. An image of a snake was wrapped around his wrist, biting its own tail. Eva wasn't entirely sure what that was supposed to prove, until she recalled the words Branka had scribbled. Something about being wary of ravens and trusting a snake? Or had it been a dragon?

Uktena seemed to read her confusion, because he sighed and pushed his cuff back down. "Jörmungandr," he explained with tested patience. "A division of Fenris."

Remaining silent, Eva again studied the man. With slightly parted lips, Eva breathed in through both her nose and her mouth in order to scent the air. The man smelled of cold, stagnant water, like a darkly-shadowed bog. It did nothing to ease her worry; past experiences proved nothing good came from bogs. Well, except cranberries. But no good *supernaturals* came from the dark, murky depths of bogs.

"Look," he said, "if I meant you any harm, you'd already be dead." It was such a cliché line, but Eva knew that he was telling the truth. There was no change in the pace of his heartbeat, no scent on the air of nervous sweat. "We don't have all night for you to decide to trust me." At that he glanced up at the night sky. "The ravens may have already been sent out to find you."

Slowly, Eva released her hold on the gun. "Fine."

He relaxed his stance and looked away from Eva to take in the still-smoking car. "What happened, exactly?"

With a slight flick of her hand towards Lucy, Eva answered, "She woke up and made the internal combustion...combust more."

Uktena drew in a hissing breath and moved towards the car. "You have anything in there you need?"

"Yeah," Eva gently removed Krysti's hold so she could join Uktena by the car's trunk. "Mine and Lucy's things, plus all of the weapons I could bring." She pressed the button on the keychain to pop the trunk and pulled it open.

Releasing a low whistle, Uktena took in just how many

weapons Eva had managed to cram into the small space. "Good thing I brought the Range Rover."

Together they transferred everything over, Krysti watching from beside Lucy in the grass. All the while, the engine continued to smoke, but luckily the flames didn't start up until they were done. "This works well," said Uktena as he scooped Lucy into his arms. "We would have needed to get rid of your car, anyway."

***

"We can't be there already," Eva said, sitting up with a start when she realized that the long dirt road Uktena had been driving down was actually a driveway. According to Pulchrum, Fenris was in Pennsylvania, and there was no way they were even in Maryland yet. She was riding shotgun while Krysti huddled over the still-sleeping Lucy in the back.

Uktena didn't even glance her way as he drove. "No, but we're stopping for the night. There's no way we'll be able to drive straight through and just keep knocking your friend out to stop the engine from exploding."

Squinting at him in confusion, Eva asked, "How is stopping going to help? She'll just wake up by at least the morning, and then we won't even be able to drive anywhere."

A little cabin slowly became visible through the trees. Uktena tapped two quick honks of the horn, paused for a moment, then gave a slightly longer honk. "Maybe we'll be able to get her to calm down and stop setting things on fire by then," he explained. "But I'm not going to keep punching her to keep her under. That can do a lot of damage."

He had a point, and Eva slumped back in her seat feeling a little guilty. "So is this a safe house or something?" she asked as they pulled up beside a decaying pick-up truck on cinder blocks.

"That's exactly what it is," Uktena confirmed with a wink before turning the car off. "Tahchat's place is one of the safest stops we have set up for refugees fleeing the Gehealdan's reach."

"Refugees?" Eva paused in unbuckling her seat belt to look between him and the house. "What do you mean?"

Uktena hopped out of the SUV and smiled at her with raised eyebrows. "You think you three are the only ones who've needed to escape the Gehealdan's tyranny?"

Eva had to bite back her knee-jerk reaction of objecting to the insult against the Gehealdan. After being raised to think of the organization as good and necessary, it was difficult to fully accept the truth. Turning away from Uktena, Eva leaned into the back to gently shake Krysti's shoulder. "C'mon. We're stopping here for the night."

Blinking awake, Krysti first stared at Eva and then at the cabin through the windshield. "Where are we?"

"Somewhere safe," Eva assured, before slipping out of the Range Rover.

"I'll get Lucy," Uktena called out to her from the other side of the vehicle. "Grab whatever bags you need."

Krysti got out and walked close to Eva as she retrieved two duffels from the very back. After shutting the hatch, Eva turned to see Uktena holding Lucy in his arms like a sleeping child. "All set?" he asked. At Eva's confirming nod, he started towards the door of the cabin. Then he seemed to realize that his arms were occupied and he didn't have a free hand to knock.

"I got it." Eva carefully shouldered past him and knocked on the door. Behind her, Krysti pressed close as if trying to hide.

Barely a few seconds passed before the door swung open to reveal a short, round Native American woman who appeared to be in her late fifties. The woman studied Eva's face with an intensity bordering on frightening, glanced at Lucy in Uktena's arms, and then stepped aside with a beaming smile. "Come in, children."

The inside of the cabin didn't look a thing like the exterior. Whereas the outside was tiny and in shambles, the inside looked like one of those new-development designer homes that start at half a million. Only, instead of the stark white Eva typically saw in such homes, the walls were painted different warm tones that could have been pulled right out of a desert sunset. Paintings adorned the walls depicting open prairies with roaming bison or sprinting spotted horses. There were also different kinds of artwork that Eva thought looked Native American in design, comprised of beautiful patterns made of beads or woven threads.

As the woman led them into a large living room, Eva was able to get a better look at some of the patterns and noticed that most of them had a wolf-like figure incorporated into them. "Set the sleeping one here," the woman commanded of Uktena, not even looking at him and just waving her hand towards a large, burnt orange couch. "Poor dear," she then tutted. "I'll fetch some medicine." With that, she was bustling out of the room.

Uktena took a seat in a plush recliner once he had Lucy situated. He seemed utterly unconcerned with everything, and content to just relax. Eva envied him for that.

The woman quickly returned with a basket full of different jars and rolls of gauze. "Sit, sit," she ordered Eva and Krysti, when she saw they were just standing there awkwardly in the middle of the room. So Eva took Krysti's hand and led her to the love seat where they curled up together. They watched as the woman unwrapped Lucy's hand and proceeded to clean the wounds.

"Any rooms available tonight?" Uktena asked. "Or should we just settle here?"

Not even glancing up from her task, the woman said, "You're in luck. No one until Thursday." Then she seemed to realize something and straightened up a bit, her hands pausing where they were wiping. "Speaking of...who are these strays you've brought to my door, you old snake?" Still she did not look his way, staring instead at Lucy's face as if she'd find the answer there.

A little smile came to Uktena's lips as he replied, "The child you're working on is the Vice-chairman's daughter."

"That right?" the woman murmured, resuming her task. "I'd heard there was a chance she'd pass through at some point. These other two?"

"Friends," was all Uktena offered.

"I'm Eva. Eva Kuntz-Tenno."

"Ah," said the woman, ducking to rummage through her basket. "I'm Tahchat." She pulled out surgical thread and unwrapped a fresh needle. "There's food in the kitchen, if any of you are hungry. Otherwise, feel free to find a room on the second floor. Only the first floor master is off limits." Then she seemed to dismiss them as she went about stitching up the deepest of Lucy's gashes.

***

Eva waited for Krysti to fall asleep before untangling herself from the blonde's arms and slipping out of bed. She wanted to check on Lucy and maybe get a few more answers from either Tahchat or Uktena. They could be heard still awake downstairs, chatting quietly.

Neither of them seemed at all surprised when Eva joined them. Tahchat sat on the couch Lucy had occupied, and she patted the seat next to her in invitation. "Your friend is all patched up and resting in her own room. I saw she had a bump on her head, and Uktena just explained why."

Trying not to feel guilty, Eva sat where directed. "I had to."

"I know. When she wakes tomorrow, we can reassess. How are you and your friend?"

That was a difficult question to answer. "We'll manage," was all Eva could come up with after a long, considering moment. "We'll have to."

"Spoken like a true wolf," Tahchat praised, eyes twinkling. "And it'll be the tengu in you which will help you manage best. Tricksters are the most resourceful." Pride coated her words and widened her smile.

Tilting her head, Eva looked closely at Tahchat and thought again of the animal in the patterns on her wall. "What folk are you?" she asked.

"Can you not see?" asked Tahchat, her smile wilting a little in confusion. "Tengu can usually see through illusions."

"Illusions?" Eva's brow furrowed. "What illusion?"

That seemed to amuse Tahchat. "I don't go from animal to human like your father does, child. This is just a disguise." She seemed to realize that Eva was still a bit lost, so she gently suggested, "Maybe try making your eyes those of a tengu."

So Eva did. Nothing really seemed any different. Sure,

everything was sharper, clearer, tengu eyes being so much like those of a hawk's. Eva couldn't really figure out what minute detail Tahchat had needed her to have tengu eyes to see, though. Reading Eva's expression perfectly, Tahchat then urged, "Look at me with a desire to see the truth."

Which was a weird command, but Eva squared her shoulders and gave it a shot. *The truth,* she thought to herself. *I wish to see the truth.*

She nearly fell off the couch in shock, because sitting beside her was not a plump, kindly woman, but a coyote. Then curiosity pricked at her, and she wondered what she would see if she turned her head to look at Uktena on his chair. Right as she started to do just that, however, the coyote reached out a paw and placed it upon her cheek. It felt like a hand, and made Eva nearly dizzy with the clashing sensory inputs.

"Some illusions are best not broken," Tahchat softly explained.

Chapter 2
Alone

Günter woke up haunted by dreams filled with blood and his sister's broken body. For a long, dizzy moment all he could do was pant harshly and stare straight ahead until his brain could process what was real. His room still smelled a little like her, from all of the times the four of them crashed at his place after an execution. Stomach heaving, Günter stumbled out of bed to run across the narrow hall to his bathroom.

She was gone.

His sister, the person who understood him better than anyone else in the whole world...was gone.

After dry heaving a few times, Günter tried to calm down by telling himself that it wasn't forever. At least she was alive. Maybe she'd even come to Japan that summer, per tradition. Japan was a neutral territory, none of its populace having signed the Treaties, so the Gehealdan wouldn't be able to touch her there. It was that sliver of hope which helped slow his breathing and settle his stomach.

In the stillness left after his heart stopped pounding in his ears, Günter heard a strange scritching sound and something like the patter of tiny feet. Switching to high alert, he pulled himself off the bathroom floor and proceeded slowly towards the source of the sounds. It was in his kitchen, whatever it was, and the thought of something invading his space had Günter on the verge of a growl.

Once in the living room, he thought he could almost smell it. Something that smelled like wood smoke and lye soap. Shifting his eyes to those of a tengu, he took in the heightened details of the room, attempted to see even a trace of what could be the source of the sounds and smell. "I know you're there," he growled out, feeling his teeth lengthen and sharpen, his nails thicken and grow into talons. "Come out."

All skittering sounds stopped, so Günter listened even more closely in an attempt to detect a heartbeat or breathing. It was there, faint and small, in one of the lower cabinets in his kitchen. Something was breathing gently, its heart beating fast with fear. It wasn't a rat, not in the way it smelled or sounded. Lips pulling back into a silent snarl, he crept closer. He'd barely made it to the breakfast bar when there came a sudden knock at the door.

Hastily shifting back into something that looked perfectly human, Günter took a few deep, steadying breaths to calm himself. On one particularly deep inhalation, he drew in what scents he could, trying to identify whoever would be calling on him in the middle of the night. The scents he picked up weren't what he expected, and he scrambled to answer the door.

"Father?"

Hartmut Kuntz stared back at him from across the threshold with hollow, sorrowful eyes. "Did I wake you?" he asked, looking Günter over in concern muted by a grief that made his actions slow.

"No, I was up already." When his father gave him a confused look, Günter explained, "I had a nightmare."

"That's fitting," Hartmut murmured, nodding. "May I come in?"

Günter jolted, suddenly realizing that he was just standing there like an idiot and hadn't even thought to invite his father in. "Of course." He hurried out of the way and waved Hartmut inside, closing the door once he'd passed.

For a small moment, Hartmut paused to glance at the kitchen with a wrinkled brow, but then he was shaking his head and moving to sit on the couch. He looked over at Günter, then patted the seat beside him. "Sit. There are some things we need to discuss."

Trepidation flooding his thoughts, Günter did as his father said. "What's the matter?"

Hartmut blinked down at where his hands rested between his own knees, before turning to give Günter a searching look. "Your sister is missing. The Gehealdan say she killed an agent and fled."

It wasn't new information, but it still felt like a punch in the gut to hear it said out loud. Especially in his father's voice. "Why? I don't..." Günter allowed the tears to gather that he'd fought against all night. God, he'd spent hours at the shop after Eva left, pretending like he didn't know, pretending like he wasn't losing her.

"They will suspect you of being involved, because you are her brother," Hartmut went on to explain. "Answer whatever questions they may have. Be truthful. Do not give them reason to take you away from me, too." He looked more afraid than Günter had ever seen him. There was a haunted shadow over his usually warm features.

"What will happen to Eva?" Günter asked.

Hartmut closed his eyes and lowered his head. "She will be declared officially among the Grin Reaper's victims, pronounced legally dead. Our Eva can never come home, now."

Günter had suspected something like that would happen. Had braced himself for it. Just as he was pretty sure he knew the answer to the question he was about to ask, scenes from his nightmare flashing through his mind. "And if the Gehealdan ever finds her?"

"Why did she do this thing?" Hartmut rasped out instead of

answering, his voice raw with grief. "She knows the Gehealdan does good for us, for our kind. She knows the importance of maintaining the Treaties. I just don't know why she would *do* this."

"She must have had her reasons," Günter offered softly, a tear escaping his flimsy restraint. He wrapped his father up in a hug, pulling his bowed head to Günter's chest. For such a tall man, in that moment Hartmut seemed so small. "We'll see her again," Günter soothed, repeating aloud the same words he'd told himself earlier in order to calm down. "Maybe she'll go to Japan this summer, like always. We'll see her at Yemon-jiisan's, don't worry."

"She is my daughter," whispered Hartmut, before his body jerked with a small sob. "My little girl."

"She's tough," Günter assured. "We were raised to be warriors. She'll be fine."

"I did not want this for either of you. It is why I moved away from Germany. My family, their ways do not have to be mine. It is your mother's people who mold soldiers beneath the shadows of Bodhisattvas"

Günter hooked his chin over his father's head and held him tighter. "You'd take us to Germany every year, too." Though perhaps that wasn't exactly the right thing to say in that moment. Still, his father's words confused him. All of Günter's life he was trained by one family or the other on how to be strong, be a warrior, never back down.

"To know your heritage," objected Hartmut, pulling out of Günter's embrace in order to look him directly in the eye, "not to make you what they are."

His confusion simply grew. "Are you saying you don't want me to be of the Úlfhéðinn?"

"Your mother and I both meant for America to be a new start for each of us. And you, our children, were meant to find your own paths. It is important to know where you come from, but that does not mean you need to go backwards."

Günter studied his father's face, seeing a youthful-looking man with centuries of life and hardships weighing down his soul. The make-up and hair dye could only mask so much, and not even that well. It wouldn't be long until Hartmut was the one officially declared dead, forced to relocate and assume a new name. Just like Eva. "Maybe this is just the path Eva has chosen," Günter eventually said, voice soft and heart heavy. "She had to have had a reason for what she did, and I'm sure she didn't come to the decision lightly."

Hartmut shook his head, squeezing his eyes shut. "She has chosen her own death, and a path that could damn us all."

***

Shortly after his father left, Günter decided to forget about the creature in the kitchen and just get on with his day. After all, it had seemed that Hartmut had noticed the thing in the kitchen but didn't express any concern. Whatever it was, it obviously wasn't a threat.

In the shower he went over potential questions Czar may ask, and what the best responses would be that wouldn't be flat out lies. If he cried a little more over losing his sister, well...no one was there to witness it.

Back in his bedroom, a flickering on his computer caught his eye while on his way to the dresser. Curious as to why it wasn't in sleep mode, he threw on some clothes before moving to inspect the source of the flicker. A messenger window was flashing in the middle of the screen.

Here's a link to that video you wanted.

Figuring it was spam at best and a virus at worst, Günter reached out to grab the mouse and close the program. Then the sender's handle registered, and he stopped short.

PaintItBohemian. Even though it wasn't a handle Günter had ever seen for him, it *had* to be Mick. One of Mick's favorite things to tell people was how he and his siblings got their names. Mick himself was named for Mick Jagger and Freddie Mercury, resulting in his full name being Mick Mercury Kincade. The handle was an obvious combination of The Rolling Stones' "Paint it Black" and Queen's "Bohemian Rhapsody."

Günter clicked the link, feeling even more hollowed out at the thought of losing not only Eva, but Mick. If this was one last connection to his best friend, he'd take it. The link opened his browser and took him to a blank white page with a single download button. Hoping to hell he was right about it being Mick, he went ahead and clicked it. As soon as it finished downloading, he obligingly installed the mysterious program.

Then...nothing happened.

"Shit," he muttered under his breath, feeling certain now that it had all been a virus after all.

"Such *language*," a familiar voice scolded playfully from the speakers.

Before he could process what he'd heard, he watched in stunned silence as his computer's camera program opened on its own. Instead of seeing himself in the demo window, however, he saw Mick. Shocked, he pulled out his desk chair and sat down. "How...?"

Mick made a face. "You really wanna waste this time talking computer languages?"

"Why not just use Skype?" Günter asked, bemused. Mick looked washed out in the glow of his computer screen, and Günter wished Mick's glasses weren't obscuring his eyes with how they glinted in the monitor's glare.

Leaning back in his seat with a lopsided smile, Mick lifted his hands to motion around himself. "I figured since I was spirited away to a secret location for some mysterious organization of god-like beings, I should maybe leave as little trail as possible. Plus I was told you work for an opposing team." There he tsked and shifted closer again. "Working for the villains, Gyun-gyun? Really?"

Unable to tell if Mick was only teasing, Günter felt shame burn through him. "The Gehealdan aren't villains," Günter objected. "Secrecy is necessary, and the Treaties must be enforced."

Mick stared at him for a moment, his lips pressed in a tight line. "I don't know about all that," he admitted with a foreboding quietness, "but evidently they're the reason I lived for nearly a decade under the misconception that my dad was dead."

"In a few years, my father will have to go through the same process," Günter tried to explain.

"But you'll *know*." Mick wasn't a person who tended to raise his voice. Even in that moment, when his anger was thrumming through the connection, his voice was pitched low and deceptively calm. "You'll know the truth, know he's alive somewhere."

Günter looked away, face heating. He'd know, yes, just as he knew Eva was out there still alive even if they'd have to hold a funeral for her. "It's necessary."

Again Mick fell silent, his breaths barely picked up through the computer's mic. "And lying to me for years?"

"I had to." Günter looked back at the screen, hoping Mick could read the sincerity on his face. "You don't think it killed me to keep things from you? I was always terrified you'd find out, that you'd hate me for the deception and because I'm-" Günter nearly gagged on the unspoken word. What must Mick think of him now, to know he was a monster?

Mick seemed to only cling to his anger for another handful of seconds, but then he sighed deeply and his shoulders lost their tension. "I don't hate you," he assured softly. "I could never hate you."

Unable to believe that, Günter lowered his gaze in shame. "But I'm...not human."

"So?" scoffed Mick. "Evidently neither am I. Even if no abilities manifest, I'm still the son of some Norse lesser god or something. *Christ.*" He sighed again and ran a hand back through his choppy black hair, knocking his glasses slightly askew. "This is all weird as fuck, no doubt, but it's not enough to make me think of you any differently."

Hope flickering weakly and hesitantly deep inside his chest, Günter studied Mick's grainy image. "Even if I'm Gehealdan?"

Mick's smile looked a little sad. "Even if you worked for the Devil himself." Then he paused and tilted his head. "Is the Devil real, too?"

Günter huffed a small, relieved laugh. "I don't know."

***

He picked Jim up the next morning to go to World Street, like they would any Saturday. For about the first half of the drive, Jim didn't say anything at all. Then, quietly, he asked, "Do you think they made it?"

Günter glanced at him as much as he could while still focusing on the road. "I think so. My father visited me last night, and he said that the Gehealdan had already contacted him about Eva. They told him that she killed an agent and then fled, that she's missing."

"Christ," Jim cursed, then rubbed his hand over his mouth. "Anything about Lucy or Krysti?"

Shaking his head, Günter could only offer a soft, "No clue. But I hope so."

After another few miles of silence, Jim asked, "Do you think they'll kill us?"

Fingers clenching the wheel, Günter hoped he wasn't lying when he said, "No, of course not."

Jim huffed out a skeptical laugh. "Except that we're accessories."

"We only knew they were planning to rescue Krysti and run away, we didn't know they would kill an agent."

"You're shitting me, right?" scoffed Jim. "We distracted everyone while Eva smuggled one of the burn disks and who knows what else out to her car. And you know your sister—hell, you know *Lucy*—neither one of them strikes me as the forgive and forget type."

He had a point, and Günter couldn't really argue that. "Still, we didn't technically do anything wrong."

"Günter," deadpanned Jim, "they executed a bunch of people just for playing a silly game where you run around in costumes and pretend you're a wizard."

"Well, technically it's because—"

"You bloody well know what I mean."

They were almost to World Street. "I know," said Günter, trying not to think about Mick's words from the night before about "working for the villains." "We'll be fine. There are rules, and the rules are there for a reason. We didn't break any of the Treaty rules, so we'll be fine."

"Right," Jim sarcastically agreed. "Keep telling yourself that."

Pulling into the parking lot, Günter cast Jim a worried glance. "Just answer anything as truthfully as possible, and cooperate fully," he urged. "Don't antagonize anyone."

"Don't know what you're on about," Jim objected. "I'm gentle as a lamb."

Günter snorted as he put the SUV in park and cut the engine. They shared amused smiles, before the heaviness of their situation weighed their expressions back down again. "Come on," said Günter, "we'll be fine."

When they got out of the Sequoia, Jim only took a few steps before he was stopping dead in his tracks. "Those are a bit big for crows, yeah?" he asked, voice barely audible, even to Günter's advanced hearing.

Following his line of sight, Günter spotted two large, black birds perched above the decrepit sign for the store. "They look more like ravens," Günter whispered back, frowning.

"Didn't think they were around these parts," said Jim, keeping his voice faint.

"Not usually, no."

"I seem to recall a warning recently about ravens."

Günter schooled his expression and casually put his hand on Jim's shoulder, pulling him back around to the Sequoia. He popped the hatchback and walked the both of them over there to lean in as if looking for something he'd forgotten. "She said to be *cautious* of ravens," he whispered near Jim's ear. "And it was a warning for Lucy, not us."

"Right, so then why are we hiding in the back of your car?" Jim hissed back.

"Because I think we should tell Czar about the note. About Branka."

"Are you—" Jim started, voice too loud, only to catch himself as he tried again in hushed, angry tones. "Are you *insane*?" He grabbed Günter's arm in a firm grip. "They'll kill her."

Günter opened his voice to object, to suggest they might not, but he knew *that* would be a lie. "We can't just stay quiet about it," he objected softly. "Czar works with her on things a lot; he needs to know she's not on the Gehealdan's side."

"Who's to say she's on anyone's side, really?" reasoned Jim. "She could be a completely neutral party in all this, and we'd just be signing her death warrant by implicating her in Lucy and Eva's defection."

"Maybe," said Günter, letting himself get convinced. Then he looked around quickly, but couldn't find anything to grab that would make their little huddle back there seem convincing. "Dammit," he said loudly, drawing back from the SUV and pulling Jim with him.

"I was *sure* I brought it."

"It's okay, man," Jim comforted loudly, seeming to catch on rather quickly to what Günter was doing. "We'll find it later, I'm sure."

"Right. Yeah. Sorry for wasting time like that." Günter was by no means the degree of actor Eva was, but he had enough skill from spending his life pretending to be human and straight. Hopefully it was enough to convince the ravens. Or...whatever they were.

The birds were still there when they turned back to the shop. Both Jim and Günter just pretended like they didn't even see them, walking quickly and quietly to the door.

Phil met them at the entrance, charming grin in place. "Good to see you, boys. We were worried you might not come at all."

"Aw, that's sweet that you were worried about us," Jim cooed with false affection. Then his expression turned serious and he said, "Let's just get this over with, yeah?"

Cocking his head, Phil gave Jim a curious look. "Get what over with, Jimmy-boy?"

Jim flinched at the nickname, and Günter curled his hand into a fist to stop himself from reaching out to grasp his shoulder. "Don't dick us around, Philly-boy," Jim sneered back through grit teeth. "Like there's not some inquisition awaiting us, after what Lucy and Eva did last night."

"Oh?" asked Phil, his grin looking far less charming. "What did they do?"

"Enough," Günter broke in. "If you and Czar have any questions about our involvement or our loyalties, ask."

Phil stared him down for a moment, face serious, before he

let out a chuckle and bopped Günter's shoulder gently with the side of his lightly-coiled fist. "No need to be like that," he assured with a friendly, upbeat tone and a smile to match. "We've no questions for you."

Before either Jim or Günter could respond, Phil's expression turned sober again, and he continued, "However, until further notice, you're both on a bit of a probation. And have new assignments."

Jim squinted at Phil in suspicion. "Why aren't we going to be grilled with questions?"

"Questions don't do much good," Phil replied with a casual shrug. "It's actions which reveal the honest truth. You two have remained here, presumably because you did not agree with whatever sentiment that turned Eva and Lucy against us. So, we'll give you a chance to prove your loyalty, while we closely monitor your behavior. Simple as that."

"Simple as that," Jim mumbled under his breath.

"What are our new assignments?" Günter asked, hoping to get things moving.

Phil nodded back deeper into the shop. "Come along and I'll explain everything."

Chapter 3
Reunion

The house was so dark, Lucy could barely see. Everything was just random, distorted shapes painted in colorless shadow. Moving slowly, she tried to estimate the size and shape of the room. "Hello?" she called, reaching reflexively for her machete. There was nothing there, just soft pajama bottoms.

No one answered, and Lucy cautiously crept closer to what she thought was the nearest wall. Reaching out, she tried to feel for any potential obstacles. Her fingers pressed against an object that was bumpy and cold, and something soft like spiderwebs brushed her skin. Jerking back, Lucy stumbled and lost her orientation.

"Hello?" she tried again, a little louder, a little more desperate.

"I heard 'er. This way." The voice was faint, muffled by the wall, but familiar all the same.

"No," Lucy gasped, feeling a hopelessness wash over her and drag her down like an undertow. Czar couldn't have found her already! It wasn't possible! *No!*

There was nowhere to run. Tears pricked at Lucy's eyes. This couldn't be the end. It couldn't. She hadn't even gotten to see her father again. God, she couldn't *breathe*.

A door opened to her right, allowing light to leak into the room. For a few terrified moments, she was only able to focus on the silhouette of Czar, shotgun in hand. Then the rest of the room started to register, and Lucy wanted to scream but she couldn't. It felt like she was choking, the more she tried.

"Disgustin'," Czar sneered. "Shoulda put ya down *ages* ago."

All around her, the room was stacked with corpses, most of which looked like they'd been chewed on by some sort of wild animal. Looking down, she saw that her hands were flaking with dried blood.

The choking sensation got worse, until she was doubled-over and coughing so hard it hurt. Something dislodged from her throat, making her cough even harder until it finally came up and splattered to the blood-stained floor.

It was a finger.

*

An unfamiliar ceiling greeted Lucy when she opened her eyes. She didn't even try to move or scream, already recognizing the pressure on her chest. In a way, it was almost comforting, because it assured her that what she'd just seen was only a nightmare. As per usual, she then felt the pressure shift as if rolling off of her chest, followed immediately by a dull thump and scurrying that faded quickly into nothing.

For a few long moments, Lucy simply lay there breathing deeply, staring up at a stationary ceiling fan she didn't recognize. What was the last thing she could remember? There was the Grin Reaper, Czernobog, face-down in the dirt and choking on his own black blood. Eva had arrived, then Pulchrum, and they'd finished him off while Lucy remained by the fire with an injured hand.

Her hand...

Lifting her left hand, Lucy found clean, expertly applied bandages. A few little experimental flexes had her clenching her teeth at the aching tightness in her skin.

She pushed herself up with her right arm to try to get a better look at the room. The lights were off, but the door was ajar and the hall light glowing warm and comforting. In the dim light, she found a neat and orderly bedroom decorated with a jackrabbit motif.

Movement out of the corner of her eye had her turning towards the door, and for a split second she thought she saw a coyote standing there. After blinking a few times to clear the haze of sleep from her eyes, she realized it must have been a trick of the light, because it was just a squat little woman with two long braids.

"Sorry, little wolf," said the woman. "I hadn't known one of them would sneak in. They usually steer clear of my home, so I hadn't thought to put up any extra precautions."

"It's...alright." Really, Lucy didn't know what to say. Who *was* this woman? Why was Lucy in her house?

"I'm Tahchat," the woman explained, as if she could read Lucy's mind. "This is a Fenris safe house. Your friends are also here, sleeping safe and sound." Then she stepped a foot within the room and looked Lucy over. "How's your hand? And your head?"

Lucy opened her mouth to answer the first question before the second one fully registered. Now that she mentioned it, Lucy did have a bit of a headache. She had figured that was just the results of a restless night's sleep, but felt too localized. "What happened to my head?"

Tahchat had a smirk to rival Eva's. "Evidently you nearly exploded a car. Your friend had to knock you out."

Reaching up, Lucy rubbed at the area where it smarted worst. It stung when she pressed too hard, making her cringe and hiss out through grit teeth. "I don't understand."

"Well," said Tahchat, "I don't see anything spontaneously

combusting right now. I'm assuming, from what I've been told, you need a preexisting fire source."

Lucy would have asked for what, but then she remembered the fire breathing with her just before she fainted. At least, it had *seemed* to be breathing with her. "It breathes with me," she whispered, half to herself and half as a weak explanation for Tahchat.

Tilting her head, Tahchat seemed to consider her words for a moment before giving a little nod. "Makes sense. Despite what some may think, Loki is air, not fire. A lot of the folk who are associated with fire, I've found, have actually just been manipulators of air. It's the only way to really control fire, you see."

"Because of oxygen?" Lucy asked, trying to dredge up science lessons.

"Exactly that," confirmed Tahchat. "Like how a backdraft can be created by bursting open a window or door. Control the flow of oxygen, you control the flow of fire." She offered a warm, gentle smile that comforted Lucy despite the topic of discussion. "In any case, I don't think we're in any danger of you accidentally setting the house ablaze."

"But what about a car?" If all fire was going to react to her now, would she ever be able to ride in a car with a combustion engine ever again? How were they going to get to Fenris? *Walk?*

Tahchat turned contemplative once more. "In the morning, we'll do some tests, see how much we have to actually worry. For now, just put it out of mind. Get some sleep." Stepping back fully into the hall, she rapped her knuckles softly upon the door frame. "And you'll be having no more unwanted guests tonight. I'll see to that."

***

That morning, Lucy was met with bacon, pancakes, and a candle. "We'll use it as a gauge," explained Tahchat as she worked at the stove to make more pancakes. "Though if you were really a threat, I'd be putting my life at risk working at this stove." She stepped aside enough to allow Lucy to see the tiny flames that meant it was a gas-burning range.

Not really knowing what to say about any of it, Lucy just ducked her head and ate her pancakes. Eva and Krysti soon joined her, both looking shocked and relieved to see her sitting at the table. Letting out a happy cry, Krysti threw her arms around Lucy's shoulders and nearly knocked her from her chair.

"I'm so glad you're okay," Krysti breathed against Lucy's shoulder, before pulling away to study her face. "You were bleeding and passed out and then Eva *punched* you!"

"Yeah," Eva said slowly, cringing a little. "Sorry about that. But, to be fair, you were about to explode the car."

"So I heard," said Lucy on a halfhearted laugh. "I get it."

"Well *I* don't!" objected Krysti, pulling away from Lucy and stepping so she had everyone in her field of vision. "Nothing since last night has made sense. And how could *Lucy* have set the engine on fire like that?"

Lucy looked to Eva with a start. "You didn't explain any of it to her?" How the hell were they supposed to take her to a supernatural organization if Krysti didn't fully understand what she'd been caught up in?

"I didn't really have the time to," Eva offered as excuse,

looking a mixture of guilty and disgruntled.

"The thing that killed everyone was supposedly a strigoi," Krysti broke in. She looked on the verge of tears, but had squared her shoulders and was attempting to seem composed and strong. "I'm not sure if I believe that, but I do understand it was something horrible and we have to get far away from it. Eva said our families should be fine, though." The look she gave Lucy then was a plea for confirmation.

Lucy didn't know if she could honestly offer the assurances Krysti wanted, so instead she said, "It *was* a strigoi. So was the guy who created the game."

Krysti stumbled back, eyes wide and lost. "What?"

"Everything in the game was true. All of the creatures in the book you gave me are real. Some supernaturals don't like humans knowing the truth, so that's why the bad strigoi was sent to kill everyone." Lucy didn't see a need to sugar-coat anything, to lighten the impact. Krysti deserved to know the truth, deserved to know why she'd watched her friends die and was now being whisked away from her family and the life she'd always known.

"I don't...what are you saying?" asked Krysti, voice small and fragile.

Lucy tried to exchange a look with Eva, but Eva was staring down at the tile floor, expression expertly shuttered. Sighing, Lucy turned back to Krysti. "I'm not human." Those weren't words Lucy ever thought she'd have to say, and they felt strange on her tongue.

The confession seemed to only upset Krysti more, and she cast frightened glances around at everyone in the room. Eva barely looked up from her examination of the floor, and Tahchat just flipped pancakes as if nothing was happening. "What are you, then?"

Shrugging, Lucy said, "I'm not sure. My dad is Váli, but my mom is human."

Something seemed to click in Krysti's mind, because she blinked and took a hesitant step closer. "Váli? The son of Loki, and creator of the verúlfr?"

"Yes," Eva answered softly. "My father's folk. He is one of the Úlfhéðnar."

"What?" Krysti shrieked, abandoning her slight advance and quickly moving farther away. "You, too, Eva?" She sounded betrayed, and it made Eva close her eyes in something like a flinch.

Steeling herself, Eva lifted her head and locked eyes with Krysti. "And my mother is a tengu."

"She wasn't allowed to tell you," Lucy was quick to explain, knowing this had to be killing Eva. "And I didn't know about my dad until recently."

Tearing her eyes away from Eva, Krysti shot Lucy another confused look. "What do you mean she wasn't *allowed* to?"

"Like I said, some supernaturals don't like humans knowing the truth."

Krysti's eyes widened at the implication. "So you're saying if Eva told me, she could have been killed?"

"It's very likely," said Lucy, swallowing down her own guilt. How many of the people she'd helped to execute posed legitimate dangers, and how many simply may have let it leak what they were? It was an unsettling thought, producing a sick, rotting feeling in Lucy's gut.

"Or you would have, at the very least, had your memories erased," Eva continued. "Possibly everything to do with me."

That drew a sharp sob from Krysti's mouth and she stumbled

forward to throw her arms around Eva. "No," came her muffled objections as she pressed her face into the crook of Eva's neck, "I don't want to ever forget you."

Eva wrapped her arms tightly around Krysti, and Lucy could see tears brimming in her eyes. "You won't. Where we're going, they won't let the others get us or you. They'll keep you and your memories safe."

"Flapjacks are gonna get cold," announced Tahchat, setting a heaping pile of pancakes in the middle of the breakfast table. "Got bacon stayin' warm in the oven, too. Eat up."

"Looks good," said a man from the doorway, startling a shout out of Lucy.

On the table, the candle flared, making Tahchat hum in contemplation. "Who the hell are *you*?" Lucy yelled, rising from her chair and holding her butter knife out like a weapon.

In response, the man simply held up his wrist and showed her the snake tattoo that matched Pulchrum's. "I go by Uktena," he said calmly, lowering his wrist and fully entering the room. "Pleased to meet you, little wolf."

Krysti, still clinging to Eva, looked between Uktena and her friends. "Is he something, too?" she whispered.

"Yes," he answered before either of the girls could open their mouths.

"What?" Krysti asked, then bit her lip as if worried she had just offended him.

"I'm Uktena." It was said with such finality, that no other questions were asked. The girls just slowly sat down at the table to start on breakfast.

"Candle's back to normal," remarked Tahchat, as she set

glasses out for everyone. "I think that so long as the little wolf's mood is even, there's no danger to the car. Now, who wants juice?"

***

"This is it," said Uktena, pulling up right outside the doors of a massive office building in the middle of nowhere.

They were somewhere in Pennsylvania, in the wooded outskirts of a small, quiet town. "It looks like some company's corporate headquarters, or something," murmured Eva from where she and Krysti were sitting in the back.

"Still haven't gathered yet that deception is key for our safety?" he asked, setting the SUV in park.

"But I thought Fenris was about exposing the truth," said Lucy.

Uktena's eyebrows rose. "And we are. But until the Gehealdan is dismantled, it's dangerous for many people to know where we're located."

"Makes sense," Lucy agreed, slipping out of the car. When she and Eva moved to start unloading their things, Uktena waved them off.

"Don't worry about that, it'll get handled." Then he tilted his head back towards the building. "There's some people who've been waiting to see you."

Dad, thought Lucy, heart beating faster at the thought. "Right, yes, of course." She nodded as the words stumbled over each other in a rush.

Once through the glass doors of the entrance, they found themselves in a massive lobby that reminded Lucy of a fancy bank.

Seated at a curving reception desk was a petite woman in a security guard uniform. There was a clipboard set in front of her on the marble counter of the desk, containing a rather neglected sign-in sheet. She eyed the girls with obvious suspicion, until she spotted Uktena. Then her eyebrows rose and she seemed to reexamine the girls, focus ultimately sticking on Lucy.

"No way," the guard breathed, then quickly reached forward to blindly fumble at the phone while her gaze remained fixed on Lucy's face. Eventually the guard looked down at the phone just long enough to press the correct buttons and offer a flustered sounding "She's here, sir," before once again staring at Lucy.

Uktena stepped up and drummed his fingers on the counter, effectively drawing the guard's attention. "The girls need their things brought up."

"Of course," the guard agreed quickly, reaching for the receiver again.

The gentle ping of an elevator echoed in the cavernous lobby, distracting Lucy from whatever the guard was commanding into the phone. She turned to locate the source of the sound, and then felt her mouth go dry when the elevator doors parted to reveal her father. He only managed a few steps out into the lobby before he spotted her as well, and his eyes gleamed as a smile peeked from beneath his beard. "Lucy," he whispered, though it was loud as a bell in that quiet space.

"Dad," Lucy choked out, then swallowed and tried again louder, "Dad!" She shot off towards him, boots squeaking on the marble floor. When they collided, he laughed bright and happy, wrapping his arms tightly around her and giving her a celebratory twirl.

"Sweetheart," he sighed into her hair. "You did it. You brought us all together again."

Lucy was helpless to hold back her tears, and she buried her face into the soft fabric of his black suit to wipe them away. Then she sniffled, pulled herself together as best she could, and pulled back enough to motion towards her friends. "Dad, I'd like you to meet Eva and Krysti. Without Eva's help, I never would have made it this far."

"Indeed," said Váli, turning to fully face Eva. "It pleases me that one of the Úlfhéðnar has returned."

Scrunching up her face, Lucy said, "There's that weird word again. What even *is* that?"

Her father smiled, even as Eva shifted a little and seemed a bit uncomfortable. "The Úlfhéðnar are Odin's wolf warriors. They are some of my verúlfr, who split off to join Odin." He walked over to Eva, still smiling gently. "But still, once a verúlfr, always a verúlfr."

Eva ducked her head, looking humbled in a way Lucy had never seen her behave. It must be a strange experience for Eva to meet the creator of her father's entire species. "I am not officially an Úlfhéðinn," Eva said softly, and it sounded like a confession and apology in one. "My father is, but I have not been sworn to his clan. My mother's father has fought against it."

Váli tapped softly beneath her chin to get her to lift her head and look at him, so she could finally see the warm smile he'd directed her way from the start. "I am thankful for how you have protected my daughter, and that you are here with us now." His words made Eva seem a little flustered, before she finally returned his smile with one of her own.

Then Váli looked between both Krysti and Eva. "I know you girls have had to give up much, but I vow we shall do all we can to make you feel welcome and safe here." He patted Eva on the shoulder and held an arm out to invite Krysti closer. She moved with some hesitance, but then ultimately gave in and took his hand.

"You look a little like Mick," Krysti said softly, head tilted to study his face. "Except hairier." With her free hand, she made a circling motion at her own face in illustration.

He chuckled and guided the girls back over towards Lucy and the elevator. "Speaking of Mick, let's swing by and say hi to everyone, on our way to your new apartments."

*

They were taken to a large apartment on the fourth floor that was surprisingly modern in décor for belonging to an ancient Norse deity. In the large living room Diana, Donnie, and Mick sat on a blocky black couch while chatting with a guy sitting in an armchair facing them. Lucy did a double-take before she realized it was Ren.

"What is *he* doing here?" Lucy blurted, instead of greeting her family properly. She just didn't understand why the hell Ren, of all people, would be *there*.

"You know him?" her father asked, pausing between her and the couch and looking a little stunned.

Ren turned around to face her, then broke out into a short, shocked laugh. "Well I'll be damned," he chuckled.

"Who is he?" Krysti asked Eva in a whisper.

Smirking, Eva leaned towards her a bit. "The guy Lucy has a crush on."

"I do *not*!"

Váli went from stunned to downright concerned. "Wait, what?" He spun on Ren with an accusing glare. "You're dating my daughter?"

Lifting his hands up in peaceful surrender, Ren shook his head. "Absolutely not. We've only met a few times."

"You propositioned me," Lucy reminded loudly, "when I was still *seventeen*."

He shot her a look that read *"You're killing me here,"* before plastering on a wide, placating smile when he returned his attention to Váli. "I was *joking*. Believe me when I say I have absolutely zero interest in sleeping with your daughter. Even if I didn't know she was *your* daughter."

Váli's shoulders slumped and he pinched at the bridge of his nose. "Fine," he sighed. "But I'm going to be hiring a different psychologist for her, considering you have a history."

"Totally understandable," agreed Ren.

Lucy felt her confusion spike. "Wait, *psychologist*?"

Clearing his throat, Ren rose from his chair and pulled a flat silver object from his pocket. "Here," he said, approaching her and offering a card from the silver holder. Lucy took the card and read *René Sartre, PsyD, PhD*. It also contained the name of the center where he worked, its address, and how to reach him.

"What." She looked back up at him with her eyebrows raised. "So is there a reason you hang around teen parties?"

"Technically, they're college parties," he corrected. "And yes." At Lucy's accusing glare, he quickly amended, "Nothing unsavory, I promise. It's just the perfect place to find sustenance."

"What?" Eva asked that time, eyes narrowing in dangerous

warning.

His only response was to roll his eyes as if he weren't being stared down by someone who could literally rip out his throat. "Calm down. I can't physically harm anyone or even eat meat."

"He's a good man," Donnie offered up from his place on the couch. Looking over at him, Lucy found her younger brother's expression firm, his jaw set in determination.

Beside him, Diana nodded. "He's been a lifesaver. I'm not sure how I could really process any of this without his help, honestly." Then she continued, almost under her breath, "I'm still not sure how I'm processing it all anyway..."

"Whatever he is, I'm sure it's fine," Mick waved off, then stood from the couch. "So don't worry about him, and just come here already. Christ."

Lucy couldn't help the little laugh that bubbled out of her at that. Shaking her head, she rushed to comply, giving her brother a big hug.

Behind her, Lucy heard Eva stage whispering to Krysti about how she'd honestly always had a good feeling about Ren. "Don't worry," she said, "I'm a great judge of character. Part of the tengu genes."

Krysti laughed nervously and introduced herself to Ren, who said he was looking forward to speaking with her soon. "It can all be a bit overwhelming," he sympathized.

"Lucy," Diana beckoned, reaching up from her seat to invite her own hug. "I'm so glad you're safe."

"I'm glad you're safe, too," Lucy said, nearly choking on the words as she threw herself down onto the couch to hug her mother.

Fractured Masks

Chapter 4
Lost

"Research?" asked Jim, arching a brow at Czar.

The old codger just nodded back, motioning towards the sole computer in the weird, tiny room. "Tha's right. Fer now I got it logged in under mah account, but by tha end of taday, we'll getcha set up with yer own."

Jim glanced between Czar and the computer, wondering what the catch was. "So I get to sit here and look stuff up for you, instead of run around digging up graves and watching people get chopped up?"

It looked like Czar was fighting back a smile. "Yup."

Huh. Maybe probation wasn't such a horrid thing after all. "Sure thing, chief. What do you need me to research?" he asked, sliding into the chair.

Czar moved up beside him and motioned towards part of the screen. "Head over ta this here an' look fer any an' all listed terminations due ta infraction C-54 within tha last ten years. Focus first on tha US, then maybe later we'll branch out a bit."

"Sure thing," Jim chirped, clicking on the proper link and typing in the designated infraction to the search bar. "What's C-54, anyway?"

"Excessive consumption of children."

Jim's fingers paused, hovering above the keyboard. Slowly, he turned his head to give Czar a good long look. "You're serious?"

"As the grave," Czar smirked back. Then he patted Jim on the shoulder and stepped away. "I'll be headin' ta mah office fer now.

But I'll be back later ta check in an' get yer new account all set up."

With a jerky nod, Jim turned back to his task.

There was a surprisingly high number of search results. He filtered it down to within the past ten years, opened up the computer's word processor, and began to record the results. "The hell is a *Tlanuhwa*...?" he muttered to himself as he recorded the details of two having been executed in North Carolina.

It was going to be a long, dull weekend if he was to spend it locked up in that little room. Still, he'd not trade it for his old job as executioner. He'd take dull over disgusting any day. Besides, it helped keep his mind off of his friends and all the mess they'd made.

***

"What have they got you doing, then?" Jim asked as Günter drove him home that evening.

"Still an executioner," answered Günter, sounding a bit confused. "Only now I'm assigned with Carmen and Montenegro, and we're handling things aside from just strigoi."

Jim opened his mouth to ask why Günter seemed to get the short end of the reassignment stick, when he realized it was probably because he was Eva's brother. If either of them were likely to be a secret traitor, they'd suppose it to be Günter. "Sorry to hear that," Jim offered, not knowing really what else to say. "Maybe after our probationary period is done, you'll get a better assignment."

Günter scoffed. "I doubt it. From what I can tell, executioner is typically what the lowest ranked members are assigned to anyway. If anything, this is a bit of a promotion to be working with a more elite team."

"But you'll still be killing strigoi, as well as the other baddies, yeah?"

"Well, yes. But Phil thinks that the strigoi executions will likely be on the decline. He says things have been working in waves recently."

Frowning, Jim tilted his head and studied Günter's stern profile. "What does that mean?"

"Before the recent wave of strigoi incidents, he said there were other things. Nothing quite as dangerous, just increased sightings of things. Luckily, the Gehealdan was able to get everything under control before people started realizing supernaturals exist. A few new urban legends sprang up, but that was all."

Jim considered that for a moment, and also was more than a bit curious about which urban legends they were. "Do you think it's the work of Fenris?"

"What is?" asked Günter, glancing his way as he drove.

"The waves of activity? Reminds me a bit of the velociraptors in *Jurassic Park*. Running at the fences, testing for weaknesses, that sort of thing."

Günter chewed on that for a bit before saying, "It's possible. The way Phil described it, it felt like there was almost a pattern to it, which sounds like something that could be organized."

"So if that's the case, then I wonder what the next—" As he said the words, the realization dawned on him. "Oh hell. I think I know what the next wave is. Or, at least, have some clue as to what it might be."

"What?" Günter's eyebrows came down as he looked askance at Jim. "What are you talking about?"

"The research Czar's having me do," Jim explained. "I'm looking up things that eat kids."

Günter's eyes widened. "Phil said our next Treaty breaker is guilty of killing too many local children in her area." He bit his lip before pulling into a parking lot so that he could direct his full attention to Jim. "He said it's a strix."

There'd only been a few cases Jim had come across with them so far, but enough that he could believe it. "Those are the evil owl things, yeah? The ancestors to strigoi and striga. Hell, you're going after one of them?"

For a moment Günter looked almost frightened, before his usual mask of composure clicked back into place. "Once we've determined where she's hiding, yes. Supposedly she registered and followed all the proper protocol, but for some reason she just...started going rogue, or something."

"Well, from what I've been reading, they certainly like eating the wee ones. Maybe it moved into an area near a lot of new families, and the temptation was just too much," Jim offered.

Günter nodded but didn't look convinced. "Or maybe it's like you said, and this is being orchestrated."

"Fine," allowed Jim, nodding and waving his hand. "Let's say this is all part of Fenris' big plan, or even some other group. *Why*? Why would they want to send out a bunch of things to snatch up and eat babies? What could they possibly hope to accomplish?"

"I don't know." Günter leaned back in his seat, looking defeated before the battle even began. "Maybe it's not that, then. Maybe it seems like waves just because everything sort of works in cycles? Like, the supernatural world is really big about cycles."

"Cycles?"

Shrugging, Günter offered a little nod. "Yeah. Cycle of the moon, cycle of nature, cycle of seasons... A lot of supernaturals are sort of set to be sensitive to those sorts of things, as part of their very nature."

"So it could just be something like that," Jim pondered aloud, trying to work all of the madness out. "Might not be some huge conspiracy."

"But it still might be a conspiracy," Günter cautioned. "We can't fully rule that out until we know more."

"Right." Jim nodded. "So I'll see what I can find in my research, and you see what you can find working with the others."

Günter nodded back, but he looked uneasy. "Part of me is really hoping it's just cycles." He didn't have to explain any further; Jim understood. It wasn't a pleasant thought to consider Eva and Lucy might have just run right into the arms of some horrible, baby-eating organization.

"Here's hoping," Jim offered, before pressing his lips together and trying not to cringe.

***

At school on Monday, Jim was caught off guard by the memorial taking up most of one wall in the main entry. He didn't know why he was surprised, really, considering a few of the players in the LARP were from his school.

Vaguely familiar faces stared at him in artistic black-and-white, and it slowly sank in that these people—these *kids*—were dead. Killed by the very organization for which he worked. All because they played some rubbish game and were told dangerous truths wrapped up as fantasy. Not for the first time, he wondered if he had made the right choice to stay behind instead of going with Lucy.

Then he thought about all of the research he'd done that weekend, and all of the cases where the Gehealdan had stepped in and saved untold numbers of innocent children. Maybe Günter really had the right of it. Sure the Gehealdan had rather brutal methods, but it served a much-needed purpose.

He started to turn away, intent on keeping his head down and going to class as if nothing were different, but one photo caught his eye. Krysti. Krysti was posted among them. Then, beside her photo, was Eva.

Jim's chest felt tight. He knew she was probably still alive, too bloody tough to kill. Günter had even said that his father had been told she was missing, not dead. Listing her as one of the victims was just the Gehealdan's way of effectively killing Eva in the legal sense to explain away her sudden disappearance. He knew that. Still...it didn't make seeing her photo any easier.

Lucy was trickier. He was curious to see what sort of cover the Gehealdan was going to fabricate to explain why an entire family just dropped off the map overnight. At least her photo wasn't also on the wall.

Looking back at Krysti's photo, Jim hoped that Eva and Lucy had gotten to her in time, and her inclusion was as much of a lie as Eva's. He wondered if Eva would have even gone with Lucy, had Krysti not been part of the LARP. A strange bitterness welled up within him then, and he hated himself for it. Hated the way he resented Krysti for being somewhat responsible for the loss of his best friend. She didn't deserve that, was just an unknowing victim in a game beyond her scope of knowledge.

"Jim," came a fragile, breaking voice, a second before Alice's dainty hand grasped at his sleeve. He turned towards her at the touch, felt something sharp shift within his chest at the bald look of grief and fear on her face. "What is this?" she asked, dark eyes looking at the pictures of their friends as if they displayed vivid images of their murdered corpses instead of their generic senior photos.

"Didn't you hear the news this weekend? It happened Friday night."

Alice let out a sob and leaned into him. "I kept trying to contact them all weekend, see about getting together for a movie or something. They never replied to their texts." Then she looked up at him in renewed terror. "Lucy didn't either. Is she...?" She whipped her head back towards the board, scanning each of the photos in search of Lucy's dark hair and pale skin.

"I don't know," he answered honestly. "I haven't heard anything from her all weekend, either."

Covering her mouth, Alice doubled over crying, and Jim rushed to sweep in and support her. "There now, love. Let's get to the principal's office, yeah? I think both of us could do with some time at home." He held her up as they headed down the hall. Beneath his breath, he added, "Dunno why I thought I'd be good to come to school so soon, honestly."

***

His mother brought him home, casting him worried glances the whole drive. "You could have told me," she said softly. She must have been either sleeping or working when Jim had called from the office, because her natural hair was hidden beneath a soft scarf instead of styled free and loose like she preferred when out in public. It was a garnet silk that looked amazing against her night-black skin, though Grace Lukehurst was the sort of woman who could take a potato sack and make it look fashionable.

"I thought I'd be alright," was all Jim could think to say.

Grace gave him a sad look and patted his knee before returning her hand to the steering wheel. "Stay home as long as you need. I'll get your assignments forwarded from your teachers." Then she bit her lip before quietly adding, "And if you need to see someone, to help you cope, we can take care of that. Nothing wrong with getting help when you need it, pet. You know I saw someone when your Aunt Yvette died."

"Maybe," he allowed, feeling perhaps it wasn't a bad notion. Though it'd have to be someone he found through the Gehealdan, in order for him to be able to talk freely about everything that kept him up at night and plagued his dreams.

Back at home, Grace saw that he had all he needed, asked if he wanted her to stick with him, then reluctantly retreated to her studio once he insisted he wished to be alone. Jim retrieved his phone from his backpack, intending to contact Czar about an in-the-know shrink, only to find it flooded with texts.

They were all from Kyle, frantic and rapid-fire to the point Jim could practically hear the desperation in his words.

where are u?
did u see the memorial?!
just txtd Alice she said you 2 went home

I'm goin home 2
y can't I get ahold of Lucy???
can u reach lucy?
tried calling her -goes strait to vm
alice said lucy mb was with eva and krysti?!!
jim! Do u kno?
is lucy ok??

Jim stared at the messages, unsure how to respond. *"I think Lucy is gone,"* he eventually typed out, thumb hovering over the word "send" before finally tapping it. Kyle called a few seconds later, but Jim just hit ignore, stuffed his phone in his pocket, and headed up to his room. He felt it vibrate with a few more messages as he walked slowly up the stairs, but didn't bother checking what were surely just more texts from Kyle.

Once in his room, he pulled out his phone to actually try contacting Czar again. Only then he found that while there were indeed a few more texts from Kyle—as well as a voicemail message—there was also a text from Dorian about when a good time would be for him to come model.

Jim sat down heavily on the end of his bed and stared at the tiny screen. Honestly, it would probably do him some good to focus on his art. It was as good a therapy as any, far as he was concerned. He texted back that he had the next few days free. When Dorian quickly responded that he was available that afternoon, Jim actually felt himself smile a little.

***

Strange, thought Jim, his memories of Dorian painted him as more beautiful. Maybe it was the dim lights of the party, he reasoned, studying Dorian closely and scritching out his likeness in charcoal. His studio's lights were bright out of necessity, and thus weren't the most flattering lighting for most people.

Still...

Jim cast a glance over at the easel housing a few of the drawings of Günter, where it stood beside his unfinished statue. There was even a small, to-scale model of what Jim intended to carve, which he'd formed out of clay. It stood on a nearby table, capturing Günter's preternaturally good looks that weren't hindered at all by the harsh glare of the studio's lights.

"You seem distracted," Dorian observed, even as he tried to remain as perfectly still as possible.

"There's a lot going on in my life right now," Jim offered vaguely, not really wanting to produce a lie or even half-truth. Christ, he felt so bloody tired.

Dorian hummed a little, daring a short glance before fixing his eyes back to where they needed to be. They were rather pretty eyes, Jim supposed. Sort of the color of deep ocean water, a blue-green that looked almost black under the right light. "Gehealdan business?" Dorian ventured casually.

The charcoal stick snapped as Jim's fingers jerked in alarm. For a long moment, he simply stared at the white boy in silence. "How did you know?" he finally asked through a suddenly dry throat.

That seemed to amuse Dorian, a smirk flirting with his lips before he was schooling his features once again. "I could smell it on you when we first met."

"Smell what?" Jim croaked.

"The scents of grave dirt, strigoi rot, and pyre smoke." After another glance, Dorian offered a quick, comforting smile. "Don't worry, it wasn't strong. Obviously you hadn't done it that night, but it was something you'd done enough of for it to linger on your skin, your hair. My kind have an exceptional sense of smell. It's better in water, but, well..." He gave a tiny shrug, still being careful not to move his position too much.

"So you knew I killed vampires," said Jim, muscles frozen and mind racing, "but that doesn't mean I'm Gehealdan."

Dorian actually scoffed at that. "Who else would be executing strigoi to such an extent? They're like pests, though, aren't they? Strigoi. Like vermin, the way they multiply and scurry about doing whatever they please." He scoffed again, his lips curling for a moment. In that brief glimpse, his teeth seemed too sharp. "They've always been the biggest risks to the Treaties."

"It doesn't bother you, then, that I'm Gehealdan?" Jim asked, pulse finally starting to slow as he began to assess that Dorian might not actually pose a threat. He even dared to look away, reaching for the larger piece of the broken charcoal so that he could get back to work. "You're part of the Treaties?"

"It doesn't, and I am," Dorian replied, almost smiling before forcing his features back into the imperious, god-like pose he was to maintain.

"May I ask," Jim started, then faltered, unsure of the proper way to phrase his question. Was it gauche to ask what someone was? He concentrated on capturing the exact slope of Dorian's nose in order to mask his embarrassment. Actually, the more he looked at Dorian, the more Jim was starting to see exactly why he'd found him so appealing. He really was quite striking. The most beautiful man he'd ever seen.

Wait, no.

That wasn't...

He glanced again at the drawings of Günter, then back to Dorian. The man in front of him wasn't anything particularly special, just sort of generically handsome in an honestly boring way. He might even have to employ some artistic license to make the statue look as godly as he wanted.

"I'm Lamiae," Dorian was saying, while Jim puzzled over his mediocrity.

"Oh?" asked Jim. He made a few quick sweeps with the charcoal stick, then went back to refine specific details in Dorian's torso. He stopped short, confused, as he looked between his subject and the drawing. Jim could swear he'd done as he always had, drawing exactly what he saw in front of him, filling in the shadows with perfect precision. Yet the drawing didn't seem to be doing the subject justice. Which was odd. Had he gotten it backwards in his head? Was it his depiction of Dorian that was plain while Dorian himself was a marvel to behold? No, that couldn't be right...could it?

"We are all descended from Lamia herself," Dorian was explaining, his perfect lips curving around each word even as he strove to keep his chiseled jaw as still as possible.

Blinking a few times, Jim shook his head and tried to clear the muddled mess that was his mind. "Who might that be?" he asked distractedly as he returned to trying to capture Dorian's image.

The way Dorian's face lit up was like looking at history's most stunning sunrise. "She was once a princess of Libya, thousands of years ago. So beautiful that Zeus himself fell in love with her."

"Explains where you got it from," Jim murmured idly, fingers rushing to capture every detail of Dorian. He was nearly feverish with the need to draw that beautiful man. Quickly flipping to a new page in his large sketch book, Jim shifted to another angle and started drawing anew.

"You think I'm attractive?" Dorian asked, a pleased smile flitting across his lips. Jim wanted to chase it with his tongue.

"Yeah, 'course," said Jim, completely lost in his mission to perfectly capture every glorious detail that comprised Dorian. Something shifted at the back of his mind, though. A strange, slithering sensation that made him queasy if he focused on it too much. So instead he shied away, let himself get lost in his art and Dorian's elegance.

"The feeling's mutual," Dorian confided with a slight purr to his voice. Then he was moving, stepping out of his pose and sauntering towards Jim.

Opening his mouth to chastise Dorian from breaking pose, Jim felt the words washed away by the mesmerizing way Dorian moved. With a huge grin, Dorian circled around Jim, looking briefly at the drawing before returning to stand directly in front of him. "What should we do about this, hm?" Dorian asked, leaning close into Jim's space.

Again the slithery thing writhed in the back of Jim's mind, making him feel uneasy and dizzy. This wasn't right. He tried to look towards the drawings of Günter again, as if reaching for a lifeline, but Dorian just shifted to block his view. "Come on," crooned Dorian, and Jim felt the man's hand on his cheek, thumb brushing against his lower lip, petting through his goatee. "I thought you said you find me attractive."

"Yes," Jim heard himself say without his consent. He watched in mute horror as Dorian closed the distance between them, his mind screaming how it was all wrong even as his body leaned in to meet Dorian halfway. Hands going weak, the sketchbook and charcoal clattered to the floor.

The kiss was too harsh, too stiff, just right in how Dorian angled his head, so perfect. It was the best kiss of his life, and his mind reeled at receiving it from such a gorgeous bloke. When the kiss came to an end, Jim felt himself sway towards Dorian and release an involuntary whimper.

He opened his eyes and felt his breath whoosh out of his lungs. Dorian was like something from a dream, almost painful to look at, and a craving tore through Jim. "More," he whispered, so hungry for another kiss that he felt ever more hollow the longer he went without.

Dorian gladly obliged.

Chapter 5
Purpose

Eva sat on the cold marble floor, her back against the wall beside a gleaming black door, and she waited. Beyond the door was Ren's office for the duration that he was going to work for Fenris. Krysti was in there, likely curled over herself as she cried and tried to work through all of her grief. All Eva could do was just sit there and wait for her, feeling useless. There was an anger inside of her directed just as much at herself as towards the dead strigoi who put Krysti through so much hell.

What would her life even be if it weren't for Krysti wandering in to obliterate her walls with sunshine and sugar? Outside of her family, Eva hadn't had any friends until she'd met Krysti. No one was allowed to get close enough, Eva always afraid that she just wouldn't be able to fit in with the human children. Other kids always had stories about summer vacations filled with Disney World and beaches, while Eva's experiences involved shape-shifting foxes and forbidden dark forests. What could she talk about with the other children? How could she possibly relate to them?

Krysti had taken her hand one day, called her "my friend," and refused to be deterred. She never seemed to mind that Eva only silently stared at her in utter confusion, Krysti brightly talking enough for the both of them. The next day had been much the same, and so on until Eva's walls cracked and crumbled and Krysti could step easily past the rubble into Eva's very core. Eva later witnessed her do the same with a grieving Lucy, pulling her close and wrapping her in friendship to heal the wounds caused by loss.

Now it felt like a paradigm shift had taken place, and it was Krysti who sat broken and quiet and afraid of the world. Eva wasn't certain she had what it took to fill Krysti's shoes and save the day with rainbows and laughter. Still, she'd do what she could, offer her own brand of support and love. No matter how much she felt like a failure, undeserving of Krysti's continued friendship.

At least Ren could possibly do something to help Krysti. A psychologist was far more equipped to help Krysti than Eva was. It also helped that he was supernatural and something which evidently couldn't pose any sort of threat. Ren had said he *couldn't* harm anyone, not that he *wouldn't*, a huge distinction which made him something safer than even a human.

Footsteps approaching from down the hall drew Eva's thoughts back from dark places, and she turned to see Uktena. He was dressed much the same as before, except his shirt was a simple long-sleeved henley. Still, it also seemed to have a type of fabric woven so that its color was ever-shifting and indistinguishable.

In his hand were two white folders, and he looked right at Eva as if he'd been expecting to find her there. "I have your new identities," he said once he was only a couple meters away. After glancing down at the fronts of the two folders, Uktena held one out to her.

She blinked up at him for a moment, but then sighed and pulled herself up off the floor. "That was quick," she observed as she stepped closer to retrieve the folder.

"We can be a pretty efficient organization when we want to be." Uktena seemed to be studying her closely, as if assessing something about her. Eva wondered if he was simply concerned with whether or not she'd like her new name, but it felt like something more.

Eva flipped open the folder and found a new—though perfectly aged—birth certificate, as well as a Social Security card and Pennsylvania state driver's license. The name on all of the documents read "Lea de Jong," and they evidently aged her a year to make her a legal adult. "You got the nationality wrong," she commented with a touch of bitterness. "Not all Asians are the same, you know."

Uktena snorted. "It's Dutch," he corrected. "Pronounced deh-yong."

Rolling her eyes, Eva shot him a sardonic glare. "Fine. Not all Europeans are the same, either. My dad's German. Krysti's the one with the Dutch ancestry. Van Schuyler."

He just shrugged in return. "It's close enough. We don't necessarily want your new identity to be totally obvious." Then he tipped his chin towards the door. "She'll be getting a pretty generic-sounding English name."

Looking back down at the documents, Eva tried to think about being Lea to strangers. At least it sounded similar enough to her own name that it would be easy to train herself to react to it. "Fine," she relented. "Thanks."

Instead of leaving, Uktena just shrugged and moved to lean against the wall opposite the door. Evidently he was going to be waiting along with her for Krysti to finish her counseling session. Eva closed the folder and returned to where she'd been sitting on the floor, content to ignore his presence.

After a few minutes of awkward silence, Uktena tilted his head and asked, "So what's the deal between you and the blonde? Is she your girlfriend?"

Eva shot him a sharp glare before looking away. "It's not like that."

He lifted the hand not holding the folder up, in a sign of peace. "I'm not judging. Such prejudice is a human thing."

It wasn't like Eva was ashamed, she just hated having to explain things every time people asked about her love life. She closed her eyes and heaved a deep sigh before looking back at him. "Not that it's any of your business, but the most intimate I'd want to get with her or anyone else is engaging in some primo cuddling."

Usually such a confession confused the hell out of people. For some reason, they just couldn't seem to comprehend how someone wouldn't be interested in sex. Eva was expecting the same kind of response from Uktena, maybe even accompanied with the typical questions of "Have you even tried it? How would you know if you haven't tried it?" So, she was completely thrown to find him looking at her in something akin to absolute delight.

"That's *perfect*," he enthused.

"What?" She jerked back, pressing her shoulders against the wall and wondering wildly if he had understood her or if he maybe had some sort of weird fetish. "You do get what I mean, right? I'm —"

"Asexual. Yes. And that makes you an even better candidate! I admit I had my doubts when the Chairman recommended you, despite your lineage and training." He paused and looked thoughtful, murmuring to himself, "I wonder if he knew, somehow..."

Eva stood again and had to force herself to relax her grip on the folder or risk ruining the documents it contained. "What the hell are you talking about? Candidate for what?"

Uktena's attention snapped back to her. "I was going to talk with you about it later, after your own session." He tapped the folder idly against his thigh. "Two of the Lamiae, in two different states, have been executed by the Gehealdan within the last few months."

"So?" Eva asked, confusion only growing.

"That's two more Lamiae executions than what have occurred since the forming of the Treaties. Despite their ancient reputation for being gluttonous, insatiable monsters who just can't resist eating babies, they've been one of the most well-behaved of all the folk who signed the Treaties. They've even been allowed to exert a little bit of their allure to help them out in their respective vocations, which typically include entertainment and politics. So long as they don't ever ensnare someone fully or go around using it to lure helpless victims to their doom, it's all good."

She recalled the douche Jim would act like an idiot around. Günter had been certain he was one of the Lamiae, hadn't he? Feeling a bit of trepidation start to crack through her confusion, she asked, "So what's changed?"

"That's part of what we need to find out. From what our operatives on the inside can determine, the Lamiae are being blamed for a rash of recent child disappearances in areas near water."

Memories of her childhood flickered through her mind, of being warned away from a certain lake deep within the forest near her father's clan in Germany. A day of naïve defiance, a dark, winding trail, a lake like a puddle of oil, and large, glowing eyes.

"There are a lot of things that live in water and eat kids," said Eva, trying to shove the dusty memory back to where it usually hid.

Uktena nodded. "That's what we're thinking, too. We're not convinced that these disappearances are due to Lamiae suddenly acting out of character and breaking the rules."

"So what do you think it is?" she asked, squinting across the stretch of hallway at him.

"Could be a political move on the Gehealdan's part, since the Lamiae have so much sway in governments around the world. Maybe they're trying to remind the Lamiae exactly who's in charge. Or, it could be someone else intentionally trying to set the Lamiae up. We won't know anything for sure until we investigate."

"And that's where I evidently factor in?" Eva asked, sounding only half as skeptical as she felt.

With a slight tilt of his head, Uktena said, "Potentially. The Chairman recommended I use you as my partner on this assignment."

"I just got here," she objected. Though perhaps that was explanation enough for why she'd be sent on some type of assignment. She wasn't related to anyone in the organization like Lucy was, and so she'd have to do *something* to pull her weight, earn her keep. The folder in her hand suddenly felt uncomfortably hot at the realization.

"You've been trained in a wide variety of martial arts and combat skills," he explained, sounding as if he was mentally reciting a list. "Thanks to Tahchat, we know you've inherited your mother's abilities and are able to see through some illusions. You've got some experience working within the Gehealdan, which only our spies have. We can't exactly risk their covers by using them for this. Then," he gave a little pause, and his mouth curled into a small smile. "Evidently you'll be immune to the allure magics used by not only the Lamiae, but so many other human-eating water folk."

He gave a soft, startled chuckle. "I think I just convinced myself that you're the right one, actually." The smile grew and seemed directed at someone not present. "Someday I gotta learn to stop questioning some of the Chairman's weirder ideas."

Eva shifted her weight where she stood. Part of her felt oddly proud to be recommended by the leader of Fenris himself, which was who she assumed this mysterious "Chairman" was if Váli was the Vice-chairman. Still, she didn't feel right about running off and leaving Krysti in such a fragile state.

"I can't," she finally said, quiet yet firm. "Krysti needs me here."

Uktena returned to staring at her in his intense, assessing way. "So, ace but not aromantic."

Huffing, Eva forced herself to not look away. "She's a human thrown into a supernatural conflict by way of watching a lot of her friends get slaughtered in front of her. I can't just abandon her."

The folder tapped against his thigh again as Uktena looked between her and the door. "She'll be fine here. Not just safe, but in the company of friends. The Kincades are here. Plus she'll be receiving regular therapy with one of the best in the business."

"Lucy will be too busy training to control her powers," Eva objected. The manifestation of Lucy's abilities had sent Váli over the moon in excitement, and he had insisted that she start training with her grandfather soon so that she could have full control. There was no way Lucy would have much in the way of free time while wrapped up in all of that.

"There's her brothers, her mother. Are you telling me Krysti never stayed over at Lucy's house, never befriended her family?"

She didn't like how he was trying to outwit her, using words the way a fencer used footwork. "I'm her best friend," Eva parried.

"So help her in the best way a warrior like you can," he

jabbed, finding a chink in her armor and exploiting it. "Can you honestly tell me that you'll feel like you're actually doing anything for her by just sitting around and holding her hand? She's got plenty of people to do that here. What she needs is justice for the friends who have fallen. Investigating the actions of the Gehealdan will bring us all one step closer to achieving that justice."

Eva stood there, feeling run-through and bleeding. No words came to counter his blows, and defeat felt dizzying. "I'll think about it," she eventually forced her mouth to say.

After studying her for another long moment, Uktena nodded, then held out the folder. "Give this to your friend once she's done. I'll be in my apartment, if you need to reach me. Ground floor, door marked 47."

She reached out and took the folder, unable to meet Uktena's eyes anymore. In her peripheral, she watched his snakeskin boots as he walked away.

*

"Iris Clarke," Krysti read, scrunching up her nose. "Do I really look like an Iris?"

The session seemed to have done her a lot of good. It was the first time since before the LARP that Eva had seen Krysti acting anything like herself. Somewhere in the back of Eva's mind, a voice that sounded suspiciously like Uktena pointed out, *"See, Krysti doesn't really need you around in order to get better."*

"They could have at least given me a name that sounded a little like my real one," grumbled Krysti. Then she looked over and eyed Eva's folder with obvious curiosity. "What name did you get?"

"Lea de Jong," said Eva. "And Iris is a pretty name. I think it's from Greek mythology or something. Like, having to do with rainbows."

"Can we trade? Your name sounds way better."

Eva laughed a little, more out of continued relief at Krysti's improved state than anything. "No, sorry, I think we're stuck with what we got."

Krysti closed her folder with a huff. "Fine."

"Hey," said Eva, soft and comforting as she stepped closer and cupped her hands over Krysti's shoulders. "You'll always be you, no matter what some piece of paper says."

Smiling, Krysti leaned in and gently pressed their foreheads together. "And you'll always be you."

The door beside them slid open, and Eva jerked back from Krysti with a start. Clearing her throat, Eva dropped her hands, but Krysti just reached out and snatched one up with her own, giving it a little squeeze.

Ren looked between them before cocking an eyebrow at Eva. "You ready?"

"Yeah," she said, shooting for casual.

Krysti squeezed her hand once more before releasing it and stepping away. "I'll wait for you," she said with an encouraging smile.

Eva just nodded, then followed Ren back into the office. He was wearing a pretty typical combination for him, pale teal shirt and khaki pants. It was a little surreal to see him surrounded by the stereotypical trappings of a therapist's office instead of amongst a sweaty crowd.

"So what type of sustenance do you find at college parties?

Beer and chips?" Eva snarked as she moved to sit on the couch he was waving her towards.

"Something a bit more satisfying," he replied calmly. He then took a seat in a plush armchair beside the couch.

"You said you couldn't hurt people," pressed Eva, trying to prompt him into further explanation.

Ren gave a little nod. "I can't even eat meat. Well, I *can*," he corrected himself, "but it wouldn't end well."

"So what folk are you?" Eva asked, growing tired of the way he danced around the topic.

"That's not really what this session is about," said Ren. "We're supposed to be talking about you, not me."

Frustrated, Eva leaned her head back against the couch cushion. "There's nothing really to talk about, then. I don't need trauma counseling."

"Well then," he prompted gently, "we can talk about whatever you need." When Eva continued to remain silent, he tried again. "Maybe talk about how you felt seeing Krysti so upset, at the LARP?"

"Fenris wants to send me out on assignment," Eva dodged. "I'm not sure if I'm flattered that they see me as an asset, or upset that they couldn't at least wait until I've settled in."

"It's understandable to be upset. Especially after what you went through before arriving here."

She closed her eyes and saw flashes of the dead and dying, dressed in ridiculous costumes, bodies torn apart, jagged bite wounds down to the bone. "I was raised to be a warrior," was all she said. "Warriors aren't affected by that sort of stuff. Not like civilians."

"As a former soldier, I can tell you that's not entirely true."

Eva didn't open her eyes, too worried that she'd see something like pity or concern reflected back in Ren's face. "Soldiers aren't warriors," she objected mildly. "There's a difference between someone brought into something and trained for a few months before being dumped onto a battlefield, and someone who was raised from childhood in the ways of war and combat." She peeked at him in suspicion. "How can you be a soldier if you can't hurt anyone?"

"Why would your family raise you to be a warrior?" he asked, instead of answering her question.

Closing her eyes again, she saw a flicker of a memory. Yemon-jiisan carefully holding his drooping sleeve back as he ran an ink-soaked brush across paper. His voice was soft and crinkled like dry leaves as he explained to her about their noble lineage. "It's in my blood. On both sides," she explained.

There was a short silence, and then Ren asked, "Do you want to take the assignment?"

Eva opened her eyes and stared up at the ceiling. It was as cold and grey as the marble hallways. "Maybe. I have to do *something*, ya know? I'm not meant to be cooped up in a cage."

"So you view Fenris as a cage?"

"No," she said, frowning at herself and her words as she tried to think of a better way to phrase it. "Not the organization, but this place. It's nice, but it's not for me. I'm not built to stand behind the castle walls while the war rages."

"You feel you're at war?"

"Yes." She lifted her head and looked at him then. "Can't you feel it? You said you used to be a soldier. Can't you tell?"

He looked strangely sad, even as he smiled blandly at her.

"Wars haven't really been any of my business for a long time."

Eva studied him for a moment, wondered if he was older or younger than her father. "Well, it's here. Or at the very least, it's coming. I feel it like it's a rainstorm on the horizon. You know *that* feeling at least, yeah? The buzz in the air from the lightning, the strong, sharp scent of rain." At his confirming nod, she continued, "It's like that. Something looming and inevitable."

"And you feel you have to play a part in it. That you have to fight."

"It's what I'm made for," she reiterated. "What I was crafted to do."

"Do you truly believe that? You told me before that you were into theatre."

His words reminded her of the party where she'd said it. Lucy's birthday. That guy had been there, the one who was of the Lamiae. Jim had acted strange, her brother had gotten angry, and evidently a few houses down the Grin Reaper had been carving up another victim.

"I'm not sure what I believe," she admitted, even as she could feel her resolve settling into place. "But I know I can't just sit around, if there's something useful I could be doing."

DL Wainright

Chapter 6
Framed

    Günter felt strange and uncomfortable from the moment they stepped foot into the forest. Something smelled off, but it was more than that, a bone-deep wrongness that had him clenching teeth that tried to lengthen and sharpen on instinct. All around them, the forest was unusually quiet. It may have been autumn, but it was Georgia and still warm enough for there to be insects and creatures running about. Instead, the trees and underbrush were all still as stone.

    As he sniffed at the air, Günter let his eyes shift to those of a wolf, so he could see in the darkness beyond the limited range of the flashlights. "I smell blood." After another few sniffs, he wrinkled his nose. "And something musty. Like a damp room that's been closed up for a long time."

    "That's weirdly specific," said Carmen, glancing askance at him while she remained mostly focused on the forest around them.

    "It's just the best way I can describe it. It's sort of like a moldy, rot smell, but not rot as in carrion. More like...maybe how a pile of leaves starts to smell after a while?"

    Releasing a low hum, Carmen drew her Beretta 92FS and held it alongside her flashlight. "You know, I don't think I've read 'bout their scent in any bestiary I've ever seen. It would be interesting to add those sorts of details to entries, though. Might be useful."

    Montenegro stopped suddenly, cocking his head to the side as if he'd heard something. Which was odd, since surely Günter would have been the first to hear any strange sounds. Of course, he could hear even better if he were fully shifted.

    Mildly frustrated, Günter set down his bow and pulled his

quiver off. "I'm going to transform," he explained quietly, when Carmen gave him a questioning look. Then he stripped off his shirt and unfastened his belt. He waited for Carmen and Montenegro to politely turn away before he carefully lowered his pants, mindful of his katana and wakizashi.

Once he was fully nude, he closed his eyes and tried to focus on the exact combination of shift he wanted. Sometimes he wondered if it was easier for his father when he shifted, having only one form he could take. Günter's very bones began to change, and as always it was accompanied by a glaring buzz along his nerves that left him feeling almost numb. Like when a limb falls asleep, only severely more intense.

When it was finally over, he stood there in full tengu form, save for his eyes, ears, and muzzle, which were those of a wolf. Günter stretched his wings out, trying to shake off the last tingles running through his body. With his lupine ears he could hear a light scritch-scritch sound, and the faint, rapid heartbeat of something not far off. It was the only heartbeat he could hear aside from his group, so he decided to set off towards it.

"Got her," he husked out in a voice more like a growl, before bending down to fetch up his katana.

"Which way?" asked Carmen, turning back to face him but keeping her eyes above his shoulders.

When Günter motioned towards the heartbeat, Carmen glanced at Montenegro and awaited his confirming nod before she said, "Fine, let's go."

"No," Günter objected. "I'll go first. I can track her and move in more silently."

Carmen snorted and rolled her eyes. "Sure, rookie." He could tell she was being sarcastic, but he decided to interpret it as permission anyway.

Taking another quick moment to confirm the direction he needed to focus on, Günter took flight and broke through the canopy. If it had been daylight, he'd use his tengu eyes, so nothing could escape his view. Wolf eyes were better at night, but they weren't made for stalking prey from above. He'd have to make do.

As Günter began to fly closer to the source of the sounds, they suddenly just stopped. There was nothing. No scritching, no pulse, just the gentle rustle of trees. He pulled up short, flapping his large wings to hover for a moment before swooping in wide loops to scan the forest.

"Günter," he heard whispered in Jim's familiar voice. "*Günter*," he called again, a little louder, fear stressing the word.

His first instinct was to rush to Jim's aid, and he turned mid-flight to change course towards the call. Then reason set in, and he was pulling back. Finding a large, sturdy tree, Günter landed amongst its branches as quietly as possible. There he sat and listened again, straining to hear whatever he could.

Phil had made certain Günter read up on strixes before going out on the mission, and so he sat there and thought back to what he'd read. Strixes weren't entirely unlike tengu, in that they were bird-people with the ability to weave illusions. This one seemed to be trying to trick a son of a trickster. Which, really, was a very foolish thing to do.

Jim's cries began to turn from scared to terrified, then he began to scream as if in pain. The sharp scent of fresh blood suddenly came from that direction, and Günter's talons sank deep into the branch as he reminded himself it was fake. The cries and smells were coming from the southwest, so Günter figured that she was probably hiding in the opposite direction.

He took flight again, soaring above the trees and away from Jim's cries. The farther he flew, the louder and more pained the screams became. There were no sounds ahead of him, yet he felt in his gut that he was heading in the right direction.

Then, just as suddenly as before, everything went silent.

"Why are you here?" a woman's voice asked as if whispered right into his ear. It sounded young and gentle, and not at all like he'd imagine the voice of an owl-woman.

"You've been found guilty of breaking Treaty law," he explained, changing course to circle the area just beneath him.

When the voice spoke again, it still sounded so close it was practically within his head, and seemed sad and confused. "I registered with the Old Man. I did what I should. I'm allowed to use some powers to keep people from my woods. I'm *allowed*."

"That's not what you've been found guilty of." He tried desperately to pinpoint where she could be, but whatever magic she was using to hide her heartbeat was too powerful.

"Leave," she sighed into his mind. "Do not make me kill you. Though," her voice lilted in consideration, "you'd likely be a tasty one. So special. So pretty."

Something felt as though it was wrapping around his wings, like a giant hand. He had a split-second of panicked realization before the invisible force tightened and he was falling. As he fell, he managed to release a short, desperate howl that would hopefully alert the others to where he was.

The branches broke beneath his plummeting weight, and felt to be clawing every inch of him. At least they slowed him down enough that he didn't fly apart when he finally landed on the hard forest floor.

Everything hurt. He had landed on his back, directly on top of his crushed wings. His katana was clutched protectively to his chest, so at least he'd not lost that. For a moment, he wasn't sure he could move, thought maybe his very spine had snapped. Then he forced himself to try curling his taloned feet, and was relieved that his body obeyed the command and he could feel them move.

"Should have left," whispered the voice. "Now you never will."

"I'm from Gehealdan," Günter warned through pain-clenched teeth. "Kill me and you'll definitely be executed."

"You lot wish to execute me, anyway," she reasoned. "Might as well just protect myself from your wrongful accusations."

Günter sat up, despite the blinding pain the action brought on. "You haven't been acting terribly innocent," he ground out. Yeah, he definitely had a few broken ribs, at the very least. His wings had suffered the most, and he moved to a kneeling position so he'd no longer be lying on them. The pain was excruciating when he tried to move his wings and he swallowed back his scream.

Yemon-jiisan had taught him how to block out a lot of his pain, but he'd never experienced something this bad. *Maybe*, he thought, *maybe if I get rid of the wings. Shift to another form.* So he tried, willed his bones to alter again, to draw the wings back into him.

That time, he was unable to withhold his scream. He nearly fainted, his vision going white. When his wits finally returned, he realized two things: one, he had shifted completely into a wolf; and two, his broken bones felt healed.

"Impressive," cooed the voice.

Günter stood up on all fours and looked around, trying to find the source of the voice. In his wolf form he could feel a thrum of something in the air around him. It was strange, but not entirely unfamiliar. He could recall feeling something similar a few times in his life. When he'd go exploring a little too far into the woods near his father's clan in Germany, he'd feel that same kind of thrum just before realizing something was watching him from the shadows. Sometimes it was an animal, sometimes a person, but it always smelled of blood and was gone again if he blinked his eyes.

He used that feeling like a divining rod now, moving closer to where the thrum grew stronger. It was impossible to speak in full wolf form, so he just snarled to let the strix know what he had planned for her.

"Why don't you just leave me be, child?" The voice was scratchier now, less pleasant. It no longer whispered in his ear, but echoed around him.

"Because you broke the rules, ma'am." Carmen's voice startled Günter, not having smelled her or heard her approach.

"Lies," hissed the voice, and it finally seemed to come from one specific direction.

Carmen tutted and came closer only holding a flashlight and what appeared to be a rock. "We ain't the liars here, ma'am, and you know it."

There was a rustling in the branches to Günter's right, and he turned to see a face in the darkness. At first he thought it was just a normal owl, but then he realized there was something wrong about how it was perched. The wings weren't folded at its sides, but wrapped around it, like how a bat enfolds itself.

"How dare you," the owl rasped out. Then it unwrapped its wings, revealing two little talons partway up that it used to crawl along the branch. Its body was that of a petite naked woman with the feet of an owl. Unlike with tengu, who had human arms as well as wings that sprouted from their backs, the strix's arms were its wings. They were long, not jointed like any bird Günter had ever seen. The strix clung to the branch and watched them with her wide, yellow eyes.

"Aw, what's wrong? Can't use your magic on us?" asked Carmen, voice dripping with sarcastic sympathy. She tossed the rock in her hand and caught it, grinning.

The strix opened its mouth—far larger than its deceptively small beak, gaping wide enough to swallow a baby whole—and screeched at Carmen. Long, needle-sharp teeth gleamed in the faint light as the strix continued to draw out its cry. It reminded Günter of the Grin Reaper, and his mouth crammed packed with teeth like knives.

Rolling her eyes, Carmen looked less than impressed with the strix's display. "That's enough," she shouted over the shrill screeching. Then she whistled and motioned towards the strix. Immediately a crossbow bolt shot through the darkness and sank deep into the strix's head.

It ended the screeching instantly, and the strix fell limply off the branch, falling with a dull thud upon the ground. Günter crouched there for another moment, waiting for something more to happen. "That's it, Fido," said Carmen, stepping past Günter to find the corpse. They'd need to burn it to make sure no one would find the remains.

There was a rustle of leaves before Montenegro approached,

and he walked over to set Günter's clothes down beside him. "Good effort," Montenegro offered softly, before stepping away and inspecting the surrounding area with cautious eyes.

Bracing himself in case there would be pain again, Günter shifted back into human form. Thankfully, it felt like it always did, and the transition was smooth. As he tugged back on his clothes, he asked, "Is it really that easy?"

"Yep," replied Carmen, dragging the corpse over by its feet. Up close, Günter could see that the strix was about the size of a twelve-year-old human. "They're not like Romes, and can die any ol' way, so long as you get around their magic."

"About that," Günter started, thinking back over everything. "What happened? How did you cancel out her magic?"

Pausing in her task, Carmen retrieved the stone from her pocket and tossed it for Günter to catch. He did so easily, turning it over in his hands and studying the carvings all over its surface. There were runes worked in around an image of what appeared to be a long, stretched-out bird, its body tied in complicated knots. Typical Norse artwork, similar to things owned by his father's clan.

"So this prevented her from using magic? How?" There was a thrum from it, too, sort of like what he'd felt coming from the strix but not quite the same frequency.

"Best way to fight magic is with other magic," Carmen explained. "Also, in the future, don't go zipping off on your own. Do that again, rookie, and we won't come to save your ass."

Before Günter could apologize for his actions, Montenegro was snapping his fingers and pointing to the sky. Günter cocked his head and listened, catching the sound of large flapping wings before a screech similar to the strix's pierced through the night. The flapping grew louder until something was swooping down to land near them. When Carmen turned her flashlight on it, they saw a naked woman with wings for arms and a beaked nose. She looked a lot like the strix, except she had a woman's head instead of an owl's, and was the height of an adult human.

"*Branka?*" Günter yelled, confused to find her there. The curly brown hair gave her away, but she was otherwise unrecognizable with her features shifted to something crossed between human and avian.

Hearing her name seemed to throw her off a bit, and she stared at him wide-eyed before snarling, sharp teeth bared. "How could you?" she cried. "The Old Ones are sacred!"

"This *Old One* was a Treaty breaker," Carmen shot back, a sneer on her lips.

Branka reeled back in disbelief, then rallied herself and stepped closer. "That's impossible. She would never have broken Treaty law."

Günter was rather skeptical of that, considering how the strix had treated him. He also wasn't keen to believe Branka, considering the message she had slipped Lucy and the implications of where that put Branka's loyalty. "She was *eating kids*," he seethed, incredulous. "You can't honestly say that's okay."

Looking at him as though he were insane, Branka said, "Interesting how one predator speaks ill of another." Then her eyes seemed to flash in the low light. "Your information was wrong. She was innocent."

"The disappearances all happened within her territory's range," Carmen explained with more than a little exasperation.

"And no one else could do it, then, is that it? *That's* all the evidence you need?" Branka scoffed.

"Czar confirmed—"

"Ooooh, *Hayes* confirmed," mocked Branka. "Well, if the great Caesar Hayes says so, it surely must be true. Because he was certainly *never* wrong in the past, surely *never* punished anyone for a crime they didn't commit."

"Careful, Branislava," Carmen warned. "It sounds a lot like you're not very appreciative of all the Gehealdan does for you and your kind."

Branka's mouth opened and closed, her words having escaped her. "In fact," Carmen continued, "now that I think about it, didn't the rookies visit with you shortly before half of them turned traitor?"

Terror trickled across Branka's features, and she glanced pleadingly at Günter. Carmen read the fear easily and tilted her head as she drew her gun. "What exactly did y'all talk about, Branislava?"

"She told us how important the Gehealdan was, and how she and her kind owed a lot to us for keeping everyone safe in secrecy and maintaining order." The words were out of Günter's mouth before he even thought about it. All that flashed through his mind was his conversation with Jim about how they'd kill Branka if they suspected her of being involved with Eva and Lucy's defection.

Branka cast him a grateful glance, then stood taller, head held high. "He speaks true," she said, clear and proud. "You know I have always been a strong supporter of the Gehealdan. I've helped the Old Man out many times, you know this." Then she motioned with one long wing to the dead strix. "So you should know when I object to this, it is for good reason. She was *innocent*."

Carmen eyed her suspiciously for another moment, but then

slowly sheathed her gun. "Then who do you think was responsible?"

Looking around at the silent forest, as if making sure they were truly alone, Branka leaned closer and whispered, "I have heard things. Rumors. Children getting lured to water, the fins of sharks spotted in lakes and rivers."

"Sharks?" asked Günter, trying to figure out what that had to do with anything.

Carmen groaned and shared a look with Montenegro before focusing again on Branka. "You're buying into all that conspiracy theory junk, too? That suddenly, for no apparent reason, the Lamiae have just snapped and are gobbling up kiddies left and right?"

The shark fins made sense at that. Günter knew Lamia had been turned into a shark-like monster, and her children supposedly inherited the ability to change their appearances from that to a beautiful and enticing human at will. "A Lamiae has been sniffing around Jim," Günter told Carmen, heart racing at the implication.

Carmen's jaw clenched, and she looked between Günter, the corpse, Montenegro, and Branka. She seemed to consider something for a long while, until giving a tight nod and saying, "Branka, come by tomorrow afternoon. We'll sort this out civil-like, okay?"

All of the tension seemed to drain out of Branka, and she nodded back. "Fine. It would be good to put a stop to any malcontent in the streges community that may come about due to this...mistake."

Chapter 7
Chairman

"Shouldn't you be *un*packing?" Lucy had come to check in on Eva, only to find her stuffing things into a duffel bag beside a few of her weapons.

Eva gave a halfhearted smile. "Change of plans. Seems the Chairman hand-picked me to go on some sort of fact-finding mission with Uktena."

Lucy furrowed her brow. "You met him? Pulchrum mentioned him before, in that my father's second in Fenris only to him, but I haven't heard anything more about him or seen him since we arrived."

"No, the order was passed to me through Uktena."

"Oh." Lucy bit her lip, not really sure how she felt about any of this—of Eva going off on some mission as soon as she arrived, or how Fenris' leader had directly selected her. "Why so soon, though? You just got here."

With a shrug, Eva zipped up the bag and stood. "Some shady stuff is going down, and they think I'll be good at helping Uktena investigate."

"What about Krysti?"

"What *about* Krysti?" sighed Eva. "Ren will be able to give her more help than I can, plus she'll have all of you."

"But she needs you, too," Lucy objected.

There was a heartbreaking sadness in Eva's eyes when she smiled then. "She really doesn't."

Lucy opened her mouth, but couldn't think of what more to really say. Eventually, she just asked, "Is it dangerous? Whatever this mission is?"

Eva seemed to consider for a moment before shaking her head. "I don't think so. Like I said, it's just information gathering."

"Why you?" Lucy then hurried on to add, "I mean, yeah, you're absolutely badass, but there's gotta be a ton of people working for Fenris who could potentially do it. Let you settle in first."

"Maybe," Eva allowed, "but I don't mind that they asked me. I'm glad, actually. I like having something to do."

Yeah, Lucy could understand that. Honestly she had started to feel a little antsy herself. She wanted to train with her grandfather, but she hadn't even gotten a chance to meet him yet. Evidently he'd been out of town for a while, but would supposedly be back soon. So, really, Lucy just had to be a little patient. "Just be safe, okay?"

"Aw, where's the fun in that?" Eva smirked, then reached out and gave Lucy's shoulder a playful push. "Speaking of fun, I bet you're excited Shaggy-hair is here."

Lucy rolled her eyes so hard that her entire body moved with the motion. "Don't start."

"Whaaaat, I'm just saying."

"Well *don't* say it."

Eva sobered up and looked away. "Sorry. I know this isn't easy for you, either, even if you still have your family."

Oh, hell. Lucy pulled Eva into a tight hug, feeling arms wrap slowly around her in reciprocation. "I'm sorry," she whispered, heart feeling heavy at the thought of everything Eva had given up.

"Don't be," Eva insisted, quiet and fierce. "I can't even *think* about the alternative."

"Hey, Eva, have you seen—oh. There you are."

They turned to find Mick standing in the open doorway to

Eva's apartment, a lazy grin on his face. "Guess who's back from his business trip," Mick sing-songed, then waggled his eyebrows. "C'mon, it's time to meet a real Norse god."

Eva snorted. "Your *dad's* a Norse god, technically, you dork."

"Yeah, but he's not in any of the stories, really," Mick objected mildly, giving a little shrug. "Like, there's not even a Marvel character named after him."

"No, he only created my father's entire *species*," deadpanned Eva.

"Yeah, but, Eva," Lucy snarked, "that's not nearly as important as having super villains named after you. Which, wait." Lucy dropped her sarcasm and turned back to Mick. "Why are you even referencing *that*?"

"Honestly," he shot back, eyebrows raised, "I can't think of anything where he's *not* depicted as a villain."

"That...might be intentional," Eva explained hesitantly. "Like, my father's kind mostly pass down stories about Loki being a cruel trickster, but there are a few older tales of him being best friends with Odin, practically brothers. It might just be bad PR, after they had a falling-out."

"What was the falling-out about, though?" asked Lucy.

"A murder," answered another voice from the hallway. It was lilting and tinted with an accent that reminded Lucy a little of Dr. Kuntz's. They all turned to see a pale stranger with fiery orange hair that clashed with his red suit. He looked young but in a vague sort of way, Lucy unable to say with certainty whether he was twenty or forty. Likely, he was much, much older than he appeared, as Lucy suspected he wasn't at all human. There was just something in the way his tall, slender body carried itself, and the way his pale blue eyes seemed to shine brighter than the hall lights.

Mick's entire face lit up with a smile. "You're him, aren't you?" he asked, practically bouncing on the balls of his feet.

The stranger tilted his head in a nod, an amused grin playing at his thin lips. The motion revealed that his sunset hair was far longer than Lucy had originally thought, with thin braids slithering through the vibrant locks, all of which was held in check by only a simple leather cord. "I am your grandparent, Loki, yes." His wording was odd, but Lucy was willing to chock that up to language issues.

So that was Loki, Norse trickster god. Lucy blew up a car's engine because of the powers inherited from him. There were ancient carvings of him, stories thousands of years old, and there he stood...looking almost normal. It was difficult enough to try to figure out how she was supposed to react to meeting a grandfather she had never known, but one who was once considered divine? Should she bow or use formal speech? How was this done?

After everyone just stood there staring at him, Loki held his arms out to his sides and gave Mick an expectant look. "Can I have a hug?"

Mick laughed and threw his arms around Loki, rocking him a bit with the motion. Laughing along with him, Loki hugged Mick tightly and patted him heartily on the back. When they parted, Loki turned to Lucy and opened his arms invitingly. She hesitated for a moment, but then stepped around Eva to join Loki in the hall and hug him, too. "It is good to finally meet you, Lucy," he whispered into her hair.

"It's good to meet you, too, Grandpa." So the godliness didn't matter. He was family. That was all. Lucy smiled as her anxiety left her and she felt a sense of home settle in its place.

As they pulled back from the hug, he was looking at her with so much warmth and happiness. Then he looked over Lucy's shoulder at Eva, and his expression shifted to a polite smile. "You must be Eva," he said, reaching a hand out for her to shake. "I swung by here on my way to meet up with my family, because I wanted to catch you before you left. I'm sure you have your reservations working for me, considering how your father's clan perceives me. I thought I'd answer any questions you may have."

"Working for you?" Eva asked, face mirroring the shock Lucy felt.

Loki's eyebrows rose and his smile seemed to tilt in an almost mischievous grin. "Who did you think was the Chairman?"

"Wait, seriously?" Lucy asked, drawing Loki's attention back to her.

"You didn't know?" Now Loki seemed to be the confused one, and he looked between the three of them there, realizing that none of them had been told. "I thought surely Váli would have—" he broke off on a sigh and shook his head with an amused exasperation. "That boy. *Honestly.* He gets so easily distracted..."

While everyone seemed to still be processing it all—at least, Lucy definitely still was—Loki clapped his hands together and smiled wide. "In any case, I wanted to help assuage your concerns about me," he told Eva, slipping around Lucy to move a bit closer to the threshold.

"That's not necessary," Eva said quickly, looking worried that she might have offended him.

"Perhaps," he conceded with a little nod. "When I approached, it sounded like you already had it figured out." Then a smirk slowly spread across his lips. "For the most part."

"Ah," Eva said, smirking right back. "Bad PR?"

Loki reached out and tapped the tip of her nose, grinning. "Exactly. I was framed for a murder. After the true culprit was already punished, no less." He lifted his hands up in front of himself, spreading his fingers wide. "If you've heard the stories from before all that, you know I wasn't prone to such things. There was nothing to gain from Baldr's death, as far as I could tell. Höðr did it for whatever reasons he possessed. Jealousy, most likely. But Baldr was Váli's best friend, and I would never have put my son through such grief."

"Wait," Lucy broke in, glancing at her brother before pulling cautiously at Loki's arm. "Someone killed our dad's friend and then blamed you? And that's why you got a bad rap?" She could remember her father telling her stories about the death of Baldr, but he had never mentioned that little detail. Then again, she supposed that made sense, considering he hadn't been allowed to tell them the truth about who he was.

"Pretty much," Loki confirmed with a nod. "There's some complicated politics mixed up in it, but that's the basics. Oh," he added, turning to Mick, "and you're wrong about your father. He's in the stories, and there are *two* Marvel characters very loosely based on him, who both share his name."

Mick bounced a bit again. "Seriously?" he asked with a wide grin. "I'm totally looking into that later and finding whatever comics I can with both versions of him in them."

Again looking highly amused, Loki said, "Who knows, maybe someday they will make *you* a comic book character."

Eva snorted. "Why? *Lucy's* the one with spontaneous combustion powers."

"About that," Loki cut in before Mick could retort. He faced Lucy with a proud smile. "I look forward to helping you realize your full potential and have absolute mastery over your abilities."

Pride washed through Lucy, her face heating in what had to be a dark blush on her pale cheeks. "Me, too."

The intercom beside Eva's door suddenly buzzed, followed by Uktena's voice. "What's the hold up?"

Loki held up a finger for Eva to be quiet, then stepped inside the door and pressed the reply button, saying, "My fault, Agent, sorry. She's on her way."

"Sorry, sir," Uktena was quick to apologize. "I wasn't aware you were—"

"It's fine, Agent. Thank you for your patience, and may the both of you be safe on your mission."

"Mission?" Mick barked, incredulous. "Wait, Eva's *leaving*?"

"I'll explain on the way to Mom and Dad's," Lucy whispered, putting her hand on his chest to calm him. Then she turned to Eva as Loki stepped back out into the hall. "Will you have a phone with you? Can you call while you're out there?"

Eva looked to Loki for the answer, and he nodded. "In fact," said Loki, "I insist upon it. Not just so we can get up-to-date information, but also to ensure your safety."

With a quick nod, Eva thanked him, then moved to get her things. "I'll miss you," Lucy called after her.

Returning to the door, Eva smiled and pulled Lucy into a half-hug. "I'll miss you, too. But don't worry; I'll be back sooner than you think, I'm sure."

***

Fractured Masks

When they got to her parents' apartment, they were greeted at the door by a tall woman with striking, chiseled features and hair the color of snow at sunset. After her pale eyes took in the new arrivals, the woman moved aside with an effortless grace and warm smile. "Welcome," she said, soothing and kind.

I see you beat me here," Loki said to her in greeting, before leaning in to kiss her cheek.

Once they had all stepped inside, Loki turned and motioned to first Mick then Lucy, introducing them to the woman. "And this," he addressed his grandchildren, "is my amazing wife, Sigyn. She's as loyal as she is beautiful." He turned to look at her again, his eyes filled with adoration.

Sigyn held her arms out for a hug, much like Loki had earlier. "I'm so glad to meet you, my darling grandchildren." Both Lucy and Mick moved in for a hug at the same time, so they all squished together while Sigyn chuckled sweetly.

Once the hug ended, she took her husband's hand as she led them all deeper into the apartment. "We were just discussing how it would be advantageous to have Dr. Sartre stay next door, so he can be as close to Donnie as possible."

"Why would he need to—" Mick started to ask.

"He keeps the shadows away," Donnie said simply, as if that really explained anything at all.

"How?" asked Lucy, moving quickly to Donnie where he sat on the couch. She knelt in front of him and took his hands. "You mean the shadow that tells you things?"

Donnie nodded, but Lucy could hear the adults talking in hushed voices behind her. "He's not going to be able to do that for long," Loki was insisting with regretful tones. "He's already messaged me that he'll need to move to a more populous town soon, find more sources of sustenance. We can't just keep him confined in here."

"But without him, there's.... Father, Mother thinks it's someone from Hel."

"Hell?" Lucy yelled with a start, spinning back around to face the others.

Her mother quickly swept her up in a hug and pulled her down to sit between her and Donnie on the couch. "Not H-E-L-L, just H-E-L," Diana explained gently. "They think it's someone from the realm of the dead." Despite her efforts to comfort her daughter, Diana's voice shook a bit, and Lucy felt her hand trembling where it was resting on Lucy's arm.

"Like a ghost?" asked Mick, moving to join them, sitting on his mother's other side.

"Not quite," Sigyn offered with slow hesitance. "It isn't fully in this world. Also," she seemed even more reluctant to say her next words, "it is not alone. There are others."

"How long has this been going on?" Mick asked in shock.

"I think since I was born," Donnie said quietly. "He's always been there. Sometimes the others, too."

"And Ren makes them go away?" Lucy looked at her little brother, heart hurting at the tired sadness in his eyes. "I mean Dr. Sartre," she corrected. "He makes them go away?"

Donnie nodded. "I think they're scared of him."

"For good reason," Loki murmured under his breath.

Váli looked furious. "They should be afraid of *me*," he grit out between clenched teeth. "Shadows are *my* domain."

Which wasn't something Lucy had known. Come to think of it, she couldn't really recall having heard or read anything about what her father's place was in the pantheon of the Norse gods. All she knew was that he was considered one of the Æsir and he had created Dr. Kuntz's kind. But didn't gods typically have specific areas of focus? Was her father saying his was shadows? How did that even work?

Sigyn looked infinitely patient as she rested a hand on her son's arm. "I've explained, sweetling; they aren't actual shadow. They merely look like shadows to those who can see them."

"They need the darkness, though, do they not?" Váli looked to Donnie for confirmation, then waved his hand in a there-you-go motion upon receiving a nod. "See? He said that light keeps them away."

"And you aren't light, you are darkness," Sigyn corrected calmly. "What could you do, but to give them more room to lurk?"

Váli huffed in frustration and began to pace a little. "So why not simply set Sartre upon them?"

"In the state they are in, that would be akin to killing," explained Sigyn. "You know very well he cannot do such a thing."

When it looked like her son's frustration wasn't fading any, Sigyn offered, "I will look into it as best I can. There may be others in our organization who can help. I'm sure we'll find a way to banish them."

That at least seemed to placate Váli, and his shoulders lost some of their tension. "Thank you, Mother."

"Of course, dear. He is my grandson."

"Is any of this related to the other shadow-man that's haunted our house?" Lucy asked. She knew Donnie told her before that they were different, but this seemed like an opportunity to finally figure out what that thing was. She didn't buy for one second that it was the Black Dog that Branka had claimed it to be.

Diana's eyes were wide with fear at Lucy's words, and Mick just looked confused. Part of Lucy felt guilty for bringing it up in her mom's presence and giving her one more thing to worry about.

"What do you mean, Lucy?" Sigyn asked softly, tilting her head.

So Lucy told them about having heard something downstairs one night, and how she went to investigate. How whatever it was turned off the lights. Then how she'd had Eva over the next night, and the thing returned but didn't come inside. "It looked like a shadow just standing there outside," she explained, watching the realization dawn on her mother's face as she must have remembered that night with Eva. "Then immediately afterwards, it gave a really sad howl, and it nearly compelled Eva to return the howl. She had even partially shifted."

Loki looked like he was trying very hard to hold back laughter, Sigyn was pressing her lips tightly together to stop a smile, and Váli looked embarrassed. "Czar in the Gehealdan sent us to a striga," Lucy continued, eyeing her father and grandparents curiously, "and she tried to tell us it was a Black Dog."

A snort escaped Loki's restraint, and he had to turn away as he snickered. Váli cast him a dirty look, then sighed and turned back to face his wife and children looking like a man about to approach the gallows. "She wasn't exactly accurate in her assessment," Váli started, only to be interrupted by Loki.

"Well, she's not wrong."

After shooting his father a pointed glare, Váli cleared his

throat and tried again. "Whenever I could, I would try to visit."

Lucy could feel her mother tense beside her. "You what?" Diana asked, quiet and low.

Váli bit his lip, looking guilty as hell. "I missed you all, and so would try to visit in the night, whenever I could." When he saw his wife start to look somewhere between outraged and repulsed, he hurried on to say, "Only for a little bit. Only to check in and make sure everyone was safe."

"So you...all this time, you were near me and you *never* said..." Diana's voice was teetering on the edge of tears, and Lucy quickly took her mother's hand in comfort.

"I couldn't," Váli insisted. "We've discussed what would have happened had I made actual contact with you. All I could do was *see* you. I couldn't risk anything more, because the Gehealdan would have taken you all away from me for good. Or they'd—" Kill him. Lucy knew that leniency wasn't in the Gehealdan's vocabulary.

Diana stood up abruptly, Lucy's hand slipping away from hers. "I'm going to go have a visit with Dr. Sartre now. Donnie, would you like to come sit outside his room?" Trying to summon a smile, Diana turned to her youngest and held out her hand.

Donnie was quick to nod and stood, slipping his hand into hers. "Yes, thank you."

Looking devastated, Váli tried again to explain himself, but Diana just walked right past him. Donnie, at least, looked up at him in sympathy as they passed. As soon as the door closed behind them, Váli slumped where he stood and rubbed at his forehead.

"Well, I mean...Dad, you gotta admit that's kind of creepy of you," Mick said, leaning back into the couch.

"I thought you were a supernatural intruder who was going to kill us in our sleep," Lucy groaned, feeling a mixture of frustration and annoyance. "You scared the crap out of me!"

"You weren't meant to be awake," Váli objected. "No one was."

"Dad, that's even creepier," supplied Mick.

Sigyn gave a little sigh. "It's certainly not ideal. But as your father said, he had little choice. I cannot imagine how horrible it is to be separated for so long from those you love."

Loki, seeming to finally be over his giggle fit, stepped up to his wife and kissed her cheek. "So very true."

"Okay," said Mick, "then how do you think *we* felt?" He crossed his arms and eyed the others from over the frames of his glasses. "We thought he was *dead*."

Part of Lucy wanted to agree with Mick, to rage against her father for having put them through all of that hell, but she knew it wasn't his fault. "That's because of the Gehealdan, Mick. Not Dad."

Mick let out a frustrated sound and stood up. "I know," he practically snapped. Then he took a breath, walked up to Váli—who looked worried about what Mick might do—and pulled him into a tight hug. "I know," he repeated softly, sadly. "I hate them for it. For taking you away from us, for making it so you couldn't come back for real, making it so the best you could do was watch over us from the freaking shadows. I *hate* it."

Looking on the verge of tears, Váli wrapped his arms around Mick and held him close. "I hate it, too, Son."

Chapter 8
Muddled

"This is everything?" Dorian asked, taking the flash drive from Jim. At Jim's confirming nod, he tapped the plastic against his chin and offered a charming grin. "Beautiful."

Something niggled at the back of Jim's mind and his stomach felt tied up in worried knots. "Why do you need it?" Jim asked, fingertips tapping against his thigh as he stood there staring at the flash drive in Dorian's hand.

Dorian's grin melted into a sweet smile, and he danced his fingers down Jim's chest. "Never you mind that."

The contact sparked along Jim's nerves and made him feel a little dizzy. "It's just," Jim tried, though the words felt thick and clumsy on his tongue, "I don't see how any of it can be useful."

Letting out a little hum, Dorian caressed Jim's cheek and looked into his eyes. "Anything you can get me is useful," he corrected. "Just keep bringing me whatever the Old Man has you research, okay?"

"Sure," Jim nodded, unable to look away from Dorian's eyes to the point that he didn't even want to blink.

"Jim," Dorian purred, setting the flash drive on the table beside him so he had both hands free to run along Jim's torso. "I want to thank you for helping me like this. It really means a lot."

"Think, ah, think nothing of it." Honestly Jim forgot what they were even talking about. It felt as if he was seeing and hearing everything through a thick fog, his senses growing ever duller. The last thing he was fully cognizant of was a wide grin with too-sharp teeth.

***

When the world bled back into focus, Jim didn't know how much time had passed. He was just sitting in one of the chairs in his studio, not even sure why he was there. As he stood up, he felt something on his face, and his hand came away wet when he wiped at his cheek. For a long moment he just stood there staring at his hand, trying to figure out if he'd been crying and if so why.

There was no reason to cry.

Fine, but what had he just been doing? Maybe he'd gotten hurt, stubbed a toe...

No, he felt fine. Better than fine.

That wasn't true. Something felt off. Something felt—

Everything was alright.

Then why would he cry?

Cry? He wasn't crying.

Sure he was, he'd just rubbed his cheek and it was wet.

Was it? Maybe it was just sweat.

No...that wasn't...

Sure, that's all it was. It was hot in that studio, so of course he would sweat.

Right. No, right, that made sense.

Clearing his throat, Jim rubbed his hands together and looked around the room. He was there to work on his carvings, right? Of course he was. So he should probably get back to work on that.

Günter's statue would be first, since he had more work done on it. Walking around it, he tried to decide exactly where he wanted to focus first. It was still in the shaping stages, really. Turning to his table, he fetched his point chisel and the proper mallet.

When he turned back around to start on the statue, he stopped short. He was certain he'd been about to work on Günter's statue, but he found himself staring at Dorian's instead. Wait, *had* it been Günter's he was about to work on, really?

Well obviously not, he told himself with a scoff. After all, Günter's statue was way over there. Shaking his head at his silly little lapse, he got to work pitching off the unwanted bits. Honestly, where was his head? Must be all the stress of recent events, getting things all muddled in his mind.

*

Usually he was good to work for most of the day without a break, but that day he started feeling a bit peaky after barely two hours. Again, he figured it was just all due to the stress. He hadn't really been sleeping well, either. Kept having weird dreams, or just spent hours staring blankly at his dark ceiling, unable to quiet his mind.

Christ, he thought, *maybe I really should ask Czar about a shrink.*

Whatever, it was getting close to the time when Günter was coming 'round to pick him up, anyway. Might as well get cleaned up and ready. Just as he took a step to turn and set his tools back, a creaking sound drew his attention across the studio. Jim turned to spot the source, finding the door to a large cupboard open. It hadn't been a moment ago, had it?

Chisel and hammer gripped tightly, Jim cautiously made his way towards the cupboard. Holding in his breaths, he tried to be as quiet as possible. Not only did he not want to alert whatever it may be, but he also strained to hear any noises it might make. Once he was upon the cupboard, he braced himself before reaching his leg out and nudging the door further open with his foot.

Nothing.

Just a bunch of charcoal bits and large blocks of plastic-wrapped clay. Jim would laugh at himself, call himself a paranoid fool, except his skin was still prickled with gooseflesh and he couldn't shake the feeling of no longer being alone.

"That's it," he whispered to himself, hurrying to put his tools back and get the bloody hell out of there.

***

"Are you sick?" was the first thing Günter said to Jim when he picked him up.

"Well hello to you, too," Jim grumbled back as he buckled in. Then he sighed and leaned back into the seat. "Sorry, just... You're right, I'm not feeling well."

Not making any motion to drive away, Günter gave Jim a worried look. "Maybe you should stay home, then. I can tell Czar you're ill."

Jim thought about the cupboard, thought about black holes in his memories, and felt instinctively that he would be safer at World Street. "No, I want to go." He tried for a smile, but didn't feel like he fully succeeded. "Besides, my job's pretty easy. I just sit at a computer all evening."

Günter gave a relenting nod and started down Jim's long driveway. "How is that going, by the way?" asked Günter.

"Fine, I guess," Jim shrugged. "Last night I finally made it to this year's results."

"Oh yeah? Any noticeable patterns? Any particular supernaturals eating more kids than the rest?"

Mentally reviewing everything he'd researched the night before, Jim tried to spot a pattern or common culprit. "I don't think so. There are a *lot* of things that enjoy snackin' on wee ones, though. You know how we thought it was odd that the strigoi tends to prefer prey in the fifteen to twenty-five range? Well, let's just say I'm reassessing what I consider 'odd,' now."

Günter hummed, then asked, "What about water-dwelling folk? Any of them pop up in your results?"

"Yeah, a few," Jim said, thinking again of the research. "But not much within the last few years."

"Remember any of the kinds who were water folk?"

Jim squinted at Günter, sensing something in his far-too-casual tone. "Why?"

Günter just shrugged. "Last night we took out the strix, but then Branka arrived and said the strix had been innocent. She implied it was a water folk who was actually responsible."

"Ah," Jim nodded, catching on. "So you just wanted to see if maybe there were any specific water-type Pokemon it could be."

"Exactly. Yes."

"Alright, well, let's see," Jim started, mentally sifting through which results involved water. "Kappa, nixe, siyokoy, wihwin.... A few others, but I can't really recall. I suppose I can make a copy of my results and get them to you." He leaned back and lifted his hips, so he could have access to his pockets. "I have a flash drive I can use."

Günter kept glancing at him, then cleared his throat and focused on the road. "Why did you bring a flash drive?"

"I—" Jim stared at the drive in his hands, trying to remember why he'd brought it. "I'm not sure. Must have just had it on me for school stuff."

"You went to school today?" asked Günter. "That's good. Means you're doing better."

"No, I. I didn't, actually." There was a strange buzzing sound in Jim's head, so he opened his jaw and wiggled it around, trying to pop his ears and make it go away. It finally stopped, so he shrugged and lifted his hips again to pocket the drive. "In any case, shouldn't be too hard to snag a copy of my notes."

"Thanks," Günter rasped, then cleared his throat and tried again. "Thank you. That should help."

***

Czar stood there staring at Jim. Well, squinting, really. Analyzing Jim like one would a particularly vexing puzzle, more like. Jim just stared back, then spread his arms out and snapped, "What?"

"You feelin' alright, son?" Czar asked, cocking his head.

Groaning, Jim rolled his eyes and turned the chair back to the computer. "I'm fine, thanks. Just tired." He scrunched up his face. "I think I forgot to eat dinner, too."

"You do that art stuff, yeah? How's it goin'?"

What exactly was happening? Czar wasn't usually the chatty sort, and small talk definitely wasn't his bag. Jim would go along with it, though. Not like he really wanted to get on the old coot's bad side. "It's going well enough," Jim said slowly, side-eyeing Czar.

"Good," Czar nodded, then repeated, "Good." He continued to just stand there staring at Jim, before slowly releasing a breath out of his nose. "I want ya ta research all Lamiae registered within Georgia an' all surroundin' states. I want a list o' their names, addresses, vocations, an' any prev'ous addresses."

Lamiae? Wasn't that what Dorian had said he was? Jim couldn't quite recall. Whenever he tried to focus on the memory, it felt a little blurred. Well, in any case, he'd be finding out for certain in a moment when he searched the registry. As he went about clicking into the correct search feature, he asked over his shoulder, "Any reason we're looking up Lamiae specifically?"

There was a heavy, hesitant silence, before Czar finally responded, "Just some routine checks, based on incident reports from other regions." Oddly, Czar's accent seemed a little thinner in that moment.

Jim watched him from the corner of his eye, while he continued to type and search. As if made of stone, Czar just stood there beside the door and continued to stare at Jim. Nothing else was spoken between them, and Jim eventually tried to ignore the disconcerting presence.

Dorian's profile was one of the first Jim came across, and he dutifully copied all of the information while keeping his features schooled. Czar didn't need to know that Jim was familiar with one of the people on the list, especially if the Lamiae were under any sort of suspicion. After all, Jim was already on probation; the last thing he needed was to be connected with any other insurgent groups. Still, he made a mental note to ask Dorian about all of this the next time they met up for a modeling session.

An hour into his research, Jim got up to use the loo and realized with a start that he was alone in the room. His attempts at blocking Czar out must have worked better than he'd realized, because he couldn't recall ever seeing the old man leave. Shaking himself out of his initial shock, Jim slipped out of the room and headed down the hall.

Different supernatural creatures watched his progress from where they were painted upon the doors. As much as Jim admired the technical quality of the artwork, he rather hated the subject matter. It always made walking down that hallway feel a bit creepy, like something from a bizarre nightmare. Any minute, one of those creatures would come to life and jump out at him. Just the thought gave him the willies, and he quickened his pace.

No one was in the little computer room when Jim returned, which helped put him at ease. The next few hours were to be filled with tedious work, but at least he wouldn't have the added stress of a giant, scarred white man looming over him.

***

"Here," Jim offered, holding the flash drive out to Günter after getting dropped off at home. The car ride had been unusually quiet and tense, but Jim couldn't really complain. He felt dead on his feet and wanted nothing more than to crawl into bed and sleep for a year.

Günter looked at the drive for a moment before reaching across the seat and taking it. Their fingers brushed, and usually Jim would feel a warm tingle from something like that involving Günter, but all he felt was tired. "Thanks," said Günter, looking down at the plastic rectangle before meeting Jim's eyes. "Are you sure you're alright?"

"Yeah, I'm gonna head right to bed," Jim yawned. "Get some sleep. I'll be fresh as a daisy tomorrow, promise."

For some reason, Günter didn't look reassured. His expression was pinched and worry was practically radiating off of him. "If you ever need anything, call. Don't hesitate, okay? No matter what time it is. Promise me." There was a strange insistence in Günter's voice, an intensity that startled Jim.

"Yeah, sure," Jim agreed, brows coming down in confusion. "Why, what's up?"

Günter studied Jim's face for a moment before dropping his gaze. "Phil thinks he knows what the next wave involves, but Czar says it's still too early to know for sure. I can't really go into details, because Czar said I'm not allowed. Just...be alert, alright? If you notice *anything* strange at all, *please* call me." He looked back up at Jim, and something in his eyes made Jim's heart lurch. Those were the eyes of someone who felt powerless to stop something horrible, and it was killing him.

"Am I in danger?" Jim asked in an anxiety-tense whisper.

His question looked to have Günter cringing, despite the stoic rigidity of his expression. "Hopefully not."

"What does that mean?" hissed Jim, leaning back into the SUV. "What aren't you telling me?"

Günter just answered Jim's question with another question. "What's on this drive?"

Angry at the diversionary tactic, Jim snapped, "Local Lamiae. Czar had me look up details on all of them in the region."

"Exactly," Günter said softly, trying again to communicate

something purely with his eyes.

Jim drew back, tempted to just slam the door. "Not this again," he seethed. "Look, it doesn't matter what Dorian is; he's been nothing but decent to me. He's been coming over the past few days and modeling, and nothing's happened."

"Fine," Günter relented, making a slow, downward motion with his free hand. "I'm just saying to stay cautious. If Lamiae are stirring up trouble—"

"You said it was a strix."

Günter paused, then sighed and ran a hand back through his long hair before turning in his seat to face out the windshield. "That might have been a mistake."

"A *mistake*?" Jim felt like his eyes might pop right out of his skull. "You mean to tell me that you lot might have executed a completely innocent strix?"

Closing his eyes, Günter gave a small nod. "Possibly."

Jim inhaled deeply and tried to clear his head. This was all a bit too much for him to handle at the moment. "Fine, sure, I'll be careful around Dorian, but I don't think it's necessary."

"And call if—"

"—Anything weird happens, yeah. I got it. Goodnight." Jim pulled away from the Sequoia and shut the door before Günter could respond.

Load of bollocks.

Chapter 9
Web

"You know, I could do some of the driving," Eva offered flatly, rolling her head away from the window to instead arch a brow at Uktena.

He made a shrug-nod. "And you will. Eventually. When I'm tired."

Snorting, Eva turned back to the window. "Sure."

"We'll be stopping soon," he said calmly. "You can drive tomorrow."

"Right." As if he wouldn't be the Dictator of Drive again.

"Look," he sighed, "I know this isn't a fun adventure for you, but there's no reason we can't get along."

"We *are* getting along," she droned back. "Look at us. Couple of old pals, yucking it up."

"You didn't have to come."

"Thought you wanted me to come."

"I did," he agreed, flicking on his blinker and checking his mirrors. "I do. Your avian nature aside, I feel I can trust you at my back."

"My—what is *that* supposed to mean?"

Uktena pressed his lips tightly together, eyes focused on the dark road as he took a sharp-curving exit. "What I am...well, we don't really get along well with a few of the bird folk."

She studied his profile in the darkness. They were well beyond where any streetlights existed, and she was tempted to shift her eyes to those of a wolf so she could better see him. Part of her was afraid to, however, frightened of the possibility that she'd mess up and shift to tengu eyes. The memory of Tahchat preventing her from turning to look at Uktena always left her feeling uneasy. What would she have seen? What would she see then, in that moment, if she dared to look past his illusions?

"What are you?" she asked in a whisper.

"Uktena," he replied back, as he always did.

Eva finally realized what he meant, though. Unlike Tahchat, he wasn't something that humans knew. There was no non-supernatural equivalent to what he was. "What exactly is an Uktena, then?"

His lips twitched into something like a smile. "It is what the Cherokee call my kind."

"So you don't go by an actual name? That's like my mom naming herself Tengu."

Uktena chuckled softly. "It is a bit, yes. But many of the folk from this continent just go by what they are. Mostly because that's just what humans call us. Though some are like Tahchat and pick actual names for themselves." He tossed her a slanted grin and wink. "All I have to do is use the Cherokee term for what I am, however, and most American's won't know it's not just a name."

Huffing a little laugh, Eva smirked back at him. "Nice. So tell me about your folk."

Tapping his fingers on the wheel, he made a thoughtful hum. "Water snakes. Large. They call us horned snakes, but it's really more like antlers."

"And you don't typically get along with birds."

"Certain birds," he corrected with a tip of his head.

"Why didn't Tahchat want me to see you in your true form?"

At first he didn't answer, just seemed to instead focus all of his attention on pulling off into an old, rundown motel. It was only once he'd parked and turned the Range Rover off that he finally replied. "It can be...unlucky...to look at an Uktena."

"Unlucky."

"Deadly."

"Ah." Eva nodded. Great. So. She was on a long road trip around the country with a giant snake that could potentially kill her if she accidentally looked upon his true form. "So, are we staying here tonight?" she asked with obviously false cheer.

**

God, what a shithole. Still, she supposed it was best to keep a low profile. They got the same room, two twin beds. The guy at the desk didn't live up to any TV clichés of insinuating they were a couple, so that was a relief. Didn't change the fact that Eva could smell just how rarely the bedspreads were cleaned, and hear rats scurrying in the walls.

"I think I'd almost prefer sleeping in the car," she muttered while checking out the parking lot from between a thin gap in the curtains.

Uktena laughed from where he was brushing his teeth at the sink. He spit and rinsed before replying. "Before this is over, we just might be doing that a few times."

"Awesome. This mission just keeps getting better." Satisfied that the parking lot was clear of any potential tails, she turned back to face the rest of the room. "So what's our game plan?"

"Get up at dawn and drive some more. We should reach our destination by late afternoon. Then we talk to some locals around the main bodies of water in the area. See if any of them saw the convicted Lamiae actually spending time in the water or around children." Uktena leaned out of the bathroom and added, "I might have to actually get in the water. If so, I'll need you vigilant on the shore, in case of attack."

Eva nodded as if receiving an order instead of a suggestion. "I'll cover you."

He eyed her, then straightened up and stepped back into the main room. "I'm pretty resistant to most charms and enthralling magic, but if it looks like I start to succumb..." Words seemed to escape him for a moment, before he looked back at her with renewed resolve. "Kill whatever charmed me, and that should break the spell. If I try to stop you, do whatever you can to incapacitate me. Preferably leaving me alive."

After waiting a short pause to make sure there was nothing more, Eva gave another firm nod. "Should I be concerned about your bite?"

Uktena raised a brow at that, then seemed to think on it for a moment. "I'm not sure how it will affect your physiology. Best to not let it get to the point where that's tested."

Suddenly Eva missed the days when all she did was fly lookout while the others dispatched the target. Well, at least she'd been training her whole life to be able to deal with this sort of crap.

***

"This place reeks." Eva tried holding her breath, but gave up and just covered her nose with her sleeve instead.

Giving a big, deep whiff, Uktena made a considering sound

before nodding. "Yeah, that's not normal."

"You *think*?" Jesus, she felt like she was going to puke.

Despite the stench, Uktena insisted they kept heading towards the lake. The closer they got, the stronger the stench, until Eva could barely breathe. All around them was the sound of buzzing flies. Just when the lake was in view, Uktena froze, holding his hand out to Eva in silent command to stop.

"What is it?" she whispered, muffled by her shirt sleeve.

Instead of answering, Uktena shook his head and motioned back down the path the way they came. Eva was all too glad to follow that order, moving as quickly away from the stink as possible.

It wasn't until they reached their vehicle when Uktena finally explained, "I don't think I'll need to take a swim there, because I'm fairly certain the culprit wasn't a water-dweller." There was a tightness around his eyes and a tension in his posture. Still, there was no scent of fear. Eva was starting to believe she'd never smell it on him.

"So you know who was actually behind the child abductions?" Eva asked, looking back towards the path.

"There was a boulder covered in flies," said Uktena, as if that explained anything at all. While he wasn't scared, he did seem a little spooked. Still, he made no move towards getting into the Range Rover. Eyes scanning the trees, he muttered, "But that doesn't even make sense. This is too far from where she should be."

"Who?" Eva demanded, smacking her palm on the side of the SUV to get his attention.

For a second, his eyes were bright and opalescent, the pupils slit like a snake's. "She is called U'tlun'ta, and she typically stays in the Appalachian Mountains, within the territory of the Cherokee."

Which would explain how he'd recognized her so easily, Eva figured, if they were from the same region.

"Then what the hell is she doing in *Missouri*?"

"That's what I don't know," Uktena shot back with mild annoyance. He seemed to spot something in the trees, and started walking towards it at a fast clip. "We might be able to find out, though."

Staying on alert, Eva followed and kept her hand on the gun at her hip. They were barely back into the forest before Uktena was coming to a stop at a large spider web about waist high. "Tse-xo-be," he called gently. "Honorable Tse-xo-be, I am a traveler from the east."

"I know who you are, serpent," came a soft, feminine voice.

Uktena smiled as a large spider crept out from the shadows. Its body was shaped a bit like a black-and-yellow light bulb with long, dark legs sticking out from it. "I am tired," the spider sighed. "Cold. So cold."

"I know, ma'am," Uktena agreed with the appropriate amount of sympathy. "My kind is sensitive to the chill, as well."

"What do you want, serpent?" asked the spider.

"Have you seen a woman? Old and bent, looking like the humans who used to live here before, when you were still called Tse-xo-be, when you were their symbol." His eyes tracked the threads of the web and then he added, "She would have brought many flies."

"There is an old woman who brings flies," the spider confirmed, her voice sounding weak and sleepy. "She came just after I found my mate. I remember. Human children follow her to the pond, but they never come back."

"Have any children been by recently?" Uktena asked.

The spider took a moment to reply, then sighed out lethargically, "No. No, not since my eggs were all snug. None since then." Her spindly legs made infinitesimal movements on the delicate silk threads, so that Eva couldn't tell if it was the spider or merely the wind.

"And what about a younger human woman? She would have had curly hair the color of the sun, and skin nearly like my own. I am told she sings with a voice so beautiful that it makes the very trees sway in time. Have you seen such a woman come here?"

It took even longer for the spider to reply to his new questions. Eva started to wonder if the spider had simply fallen asleep, until the tiny voice finally answered, "Once, I heard of such a woman visiting the water. The birds were chattering on about her voice and how they hoped she would come again soon."

"And did she?"

"No," sighed the spider. "If she did, I heard no more about it from the birds."

"Thank you, ma'am," said Uktena, packing so much respect into those three simple words. "I'll leave you to your rest."

When he cast Eva a pointed glance, she was quick to duck her head in a small bow and say, "Yes, thank you."

"So polite," murmured the spider, sounding pleased despite her lingering sleepiness. Then she worked her way back up her web, looking like a large drop of water trickling in reverse.

Nothing else was said until they were back at the Range Rover, and then Eva eyed Uktena and asked, "So are we going to just leave her here?"

"Who? The spider?"

"No, Utl—the woman who brings flies and evidently was the

one eating children." There had to be a way to kill her, right? Everything had a weakness.

Uktena took a deep breath in through his nose, as if bracing himself for something. "I don't think there's any need to engage her in combat."

"What, are you scared?" Eva asked, scoff in her tone. Maybe she'd read him wrong earlier. Maybe he was more than just a little shaken. "Just what exactly are we dealing with, here?"

When he met her eyes, his expression was calm and serious, not a hint of fear about him. "We're not dealing with anything here, because we're leaving. Remember, our primary objective is information retrieval. You want to go around slaughtering people, you should have stuck with the Gehealdan."

Objections formed and died on her tongue as the indignation washed over her. "Back at the room, we talked about—"

"Worst-case scenarios, and killing as a last resort. Not rushing onto the scene, guns blazing, wiping out anyone who may have done wrong."

"But we know—"

"All we have is speculation. There is no irrefutable evidence that proves U'tlun'ta is the one who killed those children. Do I think it's more likely it was her instead of the executed Lamiae? Yes, absolutely. But it is not my place to kill her, especially based purely on my assumptions." He stared her down, and Eva felt an almost instinctual urge to dip her head in submission. Stubbornly she fought against the reflex, even as her cheeks burned in shame. "Besides," he continued, "she stopped."

"But how do you know she won't start again?" Eva insisted.

"We don't. Though don't you think it's interesting that she

stopped right around when the Lamiae was killed?" There was too much weight to his words for Eva to do anything other than silence all her other thoughts and focus entirely on his implied meaning.

Thinking back on the spider's words, Eva tried to compare it to the reports she read on the road. "She said the children stopped coming when her eggs were ready. When would that be?"

"For that particular species, here, in this climate?" Uktena looked back towards where they'd found the spider. "It typically happens in the summer or early autumn. Before the chill sets in."

"And the Lamiae was executed in August," Eva said, clicking the pieces into place. "So, what, do you think it was planned? That the Lamiae was framed?"

Uktena pressed his lips together, then reached for the door handle. "We won't be able to know for sure until we get more information. C'mon," he prompted, opening the door. "Tomorrow we'll head out to where the second execution took place."

With a put-upon sigh, Eva got into the SUV. "I don't suppose we can catch a plane to Montana instead of drive all the way there?" she asked, already resigned to knowing the answer.

"Nope." And there it was.

She groaned and leaned her head back against the seat. "I've just been on the road so much lately. My spine is going to permanently have a crick in it." To illustrate her point, Eva wiggled a bit in her seat in a futile attempt to get comfortable.

Uktena just chuckled and started the car. "Let's hope discomfort is the only thing we have to worry about on this trip."

Despite the levity in his voice, Eva knew he was right. She couldn't shake the feeling that they were lucky this time. If Uktena hadn't recognized the signs soon enough, it might have turned out differently. "Tell me about her," Eva eventually whispered. "Tell me about the woman who attracts flies."

After a little nod, Uktena said, "In English they call her Spearfinger. The index finger of her right hand is long and sharp, and she uses it to kill people—typically children—and cut out their livers."

"So she doesn't eat people whole? Then, if she's behind the disappearances, where are the bodies?"

"They're not usually found, where she's concerned. U'tlun'ta always hides the bodies."

"Is that the source of the stench?"

His lips twitched in something almost a smile. "No. She just stinks."

"And the rock? You said there was a rock covered in flies."

"She *is* the rock."

Well. Eva supposed she'd heard stranger things. "Shape-shifter?"

"Shape-shifter," Uktena agreed with a nod.

Chapter 10
Choked

    Günter couldn't believe he'd forgotten his lab notes in his car. Luckily the parking garage wasn't too far, so he could just pop over, grab them, and be back in time. Switching direction to head to the bridge that linked to the garage, Günter walked right into a long, hollow room. He stopped short, confused about how he'd gotten so turned around. There was something familiar about the room, but it didn't look like any of the classrooms or labs he'd ever seen in Whitehead or any other building on campus.

    Turning around, Günter found only a wall behind him. When he spun back to the rest of the room, he realized there were no doors. A few windows stretched tall in places, light pouring in that was too blinding to be able to see any features of the outdoors. Flooded with this bright light, the room itself was a featureless blur of white. Movement at the end of the room caught Günter's attention, and he squinted through the glare in an attempt to get a better look.

    Whatever it was, it quivered like a mirage, growing only vaguely more distinct as it moved closer. He thought perhaps it was a person, or at least the suggestion of a person. Suddenly the light from the windows began to flicker like strobes with discordant rhythms. The person-thing seeming more solid in the broken light, and a dread seeped into Günter's bones.

    The windows at the far end of the room went black, and the flickering slowed until the other windows were all stuck at half-light. Moving ever closer, the person-thing looked rippled and distorted, like viewing someone just below the surface of dark water. Günter didn't know what it was, but he knew with absolute certainty that he didn't want it to touch him. He tried to shift his body, tried to bring to the surface talons and fangs and eyes that see well in the dark.

Nothing happened.

It was as if his body were simply the same as any human's. Fear clutched him and he tried to breathe through it while he thought of his options. There was nothing in the room that he could see to be able to use as a weapon. Maybe he could make a break for one of the windows, but their weird light show made him reluctant to try that idea.

"Who are you?" he yelled. Or, well, he tried to yell it. No sound came out of his mouth, no matter how hard he tried to talk or scream or even howl. A strange, muffled, high-pitched sound started, disorienting him and making him shake his head.

All the while, the person-thing moved closer. In its wake, the windows would blink out into total blackness, turning what had seemed like a large room into something small and claustrophobic. The person-thing's shape became more distinct, even if its body didn't seem to be entirely solid.

Vainly trying to put more distance between himself and the thing, Günter stepped back until he was pressed against the wall. Still the thing advanced, the darkness growing beyond it. Günter didn't know what would happen when it touched him, but he knew it couldn't be anything good.

All too soon, the thing was past the last windows, all light snuffed out in the room. It was so dark that even *if* Günter had been able to shift his eyes to those of a wolf's, he'd not be able to see anything. He tried waving his hand in front of his face to no avail. A rare and crushing sense of helplessness seized him, and he felt like crying. It was like being a child again—powerless, ignorant, and scared.

Something brushed against him, and it felt cold and slick like wet flesh. He jerked away, pressing himself as flat as possible against the wall. The thing simply moved with him, until he could feel it all along his body. Then it grabbed at his face, forced his jaw open, and *flowed* into his mouth. It tasted of saltwater and blood, and Günter began choking as it poured down his throat. He tried to cough it up, but that somehow just got it into his nasal cavity, so he couldn't even breathe through his nose.

Somehow he was drowning while standing upright in a dark room, something unidentifiable caging him in against a wall. Of all the ways Günter thought he might die, that had never been even at the bottom of the list. Pushing at the thing was useless, Günter's strength now human-weak and growing weaker by the moment. His lungs burned, his heart racing with the desperate need to breathe.

"Günter?" a voice hissed at his ear, killing the high-pitched noise so that the room was suddenly disturbingly quiet. It couldn't be the thing, he knew. There was too much concern in the voice for it to belong to his killer.

"Günter, breathe," urged the voice. "Count with me. In, one two three..."

With how dark the room was, Günter hadn't even realized he'd closed his eyes until he was blinking them open against the jarring brightness of a familiar hallway. Gone was the dark room, and instead of a cold wet thing at his front, there was only a warm body at his side.

"There you go," the voice encouraged, and Günter was alert enough to realize it belonged to his friend, Tayisha. They were both crouched on the floor in the middle of the hall, her hand rubbing soothing circles on his back while her dark eyes studied his face with worry and determination. With his vision a little hazy, the soft, tight curls of Tayisha's wild hair seemed almost like a halo to him. Though, she *had* probably just saved his life, swooping in like a guardian angel.

Slowly, his lungs started to do what they were supposed to, taking in the proper amount of air and slowly releasing it back out. Tayisha nodded, smiling hesitantly as he calmed.

Just what exactly happened? Had he been asleep, and it was all just a nightmare? But he'd been so certain that he was awake just moments before it started. He was at school, about to begin his last lab of the day. Then he was going to go pick Jim up to go to the shop, and—*Jim*.

Something was wrong with Jim. Günter could feel it with so much certainty that it almost sent him into a panic attack. Or, well, judging from the way Tayisha was acting towards him, *another* panic attack. "I have to go," he rasped, his throat feeling as if he really had been choking on saltwater. "I have to—" He stumbled a little as he stood, and for a moment worried it meant he still had a human body. Allowing his fangs to grow while still facing away from Tayisha, Günter comforted himself in something he'd never found comforting before. There was nothing human about him.

"You *need* to sit down and relax," objected Tayisha, straightening up and reaching out as if to steady him if he needed it.

Günter just shook his head and fumbled in his pockets for his phone. "No," he insisted, "I have to go." Then he caught himself and turned back to give her a quick hug. "Thank you," he whispered with absolute sincerity. Part of him feared she may have saved his life, and he'd still be in that terrifying room if she hadn't come along.

Hugging back, Tayisha asked, "What happened? Are you okay?"

"I don't know," he replied honestly. "But that's why I need to leave. I need to check on someone."

She pulled back to study his face, then gave a reluctant nod. "I'll tell Dr. Misra."

Managing a smile for her, Günter gave her another quick hug before he was off towards the parking garage again. He called Jim as he ran, but it just rang until it went to voicemail. Panic growing, he kept trying, each attempt ending the same way. When he reached his SUV, he paused long enough to pull up Czar's contact info and try him instead.

Thankfully, there were only two rings before Günter was greeted by Czar's gruff voice. "Jim's in trouble," said Günter by way of salutations. "I can't reach him, so I'm going to head to his house. Can someone meet me there?"

Silence responded for a frustratingly long time, Günter using the break to retrieve his keys and get in and start up the Sequoia. "Why do ya think he's in trouble?" Czar eventually asked, tone carefully even.

"Something happened. A daymare or something, I don't know. A vision." He switched the phone to speaker and set it in his lap as he pulled out of his spot and began navigating the parking garage.

"An' this vision was about Jim?"

Günter made an impatient sound. "Jim wasn't in it, but I know it's about him."

"How?"

"I just *do*."

Czar exhaled in either impatience or frustration. "Fine," he relented, "I'll send someone over."

Even though he still felt his stomach in knots, Günter felt at least a little bit of his tension ease at the offer. "Thank you. I'm heading that way now, but I'm down at Emory."

"Drive safe, son," Czar ordered before hanging up.

It was just before five, and Günter cursed as he realized he'd likely be running into the early rush hour traffic. For a moment he was seriously tempted to just pull over, shift into a hawk, and fly. Never mind that it would mean he'd be naked when he got there, or that someone could spot him transforming. None of that really seemed to matter to him in that moment, his hands gripping the wheel so tightly it creaked and his throat so tense he felt like he was still choking from the vision. He didn't think he'd be able to forgive himself if he got there too late, and Jim was injured.

*

Montenegro was already there by the time Günter finally arrived. He just stood in the driveway, arms crossed, eyes squinting against the dropping sun as he kept watch over the area. Günter actually wished that Czar would have sent Phil or Carmen, since their expressions were easier to read. Looking at Montenegro in that moment, Günter had no idea what to expect once he got out of the car.

"Is he okay?" Günter demanded, spilling out of his Toyota as soon as it was in park.

Dark eyes studied him quietly for a moment, before Montenegro looked away and simply said, "Go check on him yourself, first. Then we'll talk."

That did absolutely *nothing* to ease Günter's nerves. He was practically growling as he rushed past Montenegro towards the house and beyond it to where Jim's studio stood. Before he even opened the door, Günter drew up short when he detected a lingering scent of ocean water. His tongue swiped along the roof of his mouth, as if chasing the taste of saltwater from the vision.

Inside, Jim was standing at a huge block of marble with only a few chunks chiseled out of it so far. A mallet and chisel were held limply in hands that dangled at Jim's sides, and his expression was disturbingly blank. Approaching cautiously, Günter reached a hand out just shy of touching Jim's shoulder and gently called out to him.

As if just snapping out of a daze, Jim blinked and turned to properly face Günter. "Hey," he started, then he blinked again and a bit of a smile found its way on his lips. "Sorry, I guess I was too caught up in my work. Didn't realize it was time for you to come pick me up."

A new dose of fear and worry stabbed through Günter, and he took a few steps closer. "No, I'm early," he explained, trying to keep his face and voice calm and casual. "I tried to call, but..."

Jim frowned at that and looked over at where his phone sat on a nearby table. "Had you? I guess my ringer's off, sorry."

"That's fine." Günter moved closer still, trying to subtly sniff for any telling scents. He nearly jerked back in surprise at what he picked up. Something inside pricked painfully before feeling as if it shriveled and began to rot. "Guess you didn't want the phone to interrupt you and your...boyfriend?" The word tripped uncomfortably off Günter's tongue, and he took a few steps back. There was an overpowering scent of sex clinging to Jim, and it felt invasive to be close enough to smell it.

Jim just stared at him like he'd gone insane. "What are you talking about? I'm not seeing anyone. Or, well," he paused, looking off to the side as he thought. "I mean, Dorian's been coming over to model, and we talk a lot. And, ah," he cleared his throat with an awkward nervousness and moved towards a table to set his tools aside while not meeting Günter's eyes. "We also kissed a few times. So I guess we might be an item, or working our way to it."

"I'd say you were up to way more than kissing," Günter shot back, angling for lighthearted teasing even if it felt like sticking a blade in his gut and slicing himself open to spill out upon the floor.

With a snort, Jim turned back around to face him and leaned his butt against the table. "Not that it's any of your business, but the furthest I've gone with *anyone* is a bit of heavy petting," said Jim. Which, wait, how could that even be? At Jim's age, Günter had been so far into the closet he smelled of mothballs, but he'd already slept with two different guys. Jim was out and proud and ridiculously attractive. How in the hell were guys not throwing themselves at his feet?

Reading his confusion, Jim rolled his eyes. "Don't give me that look," he groused. "I'm very selective, and my high school is filled with idiots."

"No, I'm not judging," Günter quickly tried to explain. "It's just...surprising. I'd have thought you'd have a horde of admirers."

Jim bit his lip and ducked his head, red peeking through his dark skin to make his cheeks glow. "Who knows, I might," he said through a pleased little smile. "I just haven't found any to be interesting enough to keep my attention."

Günter almost found himself smiling back, until he

remembered the very distinct smell. "But, so you and Dorian are together now?"

The pleasure vanished from Jim's smile, and the healthy glow he'd been sporting faded until his dark skin was almost ashen. "Yeah, I guess we are."

"And you both engaged in some—um—heavy petting?" Günter asked, brows rising. It smelled like they engaged in considerably more than that, though. And Günter really wanted to stop talking about this or thinking about it or *smelling* it. Jesus.

All of the friendliness from moments before was eradicated, Jim glaring and pushing away from the table to move and put distance between them. "Again, not your business. And again, no."

Wrong. That was wrong. Günter knew it was wrong. Why was Jim lying to him? Though it didn't seem like Jim *knew* he was lying. There was no stutter to his heartbeat, no stench of nervous sweat. The only things he gave off were anger and frustration and the clinging telltale scents of sex.

"Fine," Günter relented, then headed towards the door. "I'll be in the car out front. Shower or whatever, then come out when you're ready." And it was as he said it that he realized Jim had been freshly-showered the past two times Günter had come to pick him up. Maybe this wasn't the first day Jim and Dorian had...

Günter pushed the thought from his mind, but then stopped short at the door. He slowly turned his head and took in the entirety of the studio. It was large, white, with tall windows. The vision had been of that place, its details bleached out by light or swallowed in darkness.

Forcing back a surge of bile in his throat, Günter fled. He headed right to Montenegro, needing some sort of explanation to all the madness. "Okay, spill," Günter demanded, storming up to Montenegro. "What the hell is going on?"

For the first time Günter could remember, Montenegro openly displayed emotion on his face. Unfortunately, it was something along the lines of pained regret. "You really should talk to Czar about this, not me," he said, instead of answering Günter's question.

"Well, Czar's not here and I'm asking *you*." He was scared and angry, and he knew from experience that those were a bad combination for him. Eva had always been better at control than Günter, better at hiding what they were no matter how emotionally strained. Günter? Well. There was a reason he strove for stoicism. Even though he wasn't terribly good at that, either.

Montenegro's expression became shuttered again, but he at least nodded. "I honestly don't know all of the details," admitted Montenegro. "All I know is that a shark is involved with Jim, and we are not to interfere."

"A shark? Dorian?" Lamiae had the ability to enthrall someone, and if Dorian was using that on Jim, Günter was going to *kill* the aquatic bastard. "And why can't we interfere?"

"I don't know his name, and because Czar commands."

"Is this why Czar told me I couldn't tell Jim about the Lamiae investigation? Wait, is Dorian hurting Jim and Czar knows? Is Dorian *forcing* him? Using his power to—" Günter couldn't say it, feeling sick at merely the thought.

Again an emotion flickered across Montenegro's face—a sad cringe. "I don't know all of the details, like I said. We are told only as much as we need to know."

"So then do you really think it'll do me any good to talk to

Czar?" Günter asked, a helplessness seeping in to mix with his anger and dread.

Montenegro seemed to consider for a moment before simply saying, "He is a fair man."

Honestly, Günter wasn't so sure he believed that anymore.

Chapter 11
Prophet

As Loki led Lucy through the halls of Fenris, something about the place poked at her mind. It seemed familiar somehow, but she couldn't quite place it. Then they passed an intersection, and Lucy froze on the spot as it finally hit her. Trembling, she slowly turned to look down the intersecting corridor. For a moment reality overlapped with memory, and she saw herself down that hallway, a feral beast feasting upon the corpses of her brothers.

Loki gave her a concerned look and placed his hand gently upon her shoulder. "What is the matter?"

"I saw this place in a dream. A nightmare."

He frowned at that and turned his head to follow her line of sight. There was nothing there, however, except gleaming marble and glass. "A premonition?" Loki asked softly.

Lucy shook her head. "I don't know. Maybe." God, she hoped not.

The hand on her shoulder gave a little squeeze. "I should like to hear of this dream. Premonitions speak in symbols, and perhaps I can help in deciphering them."

Nodding, Lucy tore her gaze away from the empty hallway to look up at Loki's face and nod. "I saw myself, and I was feral," she started, doing her best to keep her voice and heart steady as she intentionally dredged back up the memory of that dream. "Like a ravenous beast." She looked back to the spot from her dream and continued softly, "I was right there, eating Mick and Donnie." A lump formed in her throat and she tried to swallow past it, the choking sensation reminding her of the more recent cannibalistic dream. Her stomach flipped and she swayed a bit as a wave of nausea hit.

Loki rubbed her shoulder, but said nothing, just showing support as he waited for her to continue. His presence helped to ground her so that she wouldn't get lost in the horrific memories.

"I was scared of her. Of me. So, I ran." Looking back towards the direction they were heading, she tried to remember if it looked the same as the hallway she ran down in her dream. "Shadows rose up to try to grab at me. There were statues of gods and they were crumbling and screaming. Mirrors on the walls kept showing the feral version of myself as I ran, and her world was consumed in fire."

Taking a few breaths, Lucy then concluded it with, "There was a deafening whisper. Someone saying 'Soon.'"

"Did it sound male or female?" Loki asked, face serious and bright eyes intent.

"Female, I think," said Lucy, though she wouldn't be able to swear to it.

"Interesting," murmured Loki, staring down the hallway in thought. "And have you had any of these sorts of nightmares recently?" he asked, looking back to her again.

"The last time was at the safe house on the way here. None since I arrived."

That seemed to ease a little of his worry, until Lucy followed it up with, "It's mara."

"Are you certain?" he asked, turning them both so they fully faced each other.

Lucy nodded. "I feel them sitting on my chest when I wake up, and Eva saw one. Branka, a striga, gave me incense that kept them away, and she told me that they could be trying to warn me or deliver a message."

After thinking for a moment, Loki said, "I'll ask some people, see what we can determine. Dreams," there he paused, trailing off a bit as he seemed to consider his words. "The beings of dreams, things like mara and the like, they are from a realm not our own. It is a place outside of ours. Between existence and...well, where the shadows that follow Donnie should be."

"Hel?" Dread began to stir in her gut.

"That is one word for it. Many try to name it, as if by doing so they can define it. But, it is something beyond any true definition or understanding."

"So what does that mean?" Lucy asked, trying to process what he was telling her.

Loki cocked his head, again weighing his words before he replied. "There are reasons prophets will often see glimpses of the future in dreams," he explained. "The—ah—realm of dreams, if one would call it that, exists in a state outside of time and reality. Its inhabitants can see all possible paths we may take."

That didn't make Lucy feel any better about any of it. "Meaning that what I saw could be a potential path? A potential future?" God, just the thought of it was making the nausea return.

"Or," said Loki, voice soothing, "it is meant to be a warning of the dangers of going down a certain path. Or, they might simply be referencing you based on your father. Another thing about those from that realm is that they cannot speak in words like you or I. They can only speak in metaphors and symbolism." He cupped her cheek and his smile worked to calm her anxiety like warm chamomile tea.

Fractured Masks

"Wait, back up. What about Dad? How is that—" Before she could finish her question, she remembered something Eva had said about Váli, the creator of Hartmut's kind.

"Váli never forgave Odin for cursing him by turning him into a ravenous wolf and setting him upon his own brother."

Pressing a hand to her mouth, Lucy stepped back and out of Loki's reach. How had she forgotten that? "Dad ate his own brother," she rasped, lowering her hand. "That's what you mean by referencing me based on him. They showed me as a feral beast eating my brothers because Dad—"

Loki sighed out slowly through his nose, eyes haunted by a memory thousands of years old. "It was not his fault, and was part of how Odin thought to punish me. Odin blamed me for the death of one of his sons, so he forced me to watch as one of my sons was torn apart. For that added dash of sadism, he used another of my sons as the weapon of execution." A sad, broken smile. "Please do not blame your father. In that moment, he was pure wolf, his very nature warped by Odin's magic in such a sudden, jarring way that Váli temporarily lost himself. It was only later that my shape-shifter genetics seemed to kick in with him, allowing his human faculties to return. Still, he has ever since been of dual nature."

"Am I," Lucy paused, swallowing. "Am I like that? Tahchat and Uktena called me 'little wolf,' so does that mean I'm like Dad? And like Dr. Kuntz?"

No ready answer came, swift and reassuring. Instead, Loki studied her with his eyes that seemed to burn like the blue flames of fires Lucy used to tend on executions. "We don't know. Most of his children throughout the centuries have been human, their Æsir genes remaining dormant. Occasionally there's someone with something subtle, easily explained away by exceptional talent. None have yet displayed abilities like yours, or have seen the shadows of the dead, like Donovan. We don't know what else may be awakening, what all you may have inherited."

"So that could be what the dreams are warning," Lucy theorized, the realization sending new worry slithering through her until it wrapped tight coils around her heart and squeezed. "It could be telling me that the same thing that happened to Dad could happen to me."

Lips pressed thin, Loki stepped up to her again and placed both hands on her shoulders. "There's no use fretting over it now, making ourselves sick over one interpretation or another. As I said, I'll speak with some people, get a more expert opinion. We'll get it all sorted."

"Thanks." The word came out shaky and insufficient.

"Come on," he prompted, smiling gently as he nodded towards the direction they had been heading. "We should really go start your training."

Right, yes, good. Training meant control, which meant she couldn't accidentally hurt anyone. Through training she could maybe help prevent the sort of things she'd seen in her nightmares. Plus, training was going to be great! Maybe even fun!

*

Training actually blew.

"That's good," praised Loki, eyes intent on the small flame Lucy was making smaller, as it slowly ate away at a stick. "Keep drawing away its oxygen."

"It's hard," Lucy complained. No matter how many times he told her how to focus on the air around her, how to draw it in, command it, direct its flow, it didn't make it any easier for her to accomplish.

Loki's attention switched to her face, his scrutiny a little unsettling. "You're still linking everything with your breath," he assessed. "I can feel the rhythmic push and pull."

Holding her breath, Lucy watched as the fire rose back up from the little flicker she'd managed. It seemed to be taunting her with its average size, wiggling all about. When she released her breath, the flame flared up for a brilliant moment, then continued dancing blithely. "Dammit."

"It's an understandable mistake," Loki said soothingly, "and a natural one to make. You associate air with the function of your lungs, and so you have unconsciously been using that organ as your means of manipulation. In actuality, the air is but an extension of *you*. Think of it as something more like a limb. If it helps, try visualizing a hand smothering the flame, depriving it of any oxygen."

Lucy huffed, rolled her shoulders, and glared at the burning stick. *A hand*, she thought, *envision a hand*. That seemed simple enough, in theory. In practice, she somehow got something mixed up, and instead of smothering the flame, pushed more oxygen onto it with her imagined "hand."

"Don't worry," soothed Loki, "these things can take time." He again gave her his comforting smile.

"But I don't want to keep using up all of your time," Lucy protested.

He chuckled then, shaking his head. "Time is something our kind has in spades, dear one."

Oh. Lucy honestly hadn't even thought about that. "Are you saying that I'm—"

Loki's smile was amused, then. "The manifestation of your abilities means you are a being more like your father than your mother. Váli is half Æsir and half, well, me." At that, he motioned to himself with a flourish and wide grin.

Head reeling, Lucy tried to control her breathing. The flame rose and fell with every inhalation. "I'm...you're saying I'm immortal?"

"If you're never killed," Loki corrected with a raise of his brows. "The Æsir can be killed almost as easily as a human. It's best to keep that in mind." He glanced at the flame. "You also need to stop letting your emotions control you or your abilities."

Frustration leaked through her daze, and she huffed. "I don't know *how*."

"Then perhaps," he said, considering, "you should speak with Dr. Sartre."

"No." Lucy narrowed her eyes. "I already told Dad that I don't want to do any therapy sessions with him."

One of Loki's brows shot up at that and he tilted his head. "Yes, Váli told me you two evidently have a history. Which is...very interesting indeed."

She snorted and rolled her eyes. "It's *really* not."

His smile then was secretive, but he tipped his head as if conceding to her. "In any case, I wasn't suggesting therapy. Not really."

Crossing her arms, Lucy eyed her grandfather with a touch of suspicion. It wasn't just that it was Ren; Lucy also didn't think she really needed any kind of therapy. Mick had successfully opted out, too, but on the basis that he hadn't really experienced any traumatic event outside of getting whisked away in the night. In Lucy's opinion, she'd already had months dealing with everything, and was perfectly fine, thanks. "Then what? I don't have any creepy shadows for him to keep at bay."

"Dr. Sartre is also experienced in meditation and mental exercises that help one control their impulses and emotions," Loki explained patiently. "I'd say he's probably the best in the world at such things."

Lucy tried to picture herself learning those techniques from Ren, and could already feel her frustrations growing. "I'm not sure that's a good idea," she tried to hedge.

"Nonsense," Loki insisted. "I truly can think of no better instructor for all that. In fact," he said, smiling excitedly as he absently extinguished the flame with a tiny gesture, "I think we should call it a day with this, and you should begin your work with him. I'm confident that your control over your abilities will improve once you have a better understanding and control of your self."

Shoulders slumping, Lucy felt defeated. "You mean you want me to go to him right now?"

"Yes, exactly," he confirmed, still beaming. "I'll call him while you head to his office. Do you remember the way?"

Only vaguely. The building was like a maze in some ways. Still, she nodded and moved towards the door. "Thank you again for your help," she remembered to say before leaving, turning back to him and giving a deep nod of respect. Truthfully, she didn't really know what the proper protocol was for how someone treated their ancient, immortal grandfather, who was also their leader.

And evidently Lucy was something like immortal now, too. Someday she'd be ancient. The reminder staggered her a little, and she had to lean against the cool white wall of the hallway and just take a moment to breathe. She thought back to her time in the Gehealdan, of how they tended to refer to supernaturals as nons. Non-humans. She remembered Darin Monico's distaste of the word, how it was perceived as a slur. Before meeting with him, she had carelessly used it, just as she used any other slang term the Gehealdan tossed around.

She was a non. There were people out there who thought she was something less than human, simply because she *wasn't* human.

But, she reminded herself, straightening up from the wall, once there were people who revered her kind as gods. If Fenris was successful, someday supernaturals would again be venerated and respected by humans.

How weird would it be to be a god, she wondered. Then she laughed at herself, because she'd be a pretty piss-poor god if she never got her powers under control.

***

"This is so awkward," Lucy sighed, sinking down in her chair.

Ren smirked at her, cracking one eye open. "Would you prefer we sit cross-legged on the floor?"

"You know what I mean," she snapped, giving up on the relaxing exercise and tilting her head back to stare angrily at the ceiling.

For a moment, Ren was silent, and then he said, "I wasn't aware you hated me so much." His voice gave nothing away, was perfectly neutral, and that irked Lucy for reasons she couldn't understand.

"I hate the Gehealdan, because they are liars and murderers. As far as I know, you're only one of those things. So, I don't really *hate* you."

Making a thoughtful hum, Ren replied, "I used to be both."

That made Lucy jerk upright in her chair. "What? But I though you *couldn't* hurt people. As in, are literally unable to."

"Anyone is able to hurt people," he corrected. "It's just in my best interest not to."

She stared at him, at his dark eyes and sallow skin and face that wasn't really handsome but somehow always drew her eye. He stared back, expression revealing nothing, the same as his tone. Was that part of the great control Loki lauded him for? "Tell me," she ordered, though it came out more as a question, a request. Those eyes of his always did strike her a little too hard, make her resolve feel a little too fragile.

For a moment, he just studied her, but then he nodded and his entire posture seemed to shift into something more relaxed. "If it'll help you trust me enough to do what needs to be done," he agreed. Ren laced his fingers together in his lap, his elbows on the chair's armrests, and began.

"My entire story is too long, but the condensed version is this: I am an endangered species, because my kind was once hunted to perceived extinction. The reason being, there are two types of my kind, and one of those must constantly feed upon flesh. It is insatiable. The other kind feeds on something...less substantial, yet considerably more satiating."

"You're a vârcolac," Lucy gasped out, realization hitting almost as hard as the news of her immortality.

His black eyes twinkled and he smiled. "That's right," he said softly, "I forgot you already know what those are." Ren motioned then towards her ears, where the eclipse earrings dangled, just as they had when she came upon him in the shop on her birthday. "Of all the folk who cause eclipses, you referenced us."

"So you're a pneuma type," she surmised. "That's why you can't kill, because otherwise you'd regress to a soma."

"Exactly." He tipped his head. "Which is why I work in this field. I can only gain sustenance by having people confront their darkness and release it, so that I may consume it."

"Okay, but what does that have to do with teen parties?"

"College parties." As if that distinction really mattered. "And people that age are willing to share their deepest, darkest secrets with total strangers after a couple of drinks. Sometimes even while completely sober. Parties create a certain atmosphere where people feel as though nothing they do will have real consequence once they leave that bubble. Sitting with a man they only just met, opening up about something that's always weighed them down with guilt? It's somehow easier there."

Lucy could get that. She'd done similar with Venny, and even to a lesser extent with Ren.

"But at one point, I was a soma," Ren explained, returning to the reason they'd even gotten onto the topic. "We all start out as soma." Ren gave her a pointed, direct stare, as if trying to communicate something with his eyes. She thought she understood, though, exactly what he meant.

"That's why you said you used to be both. You used to eat people." Which, reformed pneuma-type or no, it chilled her a bit to have him sitting across from her. At one point he was no better than the Reaper.

"A *lot* of people," he for some reason felt the need to stress. Then his eyes narrowed just a bit, as if focusing on what her reaction to that would be. "Does that bother you?"

The reflexive answer was that it did but she knew he wanted her to really think about it before responding. Whatever he had been in the past, he wasn't that anymore. Just as she had once been human, but now could make car engines explode on accident. Was it fair to hate him now for what he was in the past?

When she didn't answer, he smiled ruefully and said, "You'll find that the best way to survive the centuries is to never allow yourself to get stuck in a moment. The past can never be relived, what is gone is gone. The future is never certain, no matter how many prophets you consult. All that you really have is the present. All that you can really live in is the here and now. Everything changes, and we have to—what? What is it?"

Lucy felt chilled, her breath coming in short gasps. Her vision blurred until she didn't see Ren sitting in a plush chair, but instead saw a man with lanky black hair pulled messily back from his ever-shifting face. "Death is change," she whispered. "It only hurts if you forget."

"Forget?" he prompted.

"Forget that nothing lasts forever," she replied softly, following the dream's script. "Not even gods."

"What's happening right now, Lucy?" Ren asked, his voice pitched in a way she wasn't really used to hearing from him. Gone was all the snark and sarcasm, and instead it was imbued with a rich warmth that comforted like a campfire.

"There was a nightmare," she tried to explain, shaking a little and closing her eyes. It couldn't be coincidence that she'd been reminded of her nightmares twice in one day. "I guess it was you? Only...it wasn't here. It was dark, with rock walls, and you were at a table, writing something."

"You're sure it was me?"

"No. The face kept shifting. But I think, now, that it was supposed to be you."

"Did I say anything?"

"Yes, what I just said. About changes and death and gods."

"And after that?"

Fear tried to grip her, but she mentally scolded herself. There was nothing to be afraid of anymore, because the Reaper was dead. "After that, everything went black, and then...then it was the Grin Reaper. He was there. And." She swallowed, her throat dry at the memory. "And his victims."

Then she finally opened her eyes, relieved to see that Ren looked like himself again, that her vision had cleared. "The second half of the dream's already been interpreted. That's how we found out who the Reaper was and who he was working for."

Ren nodded slowly, studying her with his frustratingly inscrutable face. "But you never determined the meaning of the first half. The memory of which was just triggered." There was no questioning inflection to his voice, but Lucy nodded in response anyway. "Can you remember anything else?"

She closed her eyes again and tried, bringing up that image. It was, thankfully, the less terrifying part of her dream. "You were writing something, but I couldn't make it out. Even when you looked up at me, you kept writing. And the table...the table had carvings in it. Stretched out animals tied into knots."

"That's a common Norse motif," Ren explained gently. "It makes sense, considering your strong Norse ties."

Lucy opened her eyes again and looked around the office, searching for such imagery but finding only the clean lines of modern chic. "Do you think it meant here, then? Loki said that those from the realm of dream can only communicate in metaphors and symbolism."

Rubbing a hand over his mouth, Ren looked away as he thought. He seemed troubled, and that worried Lucy. The only other times she could recall him looking troubled were right after she'd seen someone's face eaten off, and the night of the Halloween massacre. *Wait.*

"You knew," she said softly, realization dawning.

His head snapped back to look at her again, confusion running freely along his features. "Knew what?"

"On Halloween. You knew the Reaper was there."

"Ah." The neutrality returned, as well as a hint of his usual smile. "Finally caught on, I see."

Which, that didn't really make sense, Lucy thought. How was she supposed to know that his unease was about *that*? He'd been talking about—oh. "Oh my god." Lucy felt another wave of nausea and had to close her eyes again as she leaned forward to cradle her forehead in her hands. "Venny."

"Well, I tried to tell you that he hurt people," Ren shrugged.

"I just thought you were being weird and jealous," objected Lucy, still feeling sick. "You propositioned me right after that."

She heard Ren pull in and then release a deep breath. "It was the only thing I could think of to try to get you out of there," he explained like a confession.

That managed to pull her attention away from the disgusting thoughts of having snuggled the Reaper, and she lifted her head to look at Ren. "Why not try to get everyone out, if you knew who and what Venny was and suspected he would kill?"

Ren just stared right back at her, then sighed. "You're going to think my answer is extremely cold, and I don't think you're really at the point where you'll understand."

"Try me," she grit out, offended that he didn't think she would get it.

Shrugging, Ren explained, "The best way for me to avoid harming or killing is to avoid conflict. As such, I've spent centuries cultivating and then maintaining my neutrality."

Lucy didn't know what that had to do with anything, and her cheeks heated in embarrassment as she realized she really wanted to ask for clarification. Luckily, Ren seemed to grasp from her silence that further elaboration was needed. "Neutrality means that I don't get involved with things like what happened that night. Or that second night we met."

The vampire who ate a man's face. The incident that started it all, drawing Lucy irrevocably into this world of magic and death. "You knew someone was getting eaten in the woods. That's why you tried to stop me from going."

Ren nodded.

"But you didn't go and try to stop the vampire, because that would probably result in a fight."

"Exactly."

Lucy slumped back in her chair and rubbed her hands over her eyes. She had really hoped the giant dumps of world-shattering revelations were all behind her. Why did things just keep getting more complicated? "Okay, but then still...why did you keep trying to warn *me* about these things, when you didn't bother to warn anyone else?"

"I'm sorry, would you rather I didn't?" he asked with an incredulous scoff. "I don't really see why it bothers you that I tried to help."

"No, it's just," Lucy trailed off, not really sure how to put her scattered thoughts into words.

"It's because I know you," Ren finally explained, sounding almost tired.

Lifting her hands away from her face, Lucy shot him a look like he was insane. "*Barely*. You're saying you would have tried to warn anyone you happened to meet?"

"Why are you so fixated on this?" he muttered. Then he ran his hand back through his shaggy hair as if trying to compose himself. "Really, we should return to the purpose of your visit, and work on improving your control."

"Fine," she groused. "But I have to warn you, I'm not feeling very relaxed and meditative."

Ren smiled and settled more into his chair. "I can help with that. Just close your eyes, and listen to the sound of my voice..."

Chapter 12
Taut

"Jim," called a most unwelcome voice, and Jim clenched his jaw as he continued down the hall. But, of course, Kyle couldn't take a hint. "Jim, wait up," he pressed, running to catch up and grab Jim's arm. "You haven't returned any of my texts or calls."

Feeling too drained for patience, Jim pulled his arm free and tried to keep walking. "Hey, stop," snapped Kyle. "You can't just say something like you think Lucy's gone, and then just not explain. Look," he grabbed Jim again and pulled him until they were facing each other, "I get that you're upset, because so am I. They were my friends, too. And Lucy...you know I—"

"Don't," seethed Jim, his temper finally snapping. "Don't even fucking try to claim you cared about her. Not after you jerked her around for years, and only started really paying any attention to her the moment she began to outgrow you. And the others? You didn't give a shite about them, and the feeling was likely mutual. The only reason any of us put up with you was because of Lucy." At the harsh words, Kyle's eyes widened, and he stepped back, releasing Jim's arm.

"I thought we were friends," whispered Kyle, voice weak and whispery. To look at him, you'd think Jim had just stabbed him in the gut.

For a moment Jim almost cared, but then he remembered what a complete and unapologetic git Kyle was. "When did we ever hang out together where Lucy wasn't also present?" Jim asked, narrowing his eyes. "Did you ever really hang out with anyone in our group? Because I know for a fact that you and I never spent time bonding, and Eva thought you were an arse."

"Why are you saying these things?" asked Kyle, face crumbling in hurt and confusion.

"Because there's no reason to tolerate you anymore." With that, Jim continued on down the hall towards his class. He didn't glance back, and tried not to feel bad about what he'd just said. Honestly, they were all things that should have been said a long time ago.

***

By lunch, Jim was dead on his feet and regretting his return to school. Still, it was something he had to do if he wanted to maintain his grades. Running on muscle memory, he walked right up to the group's usual table, but then stood there when he realized that most of the people who sat there were gone. Motion to his left caught his eye, and he turned his head to see Alice walk up beside him to stare at the empty table.

"You want to eat outside today?" she asked softly, eyes moving over the vacant seats of their friends.

"Yes," he replied, relieved. He didn't think he could stomach eating lunch at that table. Not today. Not anytime soon.

All of the picnic tables were full, so they sat on the ground beneath a tree. Its leaves were a bright, vibrant red that made it look like fire, and some had already fallen to create a cushioning blanket at its base.

"For what it's worth," Jim eventually said, after they had sat there quietly eating their meals, "I don't think Lucy's dead." The others weren't dead, either, but that wasn't something Jim could really reveal. At least he could give her Lucy.

Alice didn't look at him, just took a few sips from her juice box, and then said, "But I still can't reach her."

"Her whole family sort of just packed up and left. Maybe she's too busy to respond."

That got her attention, and she turned a bit to face him, squinting against the drooping, late autumn sun. "What do you mean, her whole family left?"

"They're gone," he shrugged. "No one's home. Her mum's store hasn't been open. Maybe there was a family emergency out of state or something. It's just a coincidence that it happened at the same time as..." God, what did you call what happened? The massacre? The slaughter? Either one left a bad taste in Jim's mouth and again had him questioning his reasons for staying with the Gehealdan.

The information etched concern into Alice's features, and she leaned closer. "Do you think Lucy knows?" she asked, breathy and fearful. "Oh my god, what if she doesn't? What if she's out there somewhere, totally unaware that Krysti and Eva are—" She couldn't say the word. Not that Jim could blame her. It was difficult for him to say it, too, and *he* knew the truth.

Instead of answering, Jim just pulled Alice close into a hug. He felt her tremble against him, heard her sniffles, and wondered why she was already back in school, too. Hopefully Lucy would contact Alice at some point, just to let her know that she was okay.

"I'm sorry," Alice said, eventually pulling away. "I thought I was good to come back today, but everything still feels so raw, you know? Well, I guess you do." She studied his face with worry and sympathy. "You don't look like you've been getting much sleep, either." Her eyes were brimming with unshed tears, her voice a little choked. "I know Eva was your best friend."

And, while Jim knew that Eva was alive, Alice's words had his own eyes burning and his heart clenching. "She was," he agreed, feeling a little broken, a little abandoned. She had been his best friend, but Jim didn't think he had been hers. That honor went to Krysti, didn't it? His old bitterness resurfaced, and he tried to swallow it back down.

"It's not fair," Alice nearly sobbed, leaning back against the tree. "We were all supposed to have a great senior year. Our last year where we're all together, before we get scattered to the wind." Sniffling, Alice continued, "There's so much we were supposed to do together, so many moments and years and...it's all gone."

Jim rubbed at his forehead, then straightened his scarf headband, tugging it down to about his eyebrows. "It's not fair," he agreed. Honestly, he was starting to believe that nothing was fair anymore.

***

"Go home," Czar ordered the moment Jim stepped into the computer room. He was standing next to the lonely table, thick arms crossed across his barrel chest. "You look like death." Again Czar's accent seemed to have thinned out, or maybe even shifted into something else, something less American and more Northern European.

"Appreciate the concern," grumbled Jim, "but I'm fine."

Shaking his head, Czar stepped forward. "Please don't try to lie to me, boy. It'll never work out in your favor."

"I'm not lying," he argued, even though he honestly did feel like death warmed over. It had been a chore just getting through his day at school, and he felt about ready to collapse at any moment.

Unexpectedly, Czar's posture relaxed, his face softening. "Go to tha door with tha näcken," Czar urged gently, his Southern accent having returned full force. "Passcode is 7378. It's got some bunks fer when we need a quick nap." He looked at Jim with fatherly concern, then waved his hand towards the door. "Go," he repeated. "Stay here as long as ya need. Rest."

A wave of relief washed over Jim. "Thanks," he said, feeling rather bad about having snapped at Czar earlier. When Czar nodded and offered a sympathetic smile, Jim tried to smile back. It felt forced and brittle, and was gone in a second.

Out in the hall, the others were heading to the War Room, but Günter stopped as soon as he spotted Jim. "You alright?" asked Günter, frowning. He had been doing that a lot lately. The entire drive to the shop had involved Günter frowning silently.

"Fine," Jim assured, waving off his concern. "Czar just sent me to have a little kip. There's a room here specifically for napping, did you know?"

Günter looked past Jim, at the door with the draugr on it that housed the computer room. "Is Czar in there? Wanted to talk with him yesterday, but he was busy."

Before Jim could answer, the door opened and Czar did it for him. "We'll talk later," said the old man. "Get along now; Phil's waitin'."

For a moment, Günter just glared at Czar, but then he gave a curt nod and continued on his way. It was probably the closest Jim had ever seen to Günter exhibiting insubordination. Whatever was bothering Günter must be pretty bad, to have him act that way while they were still under probation.

Too knackered to really focus on any of that, Jim headed down the hall in search of the proper door. He stopped in front of the image of a man on a rock, dressed in nobleman's clothing and playing a violin. Squinting at the painting, Jim thought about the research he had done. "You're a bit like the nixe, aren't you?" he asked softly, tapping the painted man's face.

"Diff'rent names for tha same thing, more or less." Startled by the gruff voice, Jim turned to see Czar had followed him. Pale gaze switching to the painting of the näcken, Czar scratched his scruffy chin and continued, "Least, that's what people theorize. There are lots o' diff'rent kinds a things like 'em. If they ain't all exactly tha same, they're at least very similar species."

"Is that how it works?" mused Jim, returning his attention to the door. "I guess I never really thought about it, but I suppose that makes sense. The strigoi evolved from the strix. Günter is a new species, combining two others," he murmured, groggy mind mulling it over.

Czar nodded. "An' even nons like tengu have changed and evolved over time, what they are now bein' a product of mixin' with garudas."

"Huh." Filing away that interesting tidbit, Jim tapped at the door again. "And these folk. They typically baddies?"

Lips twitching in amusement, Czar tilted his head. "Ain't no species necessarily all bad, son. Lots o' water folk like that, an' some save people while others lure 'em to their doom. There's good'uns and bad'uns. Same as humans."

Jim stared at the painting for bit before nodding. "Would it be possible," he started quietly, hesitantly, "to add learning about all that to my duties?"

That seemed to pique Czar's interest, and he stared intently at Jim. "Ya wanna learn 'bout non lineages an' such?" he asked. "Why?"

With a little, humorless huff of a laugh, Jim turned around and leaned back against the door. "This is my life now," he explained, sounding and feeling defeated. "I need to know everything I can."

Czar nodded at that. "Definitely got tha right ta know," he agreed.

"Our initial training had us learning about different supernaturals, their names and abilities. This'll pretty much be expanding upon that."

Nodding some more, a pleased little smile came to Czar's lips. "Could definitely prove useful." He reached out and patted Jim on the shoulder. "I like tha way ya think, son." The warm, proud expression on Czar's face reminded Jim a bit of his maternal grandfather, and he felt a tension ease inside his chest.

"We'll start on that t'morrah," Czar assured, then nodded to the door. "Fer now, go get yerself some rest."

"Thanks."

***

Somehow Jim had managed to sleep the entire time they were designated to be at the shop. Though, he must not have slept well, because he still felt exhausted when he awoke. If anything, his body seemed to be aching even more than usual. It might have been the crappy mattress on the bunk, though, so he put it out of mind.

He emerged from the room just in time to witness Günter growl out a demand to speak with Czar. Literally *growl*. His usually honey eyes looked decidedly not-human, and Jim wondered what could possibly be so bad that it was causing Günter to lose control.

"T'morrah," Czar calmly replied, unaffected by Günter's display.

Günter snarled at that, his teeth growing sharp. "Stop blowing me off!"

Everyone was in the hall, Jim saw. He stood behind Günter, and further down stood the others in something like a barrier between Günter and Czar. The thought that Czar might need some sort of protective wall was laughable, really. Thick and imposing, the old man towered over the others and carried himself with the kind of natural confidence envied of kings. It didn't matter that Günter was supernatural and Czar was just a human, because Jim was fairly certain Czar would come out the victor in that battle.

"This is a complicated matter," Czar explained slowly, patiently, again losing some of his accent. "It's not to be discussed here and now."

"If he's in danger—"

"Jim," Phil interrupted, motioning for Jim to step closer. "It's time you collected your friend and headed home for the night."

Günter spun around at that, seeming to just realize that Jim was standing there. Which was odd, because Jim couldn't recall a time when Günter hadn't seemed completely aware of Jim's presence. Even when their Gehealdan work had sent them to parties, Jim would always be able to glance across the crowded room and find Günter glancing right back.

"What's wrong?" Jim asked, stepping closer to Günter and grabbing his shoulder. He watched as Günter's eyes and teeth returned to normal, but didn't feel any of the tension leave the taut muscle beneath his hand.

"Günter," Czar called out before Günter could respond, voice dark with warning. "Mind yourself, now."

Closing his eyes, Günter took a deep breath as if trying to control his temper. When he opened his eyes again, he looked on the verge of breaking. "Let's just go," he whispered to Jim, head and shoulders drooping as he turned away.

"Yeah, okay." Jim let his hand fall away from Günter's shoulder and then followed him down the hall. As they approached the others, the group parted without a word. Everyone watched them as they walked, and it unnerved Jim a bit. Carmen's expression was harsh as usual, Phil's blandly pleasant, and Czar's a stony mask. When Jim caught sight of Montenegro, he nearly tripped. Expecting to see nothing but blank, emotionless indifference, he was thrown to find Montenegro watching them with clear concern.

When they left and were on the road, Jim tried asking again what was wrong. Fingers gripping the steering wheel tightly, Günter just shook his head. "I need more information."

"Well, can you at least tell me what it's about? Nothing detailed, just the general gist?"

"I think Czar might be allowing something horrible to happen." Günter looked sick to his stomach just saying it. Christ, must really be bad, then.

"What sort of horrible something?"

Somehow, Günter started looking worse, and Jim worried he might sick up right then and there. "I'll tell you more when I get more details," was the not-answer, but Jim let it slide.

Sinking back into his seat, Jim turned the subject to lighter things, like Günter's classes and if he'd been learning anything interesting as of late. It took a bit of coaxing, but eventually Günter was nearly his old self again. For the first time in a while, Jim felt like his old self, as well.

"We should spend time outside of Gehealdan, again," Jim said wistfully, glancing at Günter before focusing on the dark, suburban road ahead of them. "Like we used to."

"That was still Gehealdan work," Günter corrected, though he was smiling a little.

"Not that first time, back before we even met them."

Günter chuckled, and Jim liked the way the corners of his eyes crinkled when he smiled like that. "I think preparing to kill a strigoi still counts as the same kind of work."

"Nah, but there were movies. That's different."

Surprise flickered across Günter's face, and his smile became almost shy. "You want to watch a movie together?"

Feeling himself grin a bit, Jim shrugged. "Maybe. Might be good for us to just relax and binge watch some ridiculous tripe. Forget about all the shite going on."

"Yeah," Günter agreed with a nod, the crinkle back at the corner of his eyes. "That *does* sound good."

"Maybe this weekend? If you don't have an assignment?"

Günter cast him a glance, and in that moment looked happier than Jim could remember seeing him in months. "I'd like that."

Even though he knew it wasn't a date or anything, Jim felt something bright and happy flutter in his chest. Hell, if that was how he felt just at the prospect of hanging out with Günter, he couldn't imagine how he'd survive a real date. Despite all of his recent pain and the lingering, unshakable fatigue, in that moment Jim felt amazing.

***

"This is the second day in a row where you haven't brought me anything," Dorian admonished, then clucked his tongue. "Don't you care about me?"

"I do," objected Jim, swaying closer and reaching out without daring to yet touch. "Of course I do. How could you even ask that?" God, it hurt just to think about. The very thought of not caring for Dorian felt like something sharp was spinning wildly in Jim's chest, shredding him apart from the inside.

Pity in his eyes, Dorian moved closer, pressed himself against Jim's outstretched hand. "I know," he cooed soothingly. "I know you care. You want me to be safe and happy."

"Yes," Jim agreed, nodding, trembling hand running hesitantly up and down along Dorian's arm. This was what he wanted, but at the same time it felt wrong. The pain increased, but was different. Burning. He tried to pull up the memory of smiling with Günter in the car less than a half hour earlier, but the pain just increased until his mind whited out for a moment.

When he could focus again, Dorian was pressed close, looking deeply into his eyes. "Then you have to help me," Dorian breathed against Jim's lips. "You have to protect me and my family from them."

"Of course." Jim felt his arms lift to wrap around Dorian's slim waist, pulling him in even closer. "Anything."

Dorian rewarded him with a brilliant smile as he wrapped his own arms around Jim. "You're so good to me."

"I love you," Jim said, as if that explained everything. Except it didn't, because the words tasted wrong. Though how could they be anything but true? Being with Dorian made him happy. Even now, the pain was fading, and he was feeling good, so good.

"I know." Dorian kissed him, soft and gentle, and Jim felt so happy. Bright and bubbly. Everything was bright and bubbly and wonderful.

Kissing Dorian felt like a release of all of Jim's tension and exhaustion, and he could just be free and content. He must have done something that Dorian liked, because he made a delighted sound and kissed Jim harder. Which was nice. Everything with Dorian was nice. Perfect, really.

The entire world was perfect, and nothing hurt. Not anymore.

Chapter 13
Fishing

"But why do they stop?" asked Eva, as she and Uktena walked through yet another forest—Montana, that time. "If it's not the Lamiae who are doing it, but some other folk, why do the actual child-eaters stop as soon as that Lamiae is executed? Unless it *is* a frame job?" A river wound alongside them like a discarded silk ribbon, nearly black in the fading illumination of twilight. Above the treetops, Eva could see huge, snow-capped mountains

Uktena shook his head, eyes focused on the lazy water. "No clue. Maybe they realize it could have just as easily have been them, so they pull back on their feeding in order to be less noticeable."

Made sense, Eva supposed. Or, well, it was at least a good theory. "Though why would they remain in the same place? If I were them, I'd have fled to somewhere else, just to be safe."

"Some people get tired of running," was his quiet reply.

Eva frowned, confused by the weird sense of empathy that had just tried to tug at her core. "That's not a luxury many supernaturals really have."

Eyebrows rising, Uktena turned away from the water to shoot her an incredulous look. "Says the girl whose family lines both have established territories where their clans can live out their lives safely."

"But not my parents," she shot back, rankled by his implication. "Not my brother. Not *me*." The rest of their lives would just be a series of temporary settlements followed by another move and a new name. Hartmut Kuntz wasn't her father's original name, and in a few years he'd shed it like dead skin. Eva already had her first alias. She wondered if the people she knew would stop calling her Eva at some point, if that name would be lost to time.

He studied her for a moment, and again Eva hated how it was so difficult to read him. "You're right," he conceded, dipping his head a little even as his eyes continued to bore into her. "Sorry." Then he was turning back to study the river as they continued with their walk. "If Fenris is successful, however, then that won't be your future. None of us will have to keep running."

Pretty words, she thought, skeptical of this Utopian future where humans and supernaturals lived side-by-side. Besides, there would always be those who felt the need to run, because there would always be those who failed to play by the rules. Somehow she doubted that humans would just sit back and be okay with supernaturals feeding on them without restrictions.

"How much longer, do you think?" she asked, wanting to get off this topic and focus back to the task at hand.

"I don't think much farther," he estimated, slowing his steps. "The water is getting deeper."

"And that matters why?" The snark in her tone was accidental and reflexive, but her curiosity was genuine.

"Typically water folk prefer deeper waters. More places to dwell and hide, easier to drown their prey." Then, without warning, he was stepping down from the path and onto the river's rocky bank. "I'll continue from below," he explained, stepping right into the river with his clothes and boots still on. "Continue on the path. If you see anything, pretend to be human, and try not to engage."

"What if it attacks me?" she asked, a repeat of the same question she'd asked him back at the car, when he'd commanded she leave all her weapons behind.

"Lethal force is only to be used if absolutely necessary."

She held her hands out to her side, as if to show him how incredibly absent all her weaponry was. "Lethal force using *what*?"

Giving her a flat look, he deadpanned, "Right, because it's not like you can grow claws or talons or sharp teeth."

That drew Eva up short. She could. Absolutely she could, and always kept that knowledge as an aside whenever faced with a potential threat. Unlike Günter, however, she'd never used anything except a weapon on anyone. The very thought never really sat well with her.

"Right," she agreed, clenching her jaw and nodding. She was a warrior, and there was no time for hesitations or hang-ups.

Uktena studied her again for another long moment, but then he kept walking into the dark water. A few steps out, and he simply dove in fully, pushing out towards the river's center. Eva stood there watching, waiting to see where he'd resurface, but it never happened. Shifting her eyes to those of a wolf, she tried to get a better look at the river in the low light.

There, just up ahead, was a long, dark shape slithering beneath the water's surface. It was a huge serpent, larger and longer than the anacondas she'd seen in documentaries. Really, it reminded her more of the river dragons she'd seen in Japan. Could that seriously be Uktena's true form? He had said his kind were large water snakes, but damn!

Well, at least now it made sense that he never seemed to be afraid of anything. She couldn't imagine what would be strong enough to fight a snake that incredibly massive. *Birds*, she remembered. *Certain birds.* Somewhere out there were beings even more imposing than a dragon-sized snake, and they were avian. A tiny part of Eva felt some sort of secondhand pride over that thought.

Not that she really had time to focus on any of that. Uktena's shadowy form was already getting way ahead of her, so she quickly started back down the trail. The sky was growing darker, but the scent of rain in the distance let her know it wasn't just the night fully setting in. She kept her eyes shifted to those of a wolf, despite Uktena's order to try to pass as human. It wasn't like anyone would be able to tell in the low light, anyway, unless they got extremely close. If he'd wanted her to keep her eyes human, then they should have brought a flashlight.

Up ahead, something slipped out of the rippling water, pulling itself onto a boulder. For a moment, Eva thought it might be Uktena, but the silhouette didn't seem quite right. She flicked her gaze back to the river, searching for Uktena's dark form, but couldn't find him.

Music started to play, something sweet and almost delicate. The figure on the rock was shifting, moving in a strange, almost jerky pattern. As Eva drew closer, she realized it was a man, and he was playing something like a violin. She stopped about six meters away, and the man turned his head towards her as he continued to play.

He smiled, and Eva felt something like the prickle of static against her nerves. It was annoying and strange, and had her scratching at her arms with a frown. The man's smile faltered, and the volume of his music seemed to increase.

Like a wave, the prickly sensation washed over her, but she was the jagged rocks over which it crashed and broke apart. It clicked, then, what she was feeling. Magic. A useless, ineffectual magic, but still magic nonetheless.

Stepping cautiously closer, Eva shifted her eyes to those of a tengu, and willed herself to see the truth. What she saw had the air freezing in her throat and her feet coming to a complete stop. For a moment, she thought she was a child again, wandering too close to the forbidden black waters where Bad Things lurked. Her vision was overlapped with the memory of large, bright eyes peeking at her, hinting at what horror she would have seen just beneath the surface.

The man on the rock was not a man, but something out of a nightmare. His body more resembled twisted, gnarled wood and water plants than flesh, except for his slick black tail that trailed down into the river. He had no instrument, and was instead rubbing together the long, thin, webbed fingers of his hands, reminding Eva of a cricket. He had large, round eyes that caught the light in a way that made them appear to glow, exactly like Eva remembered from when she was a child. But it was the mouth that was the worst, so huge it took up most of his head, and filled with teeth too large to allow him to fully close his jaw. He looked like something from the deepest crevices of the ocean.

The music came to a sudden stop, and the monstrosity spoke with a gentle, smooth voice. "I see."

Eva shifted her eyes back to lupine just in time to see his human form melt into that of a beautiful woman. Again the music started, the creature on the rock smiling at Eva with a beautiful face. The ineffectual tingle of magic grated against Eva's nerves again, and she cringed. On the rock, the illusion of a woman pouted in confusion.

"It won't work," Eva ground out, teeth clenched. "So just stop."

"I don't understand," said the not-woman, ceasing the music

and eyeing Eva with trepidation. "How are you resisting?"

"Just special, I guess." She felt better now that the music had stopped, and was starting to wonder again where Uktena had gone off to. Maybe he was further up the river, and completely missed the —näcken? Was that the right word? Nix? Neck?

Something in the river broke the surface for a second, distracting her, but by the time she looked it was gone and the ripples washed away in the current. "Don't suppose you've seen a lot of kids wandering around here recently?" Eva asked, returning her focus to the water folk.

The illusion shifted again to a handsome male, and he glared at her. "Who are you?" he demanded. Again the water was disturbed beside them.

"Just a girl out for a walk."

"I don't believe you." Some of the illusion began to fail, and even with her wolf eyes Eva was able to see elements of the being's true form peek out. "Who *are* you?" he repeated, mouth growing and stretching, teeth looking sharper by the second.

"My father used to warn me about your kind," she said casually. "You like to lure people to their doom, right? Ensnare them with your music, get them close, then drown them."

He flicked his tail, no longer bothering with the illusion of legs, and it made a wet smacking sound against the rock. "You've no way to prove it was us," he said.

"What? For all those centuries?" Eva blinked at him and cocked her head. She knew what he meant, but he'd left such a huge button exposed that it would be a real sin not to press it.

Turning, twisting, he rolled onto his belly and held himself up on his long arms. "The children," he hissed.

"Well, that seems like practically a confession right there, actually." Eva's eyebrows rose as she pressed harder on the button.

Beside them, something beneath the water was thrashing, causing splashes and churning. The scent of copper and fish grew heavy and harsh, overpowering the fresh smells of an oncoming storm.

Digging his fingers into the dirt of the shore, the being began to pull himself along at an alarming speed towards Eva. He dropped his jaw open wide, revealing just how many of those over-long teeth were crammed into his mouth. In response, Eva snarled and rushed him with her hands becoming talons.

Fear flashed in his eyes for a second before her boot connected with his face and sent him flying backwards. As soon as he landed, she was upon him, wrapping her long, curling talons around his throat. It felt slick beneath her grip, and up close he reeked like a fish market. The illusion dropped completely, and she tried not to flinch at how much worse he looked up close.

"What are you?" he gasped up at her, large fish eyes staring, unblinking.

"How many did you kill?" she growled, instead of answering him. In her mouth, she could feel her teeth elongate, even if they weren't as intimidating as his.

"You can prove *nothing*," he spat back at her, then tried to thrash and wriggle out of her hold.

Behind her, Eva could hear the water continue to roil.

"Did you *mean* to pin it on a Lamiae?" she asked, using her body to try to pin his down, even as his tail flopped and smacked at her.

He simply laughed, his huge mouth gaping open, his head

thrown back. Then he seemed to try to struggle for real, bringing his hands up to push at her and try to hit her face. Something sharp sliced across her cheek and she snarled as she tightened her grip.

It was a strange sensation, feeling her talons sink into his flesh, and the sticky wetness that trickled onto her fingers wasn't as warm as she'd expected.

Somehow he managed to finally throw Eva off, and he quickly twisted around to bite her. The sound that tore from her was something between a human scream and a hawk's piercing cry. He'd gotten her in the shoulder, and his teeth were so goddamn long. The pain ran deep, tearing through muscle and grinding at bone.

Screw Uktena for having her leave all of her weapons behind.

With her good arm, she reached over and scrabbled at his face until the tips of her talons caught on the edges of an eye. As Eva dug her talons in, the jaws around her shoulder began to slacken and cries of pain bubbled up from the fish-man's throat. Still, she did not let up, digging and tugging, until she felt the eye pop free so she could fully rip it out.

That sent him scrabbling away, screaming as he held his webbed hands up against the bleeding socket. Eva tossed the eye aside and turned on him with a piercing battle screech.

Unconsciously she began shifting into a tengu, feeling the prickle across her skin as feathers bloomed, and the stretch-pull on her face from the formation of her beak. She had just enough control to keep the wings from sprouting, not wanting to destroy her shirt and coat. Same with her feet, though she hadn't managed to stop it entirely, and could feel her half-formed talons shredding her socks.

Once the shift settled, Eva was surprised to realize that the pain in her shoulder was gone. She filed that away for later, refocusing on the bleeding fish-man. Still screaming, he had begun to try to drag himself back to the water. Well, Eva was having none of that.

Reaching out, she sank her talons into his slick tail, then dragged him back towards her. "Answer my questions," she commanded, hooking her talons in deeper.

There was a loud splash from the river, and then Uktena's voice was crying, "Eva, look away!"

She fought every instinct she had in order to obey him, releasing the fish-man and turning her head away from the river. Yet even if she could not watch, she listened. Something large moved out of the water and slid across the land towards them. The fish-man's screams somehow became even more hysterical, until the wet, squishing sounds of something being impaled heralded complete silence. In her peripheral, Eva saw the fish-man's body go limp, then slowly be dragged away.

Even after the sounds of the large thing having returned beneath he river's surface, Eva continued to keep her eyes diverted. She focused on her breaths, counting each inhalation and exhalation. Then she closed her eyes and concentrated on shifting back into a human.

After a while, there were sounds as if someone was walking out of the water and onto the shore, but still Eva kept her eyes closed. "It's alright now," Uktena assured. "You can look."

He had returned to a human form, too, and for some reason didn't even look wet. "What happened?" she asked.

Uktena's mouth pressed into a flat line, and he reached out to offer her a hand up before answering. "There had been another two

Fractured Masks

in the river. They engaged me, and we fought for a while." He released her hand as soon as she was on her feet, and looked around at the disturbed dirt from Eva's own fight. "Didn't even let me try to talk it out, explain I wasn't there to hurt them."

"The one I met wasn't much better. He tried to use an allure on me, then proceeded to attack me when he realized it wasn't working." There was so much blood everywhere. The scent of it and the stench of fish was so overpowering that Eva wondered if she'd ever be able to wash it all off. "But at least I practically got a confession out of him that they're to blame for the kids, not the Lamiae. Though he wouldn't tell me if it was an intentional frame-up."

"Huh." Uktena looked at her with eyebrows raised. "Good job with that, then."

"What did you do with their bodies?" Should they try to clean up all the blood, she wondered. And wasn't his eye somewhere...

Thunder sounded in the distance, and Uktena glanced almost nervously up at the sky. "I ate them. Now let's go." Just like that, he was heading back down the way they had come, strides fast and wide.

"Wait, seriously?" Eva boggled, rushing to catch up. Then she snickered and playfully punched his shoulder. "How can you eat so much and maintain your girlish figure? Just what is your secret?"

"Magic," he offered with unenthusiastic jazz hands and a sardonic smirk.

Eva laughed, but then the humor quickly melted away. "So do you think it's just a coincidence?"

"Might be," he nodded. "Two similar incidents don't

necessarily mean there's a pattern."

"True." Something just felt off to her, though, and it irked her that she couldn't put her finger on it.

"In any case, we need to get out of here before the storm hits." Again he glanced at the sky, and for the first time ever he actually looked a little scared.

"At least the rain will wash all of the evidence away," said Eva, trying to lighten the mood a little.

Uktena didn't reply, and they walked silently back to the Range Rover. Before driving away, Uktena looked up nearby hotels on his phone, but even then he didn't say a word. Eva changed her coat and wiped off as much of the blood on her hands as she could while side-eyeing him. As the storm drew closer, he grew more tense, turning more sharply on curves and letting his foot weigh heavy on the gas.

The next time he spoke was to the concierge of a hotel that was considerably nicer than anywhere else they'd stayed on the trip. It had a massive indoor courtyard with trees and large boulders making a waterfall and framing the subsequent stream that snaked everywhere. There was also a sitting area with a large, stone fireplace. Tilting her head to try to see down one of the off-branching corridors, Eva was pretty certain she saw an indoor pool.

"Do you have any of the hot tub rooms on the ground floor available?" Uktena asked the smiling woman at the front desk.

She clicked at her computer before affirming happily that they did, while masterfully ignoring the fact Eva's pants were coated in dirt and something most definitely not mud. "Great," said Uktena, a faint, fleeting smile passing over his lips. "I'll take one of those. She'll have whatever." At that, he waved dismissively at Eva.

The perfect picture of professionalism, the concierge turned to Eva without a single wilt in her perky attitude. "Would you also like a hot tub?" she asked brightly.

"Nah, that's fine. I'll just take whatever's next to his."

When they got to their rooms, Uktena hesitated before simply disappearing through his door. "Don't disturb me for a while," he ordered quietly, eyes staring ahead into his dark room instead of looking at her. "We're going to be staying here for at least the night, maybe longer if the storm lingers. Until then, I'm not leaving my room unless it's an emergency. Understood?"

"Sure," she acknowledged, more than a little confused.

Then he was inside and closing the door on her without any further explanation. What the hell? Was he rattled because they'd had to fight the näcken-or-whatevers? Before, he'd been adamant about this being a mission about information retrieval, and how they weren't there to fight or kill anyone. Maybe he was some sort of pacifist who hated violence, and here he had just eaten three people.

Thunder rumbled loudly over the hotel, and Eva glanced once more at Uktena's door before slipping into her own room. The storm. That's really what had been making him so cagey. Eva walked up to her room's window and slid the curtain open to look out at the dark sky as it flashed with lightning.

He was afraid of the storm.

Chapter 14
Slipping

"I have to get to class," Günter heard himself say as soon as he opened the door to his apartment to see Phil standing there. Then, realizing that Phil's arrival must mean something was wrong, Günter asked, "What happened? Is it Jim?"

Phil cocked his head, a curious smirk on his lips. "Funny you should mention him," he said with a sense of dark humor. Then he pointedly glanced behind Günter. "May I come in?"

There was only a moment's hesitation. Günter really did have to get to class, but all of that could wait if Jim needed his help, or if Phil was there to explain things in Czar's stead. "Of course," he complied, stepping aside. "So what's wrong?" He watched as Phil walked around the living room and then over to the kitchen.

"Nice place you have here," Phil commented idly, opening random cabinets, running his fingers along the counter.

"Thanks." Günter was quickly losing his patience. "What's wrong?" he repeated. "Or are you here on behalf of Czar, to finally tell me what the hell is going on with Jim?"

Phil stopped wandering, entire body going still. Slowly he turned around to face Günter, and his expression was grim. "Evidently there was a flash drive he gave you?" There was no anger or accusation to his voice, but Günter still felt a sudden low-level panic at the words. Without waiting for Günter to confirm, Phil continued, "He was supposed to give that to someone else, it seems, and that person was none-to-pleased to discover he didn't have it."

Usually Günter had his shifting locked down thanks to his constant paranoia, but in that moment he felt his teeth grow sharp and his back ached to sprout his wings. *So Dorian had done something to Jim.*

There was a strange somberness to Phil's demeanor, and he didn't even seem surprised to see Günter lose control of his shifting. "Remember," Phil continued, "we're investigating Lamiae in the area."

"Which I figured was why I wasn't allowed to mention it to Jim, since he knew a Lamiae, but—" The image of Jim's blank expression that day at his studio flashed through Günter's mind before he saw red. He felt his hands shift into paws then talons, a growl rising up from his chest. "What did he *do*?" Günter snarled. "What did that bastard do to Jim?"

That seemed to snag Phil's attention, even though he still didn't seem rattled by seeing Günter shift. "You know who it is. You know the Lamiae that's ensnared him." Phil tilted his head a little. "And you're saying Jim already knew him?"

"*Ensnared* him?" his voice was a rough roar at that, his vision changing as his eyes turned lupine without his consent. What did it mean that they hadn't known about Dorian being Jim's acquaintance? Had they only known about Dorian from the time he ensnared Jim, and had ordered Günter not to say anything because they wanted to leave Jim ensnared?

"Down, boy," commanded Phil, remaining calm and unaffected. "We're monitoring the situation."

Those words didn't make sense to Günter, and he wasn't sure if it was because he was becoming more bestial or if they truly were that incomprehensible. So they *had* wanted to leave him ensnared? "You're *monitoring* the situation? What does that mean? You're— you're *letting* him be placed under a thrall?" In that moment, it was a good thing the breakfast bar was between Phil and Günter, because he wanted nothing more than to lash out at the man. Wanted to rend his flesh with sharp talons, feel the human's warm blood flood his mouth as he closed his jaws hard on his neck.

"It's necessary," Phil said simply. Calmly. Quietly. As one would when confronted with an angry wild beast. "We need to get to the bottom of what the Lamiae are doing."

Trying to tamp down on his growing rage, Günter began pacing. "You're *using* him. You're using the fact that he's under thrall. How, though? Are you spying on him? Do you have something set up to monitor us, something that—" The strange little heartbeat in Günter's kitchen picked up, the astringent scent of fear washing through the small space. Turning sharply to the kitchen, Günter glared at Phil as everything clicked into place. "You're monitoring me, too."

"You're both under probation," Phil reminded, still acting entirely too calm. "Of course we're monitoring you."

Günter felt so frustrated that he didn't know if he wanted to attack something or cry. "Fine," he snapped. "But, we need to get him away from the Lamiae. We need to *protect* him."

"And we will, once we have enough—"

"Now!" His shirt ripped apart as his wings finally broke free. All over his body, Günter felt the prickle at his skin that meant he'd sprouted features or fur. Glancing down, he saw that his torso was a combination of both, red and grey blending together in no semblance of pattern.

There was a long, heavy pause, and then Phil was slowly moving around the breakfast bar to approach him. "I've never seen you like this," he observed softly, a question in his tone. "We pegged you for a control freak about your nature from the start, the way you always school your features, the way you rarely even speak unless spoken to. You try to blend into the background, try to make it easy for people to overlook you." Phil stopped only a few feet from Günter, and there was no scent of fear on him, not even the tang of anxiety. "What's different now? Where is all of that tightly reined control?"

Phil's words hit him hard, and Günter closed his eyes as he took a deep, calming breath. "You're right," he husked, voice rough. *Human,* he thought. *I need to be human.* Or, as human as he was able to perceive himself. As human as he could understand.

The wings retracted first, then the furry plumage, but it took a while before his hands were soft and human, even longer until his eyesight reverted.

"You still have, ah..." Phil motioned up to his mouth, then made a fake little snarl. Oh right. With a little more concentration, Günter felt his teeth flatten out.

"Now," said Phil, beaming as if nothing were wrong, "let's have a civil little chat, shall we?" He nodded to the couch before moving there to have himself a seat.

Günter stared at him, still doing his best to remain calm. "Let me grab a shirt, first." Without waiting for a response, Günter headed back to his bedroom.

As he pulled a fresh shirt from his dresser, Günter felt exhaustion trying to press down upon him. Phil was right. Losing control like that wasn't something Günter had ever done, even when he was a child first starting puberty, the magics in his blood wailing to be let free. The implications of his actions worried him, made him angry with himself.

He'd dated humans a couple of times in the past, but he never really let himself get too invested. Humans were fragile, weak. They died too early. His father had told him stories of past heartbreak, of how painful it was to outlive someone you loved so dear. Günter had vowed to himself at an early age that he'd never allow himself to fall for a human.

Part of him wanted to blame his parents for what he was feeling now. They'd obviously been trying to play matchmaker when Günter first met Jim the night his parents hosted them all for dinner. Constantly during the meal they had been doing what they could to suss out common interests between him and Günter. At first Günter had just found it endearing yet futile. It was sweet of them to try to be supportive, find him someone who might be able to make him happy. They didn't know a human could never be that for him.

But Jim was.... Jim was bold and funny and smart. The way he talked with his hands was charmingly distracting. He was the cautious one of their ragtag little group, before they were brought into the Gehealdan. Even now, Günter knew to listen to whatever Jim had to say on any subject. It was like Jim was a tether, tugging Günter back to reason and sensibility.

If Günter was good at anything, though, it was repression. So he boxed his feelings up, then buried that box deep down where it couldn't do him any more harm. He was a warrior. He was trained to be cool and calm, no matter the situation. What happened in his living room would never happen again. Günter just wouldn't allow it.

Tugging on his shirt, he went to rejoin Phil with an entirely different demeanor. "Would you like something to drink?" he asked as soon as he was back out into the living room.

Phil smiled at him and shook his head. "I'm fine. Glad to see you've calmed down."

"That was a mistake," Günter assured. "It won't happen again."

"I know." Relaxing back into the couch, Phil patted the seat beside him.

Instead, Günter leaned against the breakfast bar. Silence stretched out between them, Günter mentally reminding himself to remain calm while Phil eyed him with appraisal. "You have to understand," Phil started, sounding so damn rational, "this is about more than just you or Jim."

"I understand." He did. Really. Everything the Gehealdan did was for the greater good. It was something he had thought Eva understood, too. Maybe she had, but in the end she had let her emotions override her rationality. She'd put one person's life above the lives of countless others. Günter wouldn't make that same mistake, no matter how much it pained him.

"We'll help him," continued Phil, "we will. But first we need more information. Right now Jim's our best source, even though he doesn't realize it." He took a breath and for the first time looked concerned instead of coolly casual. "Until then, we need you to do what you can to keep him safe. I'm sure you've noticed that he's already starting to look tired, sickly."

"He says it's just stress." Günter repeated Jim's lie as if he actually believed it himself.

Eyebrows rising, Phil gave a little nod. "Well, that's part of it, actually. How familiar are you with how Lamiae magic works?"

The question made Günter uncomfortable, his mind trying to shy away from the answer even as he forced the words from his mouth. "They're a type of incubus or succubus."

"Well, yes, but that's a broad category." Phil reached back and ran a hand absently down along his braid as if checking to make sure it was all in order. "There's things classified as those, when they simply sneak in and have their ways with sleeping humans. Even Romes and owls can be classified as being incubi or succubi, in that sense."

Something rotten churned in Günter's stomach. "And Lamiae? How do they work?"

Phil idly popped his knuckles and tilted his head back as he turned his stare inward. "They use attraction and sex to put people under a thrall. Back in the old days, before the Treaties, they'd usually only exert the magic long enough to mate, then they'd eat their victim."

Günter felt his pulse start to quicken, and he pressed the feeling down. "So you're saying he's going to *eat* Jim?"

"No," Phil was quick to correct turning his head to face Günter and show the sincerity in his eyes. "We won't ever let it get to that point." When he got a nod of understanding from Günter, Phil continued, "But the reason he's looking tired and sick is because the thrall is lasting much longer than it usually does. The natural human response is to fight against it, and that's exactly what Jim's doing. Fighting."

"So the fighting is what's exhausting him."

"Yes, exactly."

Letting that sink in, Günter stared down at his shoes. "What do you want me to do? How can I keep him safe?"

"Don't let him know you know. Stop him from doing anything he shouldn't, since he won't be in control of his own actions." Phil hesitated for a moment, then added, "Otherwise don't interfere with the Lamiae's control."

Günter felt a wave of nausea, like getting seasick on a lurching boat. "But, Dorian's..." He knew exactly what he had smelled on Jim the other day, and now knew exactly what it meant. If Jim wasn't even aware it was happening, if magic was stripping away his ability to consent or refuse, then it was rape. Now Phil was asking Günter to just stand by and let Dorian continue to do that to Jim?

"No," he objected, voice quiet as he reeled from it all. "I can't let it continue."

"I thought we already covered how this is beyond you or Jim," snapped Phil, sitting forward, eyes sharp. "The information we can glean from the Lamiae could prove invaluable."

"And if it was you?" asked Günter, glaring at Phil and trying to breathe through his lingering nausea. "If you were the one under the thrall, getting used like that, getting *raped*? Would you really want us to just let it keep happening?"

Phil pursed his lips, then sighed through his nose and leaned back again into the couch. "No," he admitted, "I wouldn't."

"Then how can you tell me to just let it happen to Jim? How can *you* let it happen?" The shift tried to sneak up on Günter again, his control wavering, but he refocused and fought it back.

For a long moment, Phil had nothing to say. He looked at his knees, frowning, while he thought over Günter's words. "I'll speak with Czar," he eventually offered. "While each of us should be willing to sacrifice whatever is needed for the cause, this isn't something Jim agreed to willingly. It's different than volunteering for a suicide mission or resisting torture in an interrogation."

"It's an attack on a fellow Gehealdan member," agreed

Günter, finally starting to feel a loosening in the knot of concern in his gut. "And to just leave him under the thrall is the same as willingly leaving someone behind when we know we can save them."

"But the information," murmured Phil, seeming frustrated. "We're *so close*."

"Find a different way," growled Günter. "I'm here, part of Gehealdan, because it's a cause I believe in. But I can't abide by any organization that would treat its members like this."

Phil looked up at him, quietly studying him for a stretch. Then, slowly, he nodded and rose to his feet. "Alright," he said, moving towards the door, "I'll head to the shop now. You and Jim take the night off. Honestly, I don't know if there's anything you can do on your part to snap Jim out of the thrall, but you can try."

"Before getting approval from Czar?" Günter asked, skeptical.

With a nod, Phil confirmed, "Yes. I'll get him to agree with letting this go and switch it so that protecting Jim is our top priority."

He stopped at the door and looked back at Günter, a grim shadow to his features that seemed out of place on Phil's perpetually-smiling face. "Thank you for knocking things back into perspective. You're right; we can't just sacrifice our own like this. We exist to protect, to uphold the laws established by the Treaties...so what would we be if we couldn't even protect one of our own?"

Günter watched him go, still reeling a bit despite his efforts to reestablish his sense of calm. At least Phil had come around by the end, and they weren't going to leave Jim to the wolves. Or, well, sharks. If tossed to the wolves, the wolves would protect Jim, because the wolves would be Günter and Eva. He was certain that even though she'd jumped ship, Eva would do whatever she could to help Jim if she knew what was happening.

Giving up on going to class, Günter started to head to his bedroom in order to try to contact Mick. He stopped short just shy of the hallway, however, as he remembered the revelation earlier in relation to the little heartbeat in his kitchen. Listening carefully, he heard it again, steady and calm now, the scent of nervous fear dissipating. "Who are you?" he asked, turning towards the kitchen.

There was a pause before a small, male voice with a bit of a brogue answered, "I'm not one ta be tellin' me name."

"Fair enough," Günter conceded, knowing that for some folk their names held power that could be used against them. "I don't suppose you plan to leave, now that I know you're here?"

The voice gave a short chuff of a laugh. "Not likely, lad, no. It's the Old Man I be answerin' to, not you. He says I stay, I stay."

"Well, help yourself to whatever food you want," Günter relented, feeling too exhausted to really fight it.

"That's mighty kind of you, lad. Mighty kind."

Günter just waved the thanks off and asked, "So you've told him about my conversations with Mick, I take it?"

"Might be I have."

Not really sure if he felt frightened or angry by that, Günter slumped forward against the wall. "And his reaction?"

"Didn't seem fit ta be endin' ya, lad, if that's what ya fear."

Lifting his head, he looked back towards the kitchen again. "Why not?" Günter knew exactly what they did with people who leaked important secrets.

"Didn't say. But if ya ask me, it's likely he appreciates your words o' loyalty. Doesn't hurt that your friend could give us some tidbits, I dare say."

Well. That made sense, he supposed. "So you don't mind if I go have a chat with Mick right now? Talk to him about all of this?" he asked, waving out towards the living room to indicate his conversation with Phil.

"It don't matter much to me what ya do, lad. But if it's the Old Man you're worryin' about, just don't be givin' me anything bad to report."

"I have birthday cake ice cream in the fridge," Günter said enticingly. It had been Eva's and was way too sweet for Günter, so it wasn't like there was much point in keeping it. "You can have it all if you step out for a bit. Get some fresh air."

There was a short pause and then, "You'll not be doing anything bad, now, will ya, lad?"

"No," he assured, trying to put as much honesty and conviction in that one little word. "I just want to talk with my friend privately. It won't be any different from previous chats, but I just don't feel comfortable talking with him while I have an audience."

"Fine," the voice relented. "But only if ya promise to tell me any information he may let slip." Barely a beat, and then he continued, "And get me a real cake tomorrow."

Günter breathed a tiny laugh at that. "You have my word, I will do both."

"Very well. I'll be steppin' out for a bit, but be back before the sunset."

"Thank you," said Günter, the words heavy with meaning.

He waited until the little heartbeat was gone, and then still waited a few minutes more to ensure it wouldn't return. With a sigh of relief, he straightened up and continued on to his room.

Opening up the messenger Mick had first used to contact him, Günter shot PaintItBohemian a quick little *"free to talk?"*

Barely a minute later, his camera program was starting up on its own, and Mick was smiling at him from the screen. As soon as he saw Günter's face, though, the smile wilted away. "What's wrong?" asked Mick, leaning closer to his computer.

"Jim's in trouble."

"Jim, the guy you couldn't stop talking about a couple months ago? British artist who looks like a young Jimi Hendrix, but also jailbait high school kid?"

Günter rolled his eyes. "He's eighteen, and it's not like that, anyway."

"Right," Mick deadpanned, slumping back in his chair with a teasing grin. "You just really like his voice, and he's really talented, and he's going to go to the same college as you, and he's funny, and he—"

"Okay, okay, shut up. He's just a friend."

"Yeah, sure."

Günter glared. "He is."

"No, yeah, totally."

"Look, can we focus on the situation at hand? He's in trouble. Also, he's one of Eva's best friends, so I thought she'd like to know."

That sobered Mick real quick and he sat up a little straighter. "I'll tell her, when I can. What's going on?"

So Günter told him. By the end of it, Mick was looking just as sick as Günter felt. "Jesus," breathed Mick. "That's so screwed up." Then he frowned, chewing on his bottom lip a bit. "The guy who's doing this to him...you said he was a Lamiae?"

"Yeah." And soon to be a dead one, if Günter had any say in

the matter.

"I probably shouldn't be telling you this, since you're the enemy and all," Mick started hesitantly, eyeing the screen over his glasses, "but Eva's been working with someone on investigating some recent executions of Lamiae. Evidently, they're finding evidence that it's been someone else both times. Maybe that's why that Lamiae is using Jim to get information, because they're concerned more are going to be wrongly executed."

Günter scoffed to stop from growling. "They haven't been wrongly executed. If anything, they're trying to pin it on those others. I know, because we had a case recently where a strix was executed for something it seems a Lamiae may have actually done."

Mick's face looked pinched. "Well, that sounds all kinds of confusing, then. Who's framing whom, I wonder."

"I just told you the Lamiae are framing others."

"Yeah, you say that but your sister has seen evidence to the contrary." Then Mick hesitated for a moment before quietly revealing, "She was attacked by one of the guilty parties recently." Before Günter could really react, Mick quickly went on to add, "She's okay! All healed up, with her magical healing powers. Everything's fine. But, really, I think that helps to prove that it wasn't the Lamiae who were guilty there."

Shaking his head and trying to keep himself calm after hearing about Eva, Günter disagreed. "I was attacked by the strix, but that doesn't mean she was guilty. She was just scared and trying to defend herself. The same may have happened with Eva. Some supernatural folk are also severely territorial, so may react violently to other supernaturals invading their space." She was tough, Günter had to remind himself, calming his heart. Eva was a warrior, same as he. And Mick had said she was fine.

"Maybe," Mick allowed with a tip of his head. "But it all just seems strangely coincidental, then."

"Not if the Lamiae are trying to pin it on others," Günter insisted.

"But why would they do that? Eva said they evidently haven't stepped out of line once since the Treaties, so why would that suddenly change now?"

That stumped Günter, and he shook his head, slumping forward. "I don't know. Maybe that's why Czar was allowing the Lamiae to keep Jim under a thrall, because they were hoping to get some information that would shine a light on all of this. I mean, Phil said they were close to getting the information they needed."

"Who are Phil and Czar?"

"Czar's the boss, and Phil's second in command." Günter figured it wasn't hurting anything to tell Mick that, since it wasn't some sort of big Gehealdan secret. Besides, Eva and Lucy already knew.

"And they just *let* the Lamiae do that to Jim? Tell me again how you aren't working for the bad guys." The disgust was evident in Mick's voice, and Günter felt his face burn in shame.

"It's not like that," though it was. It really was. Günter had just chewed Phil out because of it. "They realize now it's wrong, and are going to help Jim." *Hopefully*, Günter mentally added.

Mick just stared at him from the other side of the screen, eyes sad. "You ever want to come here," he said softly, "I'm sure they'd welcome you."

Closing his eyes against a wave of pain and longing, Günter shook his head. "I believe in the Gehealdan and what it does," he objected, even as doubt pricked at his chest.

"Sure," Mick acknowledged, sounding just as convinced as he'd been about Günter's disinterest in Jim.

Chapter 15
Fractures

"Why can't I go that way?"
"It leads to the gardens."
"Why can't I go into the gardens?"
"Because of the dancing bird."

Lucy stood trembling at the intersection of yet another familiar corridor. She trembled not just because that damn dream was overlapping with reality again, but because Mick had just told her everything he'd heard from Günter about Jim. Lucy had used every scrap of her recently-learned control to remain calm throughout the revelation, to not let it slip how deeply the news impacted her. She had tried so hard to make it back to her room before breaking down, but then there was that familiar hallway, and she could feel her strength slipping.

Her feet moved down the corridor, seemingly of their own accord. It was a short hallway, and all too soon she was at the end, hand shaking as it reached for the bar to push the door open. Holding her breath, Lucy shoved at the door and cringed as if expecting an attack.

Instead, all she found was a beautiful courtyard filled with trees and flowerbeds and paved pathways. With winter fast approaching, none of the flowers were in bloom, but some of the trees still had vibrant, flame-colored leaves. The courtyard was huge, and it looked as if the Fenris building wrapped around it like a giant doughnut. Stumbling out into the sunlight, Lucy looked all around her for whatever horror Pulchrum had warned her of in the dream. There were birds, but none of them danced, and everything seemed so peaceful.

Eyes pricking with the tears she'd been restraining, Lucy found her way to a bench and sat down. There she curled in on herself, burying her face in her hands as she finally let go.

God, she felt so sick, like she'd eaten too much funnel cake before getting on the fastest ride with the most spins. Everything was swirling around, making it impossible to get her bearings. She wept for Jim, absolutely she wept for him, but she also wept for herself.

Until Mick gave her the update, Lucy had been doing her best to avoid thinking about that night they'd killed the Reaper. More specifically, she had avoided thinking about what the Reaper had done to her, and what he would have succeeded in doing had Eva not shown up in time.

Phantom touches ran along her flesh, making her shudder and her stomach turn. That moment had been a hazy blur, but she could still remember his hands and lips on her, his words whispered with a stolen voice. There had been nothing she could do to break the spell herself, no way she would have been able to stop him from taking whatever he wanted.

Was that what it was like for Jim? Could he even tell what was happening to him, or was it all just a haze? Once the spell was broken, would he remember any of it? Lucy honestly couldn't decide which would be worse, to remember it all or to have no idea what had happened.

She didn't know how long she sat there, choking back bile and letting herself finally cry. At some point, she pulled her legs up onto the bench and curled up sideways, hugging herself. Eventually she fell asleep like that, feeling too tired to move.

*

When she awoke, she heard feminine voices chatting in a language she didn't recognize. Her chilled body ached as she uncurled and stretched, but she felt a little better. Still kind of hollow and a little bit fragile, but not as bone-deep exhausted.

Rubbing absently at one eye, she wandered towards the voices. She still hadn't met a lot of the other members of Fenris yet, and figured that was something she should do, considering her lineage. Hopefully her face wasn't all puffy and gross from all of the crying, and that the impromptu nap had erased all evidence.

She rounded a corner to find a small pond surrounded by a trail. Beneath a weeping willow stood two women leaning close to each other with warm, playful smiles. Lucy recognized one of the women as her grandmother, but the other had her back to Lucy and all she could really make out was long, black hair. Before Lucy could call out to Sigyn, the women were closing the scant distance between them and kissing.

"What the—" Lucy blurted, eyes wide and torn between shock and anger on her grandfather's behalf.

The women pulled apart, turning to her with a start, and Lucy gasped when she saw that the black-haired woman looked weirdly like an older version of herself. "Ah," said the stranger, face relaxing in understanding, "this must seem quite scandalous." Her accent sounded the same as Loki and Sigyn's, and she wore a blue suit that seemed to not quite fit her properly, too tight around the hips and bust.

Instead of looking guilty, Sigyn bit back a smile and smothered a soft chuckle into the other woman's shoulder. "Sorry," said the woman, wrapping an arm around Sigyn's middle and offering Lucy a slanted smile. "This is how she first knew me, and I tend to take this form when we're alone together."

Sigyn straightened and then looked at the stranger, her expression a peculiar mix of sadness and love. "And after so many years where she was forced into one form," said Sigyn, continuing the explanation, "it's lovely to see her free to be whatever she chooses again."

The other woman seemed to notice that none of their words were easing Lucy's confusion, so she gently slipped out of Sigyn's arms and stepped closer. As she walked, her features began to shift and change, black hair bleeding into the colors of sunset, curves melting into lithe muscles. Only the eyes remained the same, a bright, pale blue that burned more brilliantly than the late afternoon sun in the courtyard. Actually, the eyes weren't the only constant, the suit slowly starting to fit perfectly as her body changed.

By the time the woman reached Lucy, she wasn't a woman at all, but Loki. "Oh," was all Lucy could think to say. She knew Loki was a shape-shifter, but it was still quite something to see. A little unnerving, really, considering what she had just broken down remembering. The last time she'd seen someone shape-shift into different people had been when she faced off against the Reaper.

"When we met," said Sigyn, as she too approached, "I knew her as Rindr. It was only months later when I first met him as Loki."

"Oh," Lucy repeated, thinking maybe she finally understood. "Grandparent." When Loki just blinked at her, Lucy explained, "What you said when we first met. You called yourself our grand*parent*, not our grand*father*. So. I get it now." She shrugged. Sure, it was a little strange, but she'd seen stranger recently, and it wasn't like she didn't know about humans who sort of wavered between genders. Lucy imagined it was probably even more common amongst shape-shifters, since they could easily alter their bodies to any gender they wanted. Well, depending on the type of shifter.

Before Loki could say anything else in response, Sigyn stepped around him to cup Lucy's cheek. "Have you been crying, love?"

Embarrassed, Lucy pulled away and lowered her gaze. "It's nothing."

"That's a dangerous thing to do," Sigyn cautioned, voice warm and soft as a fleece blanket fresh from the dryer. "You should never bottle up your emotions."

"I," Lucy wavered and stopped, suddenly feeling fragile and exposed. Her throat felt dammed up with reawakened grief, and she closed her eyes so her grandparents wouldn't see them glisten. It was hard to speak, but she slowly, quietly, told them everything about Jim.

They seemed suitably appalled, and before Lucy could chicken out, she added, "I also... The night I left the Gehealdan, when Eva and I went to save Krysti from their agent, he tried to—"

Fury made Loki's eyes burn brighter, and Sigyn's expression was hard lines of simmering rage. "He didn't succeed," Lucy quickly went on to clarify. "I was under his thrall for only a little bit, and then Eva came and stopped him. Still, I," she took a deep, shuddering breath, "I know if Eva hadn't arrived when she did, then..."

Gripping Lucy's shoulders firmly, Loki looked her straight in the eye. "I'm proud that you're my granddaughter," he said, sincerity clear on his face. "You're so strong, and so brave. It couldn't have been easy facing off against someone like him, and yet you fought him and you won. I'm also so proud of you for seeing the Gehealdan for what it is and having the strength to leave."

"I just wish there was something I could do for Jim," whispered Lucy, feeling so damn helpless.

He gave her shoulders a little squeeze and smiled encouragingly. "Someday you'll help us rid the world of the Gehealdan, and that will not only help your friend, but everyone else."

She squinted at him through her lingering tears, confused. "How? It's the Lamiae who're doing that to Jim, not the Gehealdan."

Loki's smile faded and he gave a little nod, eyes intense. "But it's the Gehealdan which drove the Lamiae—a group that hasn't done ill for hundreds of years—to take such drastic measures. And it's the Gehealdan which is not only allowing what's happening to your friend to continue, but seems to be exploiting it for their own gain."

Anger bubbled deep in Lucy's gut, accompanied with a touch of remorse for having ever served them. "You're right. The whole organization is rotten."

"Exactly," agreed Loki, features softening. He pulled her into a hug and Lucy fell into it with a sense of overwhelming relief. They had been the only ones she had talked to about what happened to her that night, and Loki had praised her strength, let her know it wasn't her fault. Not that any rational part of her brain thought she was to blame for what had nearly been done to her, but there had been this sticky, clinging sense of shame.

Sigyn came around and joined the hug, and Lucy felt a warm sense of happiness and safety blossom in her chest. Of course she wasn't fully safe anywhere, she knew that, but she also knew that these people would at least do everything in their power to protect her.

Footsteps came running quickly over grass and sidewalk, growing louder until they stopped just a few feet away. "Sorry to disturb you, Chairman," a young female voice hazarded softly, sounding a little out of breath.

Reluctantly, Lucy released her grandparent and allowed him to turn and face the newcomer. Sigyn kept Lucy in her arms, however, pulling her gently so that Lucy was leaning back against her chest while Sigyn held her. They saw a pretty, tiny woman—she couldn't have been even three feet tall—with dark tan skin and long black hair.

Bending down to allow the woman to speak more privately with him, Loki nodded for her to continue. With a brief glance at Lucy and Sigyn, the woman murmured, "Reports from our agents within Gehealdan have alerted us to another Lamiae target. This time in California, and rather high-profile."

Loki straightened up, frowning at the news. "Have you contacted Uktena?"

The woman quickly nodded. "He's waiting for your orders."

"I see." Turning back to Lucy and Sigyn, Loki offered an apologetic smile. "Sorry to run like this."

"It's fine," Sigyn assured, her chin brushing against Lucy's hair as she nodded. "Go."

Switching focus to Lucy, he said, "I'll see you again soon, for your training. And remember," he paused, reaching out to tap a knuckle beneath her chin, lifting her head a bit, "you are the descendant of very powerful beings, and that strength flows through your veins. You are mighty and brave, and we are all very proud."

Lucy felt her eyes sting a bit, and her smile couldn't do her feelings justice in that moment.

Then Loki was off, following the small woman. The late afternoon sun made his hair look like wildfire as he moved, and the trees rustled as if sighing over his departure.

Once they were alone, Sigyn turned Lucy so they were facing each other, and studied her granddaughter's face. "Loki has told me of your nightmares," she said, voice cautiously kind.

"I haven't had any since being here."

"Good. That's good. I have been working with some others to ward you from mara or anything else of that realm."

"Thank you, seriously." Lucy huffed a humorless laugh and looked around them. "Weirdly enough, I kind of wandered here because I saw this in one of the nightmares. I wasn't allowed to come this way, though."

Sigyn's brows crinkled in concern. "You saw the courtyard in one of the nightmares?" At Lucy's nod, she asked, "Why weren't you allowed to come this way?"

"Pulchrum was there—"

"Agent Belobog?"

"Yeah. He was there, and he told me that I couldn't go to the gardens because of the dancing bird."

That only seemed to perplex Sigyn, and she looked about at the trees as if she could spot the bird. "How strange. I can't even begin to imagine what that could be in reference to." Sighing with a rueful little chuckle, Sigyn refocused on Lucy. "Then again, dreams are like that. They are often times riddles, and I've never been particularly adept at dream reading."

"But there's gotta be someone in the organization who is, right?" asked Lucy, remembering Loki's promise to help her untangle the meanings of her nightmares.

"Yes, several," Sigyn confirmed. "They don't live here, however, so they'll not be arriving for another week or so. Loki tried to find the best we have available, and contacted all of them."

"That's—I don't want to be an inconvenience," Lucy objected, feeling the blush rise in her cheeks while her stomach squirmed.

Sigyn just waved her worry off. "It's no trouble, I assure you. We're doing it not only because you are our granddaughter, but also because your dreams may hold prophecies within them."

Even though that made perfect sense, Lucy still felt a little bad about causing such a fuss. Then she remembered her last nightmare, and shuddered at the thought it could be a prophecy. "But not all prophecies come true, right?" she asked weakly. "Loki said before that prophetic dreams may just be showing us a potential future, not a definite one. Or even just a warning of what could happen if we take a potential path." Lucy swallowed back a lump in her throat, the sensation reminding her of being—

—doubled-over and coughing so hard it hurt. Something dislodged from her throat, making her cough even harder until it finally came up and splattered to the blood-stained floor.

"Lucy," she heard Sigyn cry out to her, then felt the vague sensation of hands gripping her shoulders. Everything seemed wrapped in thick down blankets, muffled and hazy. "Lucy, breathe with me," commanded Sigyn, before she started a system of inhaling for three counts, then exhaling for three counts. Lucy did her best to follow, the world slowly bleeding back into sharpness.

"What happened?" Lucy asked, voice faint and throat raw. Her body was trembling and her cheeks felt wet.

Brushing back Lucy's hair, Sigyn studied her face, brow wrinkled in concern. "You had an attack and weren't breathing properly."

"I'm sorry," Lucy nearly sobbed, feeling so pathetic. Only a few minutes ago Loki had told her she was strong, and yet there she was breaking down and having some sort of panic attack.

Sigyn jerked her head back, eyes wide. "Why are you sorry? There is nothing to apologize for, my darling." She then pulled Lucy close into another hug, rubbing her back soothingly. "You have been through so much. Tell me, why is it that you still refuse counseling?" When Lucy didn't answer, merely buried her face against Sigyn's collarbone, Sigyn gently asked, "Do you feel it will make you seem weak?"

"I'm sorry," Lucy repeated, clinging to her grandmother's dress.

"Oh, my little warrior," murmured Sigyn, hugging her tighter. "It is not weak to ask for help, nor is it weak to take care of yourself."

"I'm fine. It's fine," Lucy lied, her trembling growing worse.

For a while, Sigyn simply held her, but then she kissed Lucy's temple and asked, "Would you at least speak with Dr. Sartre as one friend confiding in another? I know you two have some sort of history, and that complicates any professional relationship, but he may be able to give you friendly advice."

"We aren't really friends," corrected Lucy, muffled a bit as she pressed her face harder against Sigyn's collar.

Sigyn ran her fingers through Lucy's hair in gentle pets. "I find that hard to believe. There is a connection between the two of you; I see it."

Pulling away enough to free her face, Lucy looked up at Sigyn with a bit of a sulky pout. It was definitely not the time for her grandmother to be playing matchmaker, and Ren was definitely not someone she wanted to be matched up with. "It's really not like that. We're acquaintances, at best. He tried to help me out a couple of times, and I think he may have saved my then-crush's life at one point, but we don't like each other that much."

"Yet he's helping you with learning meditation and control, is he not? You mean to tell me that the two of you don't talk during those sessions?"

Lucy couldn't meet Sigyn's eyes, because they absolutely did, and they'd even started to really open up to each other and build some sort of trust. "Yeah, but it's not—"

"I'm not saying you have to be in love with him," said Sigyn with an exasperated chuckle in her voice. "Merely that you talk with him about some of the things that bother you. I have seen how you and your brothers are protective of your mother, and I assume you don't want to concern Krysti while she's still in a fragile state. There's your brothers, but one is perhaps too young for such things, and is already weighed down with his own issues. Mick, I'm sure, would want to hear about everything and lend you his support. Even so, he does not have hundreds of years of experience in helping people work through their issues, like Dr. Sartre does."

Sigyn sighed and caressed Lucy's cheek. "Please. For me. Speak with Dr. Sartre and let him help you."

Ducking her head, Lucy nodded. "At our next session, I'll maybe bring some of this up. I already told him about the nightmares."

"That's good," praised Sigyn, pulling Lucy closer to kiss the crown of her head. "You must take care of yourself. Even the strongest warriors need aid sometimes."

She was right, and Lucy knew on some level that it didn't make her weak to get help. Yet, just as some irrational part of her mind felt shameful for what happened with the Reaper, it whispered dark words that fed her insecurities. Lucy couldn't help feeling like a failure of an Æsir, unable to control her powers and falling apart over memories and nightmares. She wished she could be as strong and brave as Eva and Günter, standing stoic and unshaken even if the world fell to pieces.

Maybe talking with Ren would help her get there, though. After all, he was trying to teach her how to have full control over her emotions. With practice and time, perhaps she could actually feel like she was made out of something other than brittle glass.

Chapter 16
Clinging

"What's this?" asked Jim, cocking his head at a black folder spread open to reveal papers in Japanese and a glossy photo of a beautiful woman. It had just been sitting there on Günter's breakfast bar, but Jim still felt a bit like maybe he was snooping.

Günter heaved a deep sigh and strode up to snatch the folder. "Omiai requests sent by my grandfather," he explained before dumping the whole thing into the kitchen bin.

"Oh-me-eye?"

"It's like a matchmaking service for arranged marriages." Günter rubbed at his eyes as if they hurt, and Jim felt a little twinge of sympathy. It felt like Jim hadn't slept for days, and he had a horrible headache he just couldn't shake.

"Grandfather is...very traditional. Plus he wants to form some strong alliances. All of my cousins have 'married beneath themselves,'" Günter even made the air quotes, "so he considers me —and maybe Eva—to be his last hope."

Eyebrows rising, Jim crossed his arms over the bar and leaned in a bit. "No offense, but he doesn't care that your mum may have 'married beneath herself?' Polluting the bloodline with wolf DNA and all."

"You would think." Günter huffed a hollow laugh and stepped around the bar to stand close. "But Mother was always my grandfather's favorite, so I guess that cancels it out in his mind or something. Who knows."

"So I'm guessing he doesn't know you're gay?" Jim knew that 'traditional' was often codespeak for someone who may harbor some rather outdated and bigoted ideas. He could understand why Günter wouldn't feel comfortable coming out to someone like that, even if it was family.

Glancing down and away, Günter gave a quick shake of his head. Then he softly smacked his hand on the bar and pushed away. "C'mon, let's get out of here."

"I thought you said Phil gave us the night off?"

"Well, yeah," confirmed Günter, turning to flash Jim a tentative smile, "but that doesn't mean we have to spend it cooped up in here."

Despite feeling like little more than a zombie, Jim managed to return the smile and tried to drum up a bit of enthusiasm. "Alright then, where to?"

"It's Friday, so why not the High? It's open until nine today."

Jim felt himself chuckle, a bit of warmth managing to bubble up through the fog of exhaustion that had become his constant state of being. "Didn't know you were that into art."

Günter gave a little shrug, looking almost shy. "There's some nice stuff there," he offered as if needing to come up with an excuse.

No one ever needed an excuse to view art, though, so Jim just smiled wider and waved towards the door. "Lead the way."

***

Standing in front of *The Veiled Rebekah*, Jim felt his mind to be almost peaceful, in a way it hadn't for a long while. As many times as he'd been to the High, that had always been his favorite piece. Sure, there were loads of really amazing exhibits that passed through, and he definitely loved experiencing them all, but the marble statues that were permanent features at the museum always held a special place in his heart. *The Veiled Rebekah* especially never ceased to captivate him. Jim loved the Hellenistic-inspired way the clothing seemed wet and clung to her form. Then, of course, there was the veil, so perfectly carved to create the illusion of the stone being as sheer and revealing as cloth.

"That's beautiful," Günter murmured in awe as he stepped up beside him.

Smile stretching across his lips, Jim nodded in agreement. "I love the way Benzoni carves fabric, and this piece has always been my favorite of his."

"What you do is incredible, too," said Günter, bumping their shoulders.

Feeling his cheeks grow flushed, Jim ducked his head for a second before looking back up into the statue's veiled face. "I'm not nearly at his level yet, though. I mean, look at this! The fabric looks so sheer and delicate, her features peeking out from behind it." Just looking at it made Jim feel inspired, his fingers twitching with the need to carve.

"Honestly I'm in awe of what you and all of the artists here can do," admitted Günter, eyes still intently focused on the statue. "To be able to create something out of only your mind and whatever medium you choose... It's like magic to me." He chuckled and turned his head just slightly to catch Jim's eye. "And that's coming from someone who can sprout wings."

Jim breathed out a delighted little laugh, and allowed himself to lean a bit closer to Günter. This was nice. Spending time away from anything sad or stressful, in the company of a good friend. It was definitely what Jim needed. "Thanks for bringing me here."

When Günter shrugged, his shoulder rubbed a bit against Jim's. "You were right about how we needed to spend some time together outside of work."

"Well, then thanks for taking me up on my suggestion." Jim grinned cheekily.

For a moment, Günter just stared at him, features melting from warm happiness to looking almost lost. Clearing his throat, Günter lowered his gaze and took a step away from Jim. "Have you eaten yet? We can maybe get dinner somewhere, if you want."

It was difficult puzzling out Günter in that moment, and Jim wasn't sure if this was supposed to still just be two friends hanging out. Günter always struck Jim as a bit shy, but this seemed like something else. "How about we just grab something to go and head back to your place, watch something fun?"

Nodding absently, Günter turned to start heading towards the exit. "Yeah," he agreed, voice just as distracted. "Yeah, that's a good idea, actually. Better to talk in private."

"Talk?" prompted Jim, catching him up and strolling alongside him. "About what?"

Günter glanced at him, all of his emotions getting stuffed back behind his usual stoic mask. "Stuff."

"Ooooh," Jim nodded. "Of course. Very important, that." He gave Günter a friendly jab with his elbow and tried to tease out some reaction with a smirk. "Almost as important as things."

He was rewarded with Günter unable to hold back a snort of amusement, and the slight twitch at the corner of Günter's lips like the ghost of a smile. In the next second, however, those lips were pressing flat and thin, a tension hardening Günter's features. Part of Jim itched to capture the expression in charcoal, sculpt it in clay, then chisel it out of stone. It was the face of a hero going into battle, expecting death and braving it anyway. There was something beautifully fatalistic about that face, and it seemed a pity not to preserve it just like that for eternity.

*

They ended up grabbing Chinese, Jim going for spicy and Günter going for generic. "For some reason I expected you to order something besides just garlic beef," said Jim, snapping his disposable chopsticks apart.

Shrugging, Günter separated his own chopsticks, then opened his containers. "My palate always ran more towards my German side. Besides, Chinese food isn't the same as Japanese food, and this isn't even really Chinese food."

"True enough," Jim allowed, picking out a shrimp from his own container and then following it up with a bite of rice. "What did you want to talk about?" he asked as soon as he'd swallowed.

Günter poked at his food before setting it all aside. Seemingly unable to meet Jim's eyes, Günter clasped his hands together and glared down at them. "It's about Dorian."

A coldness trickled along Jim's spine, and the spicy food lost its flavor. "Not this again," grumbled Jim, so damn sick of Günter constantly bashing on Dorian.

That, at least, got Günter to look up at him, his amber eyes looking frightened and pleading. "Jim, he's using you."

Scoffing, Jim stuffed his chopsticks into his food and shoved it away. "How do you figure that, eh? All he does is come over to model, and we talk for a bit, maybe kiss."

Günter's face looked pinched with pain and he closed his eyes. "That's not all that happens. You just can't remember, either because you don't want to or his allure prevents it."

"Oh my bloody Christ, are you listening to yourself now? You think he's pulling some sort of mojo on me?" With a roll of his eyes, Jim stood to leave. "Keep my share of the food, yeah? I'm not hungry."

"Wait," called Günter, jumping to his feet, eyes wide in alarm. "You can't—are you *leaving*? How? I drove you here."

"Yeah, and there's a magical app on my phone that'll send a driver to me," he snarked back.

"Jim, just, please. Hear me out."

That voice and those pleading eyes just weren't fair, and Jim found himself stopping at the door to lean his head against it and sigh. "I'm too tired for this right now. I get it, okay? You don't like Dorian, because evidently prejudice exists among supernaturals."

"It's not that," snapped Günter, rounding the coffee table to approach him. "I don't like him because he's ensnaring you under some type of spell, and it's *killing* you."

Boiling with rage, Jim pushed away from the door and turned to practically snarl at Günter. "Are you *completely* mental?" he asked, incredulous. "You think the only way I could fall for someone like him is if he's using some sort of magic? Seriously?" Jim's fingers curled into fists and he fought back the urge to take a swing. "I *like* him, alright? He makes me feel better when he's around."

"That's the allure magic," Günter insisted, ratcheting up the dial on Jim's anger meter. "Maybe it's like a drug or something, I don't know. But just look at you! You're always so tired, and it's just been getting worse. It's your body fighting the allure, trying to break free of his magic."

"Did it ever occur to you that I'm tired because two of my best friends got me tangled up in a murderous organization that polices supernaturals, then buggered off and left me to fend for myself? Who's to say the Gehealdan won't decide during my 'probation' that I'm guilty of something and off me? So excuse me if I'm a wee bit stressed and more than a little depressed at getting abandoned. I think I've the right!" Jim was practically panting by the end of his little rant, and feeling so depleted that his vision swam for a second.

Wilting back a little, Günter just shook his head. "Of course you have the right to be stressed and sad. You don't think I'm feeling that way, too? Eva's my sister, and every day hurts knowing she can never come home." He took a steadying breath and dared to step closer to Jim. "But what's happening to you is different. Do you even remember your time together with Dorian? What do the two of you do?"

That was an odd question, and Jim tried to figure out why Günter would even ask that. What, did he seriously think that Jim had missing ti—but wait, didn't he? Or, no. No, that wasn't right. Of course he could remember what he did with Dorian; it was the entire reason they started hanging out, after all. "He models for me. We spend most of our time together like that, talking while he poses. Some snogging, nothing serious. Then he heads home."

"But he doesn't! That's not what happens," yelled Günter, concern suddenly burning away into fury. For a moment, Jim thought Günter's eyes had gone slightly more yellow in hue. "The other day, you *reeked* of sex."

"I think I'd know if I've had sex!" It felt like something had gone rotten in Jim's gut, and he wondered absently if the shrimp he'd just had was off.

Literally growling, Günter practically tore at his own hair. "Yes, you *should*! And there would be evidence! Which there was, because I could *smell it*."

"First of all, that's incredibly invasive and creepy. Secondly, you're mental because it's never. Happened." Honestly, why was it so hard for Günter to understand that Jim and Dorian were taking things slow?

Günter rubbed both hands over his face, took a few deep breaths, then lowered his hands and looked at Jim with absolute calm. "You need to believe me, for your own sake," Günter said, voice and volume nice and steady. "He's killing you slowly while he uses you to get information from the Gehealdan."

Scoffing, Jim asked, "What information?"

"Remember that flash drive you gave me?" reminded Günter, and that brought Jim up short for a moment. Why *had* he had that flash drive on him that night? "You evidently had it for his sake. You've been saving your research on it and delivering it to him."

That didn't make sense, though. Surely Jim would *remember* something like that? Shaking his head, he insisted, "Never happened. He wouldn't ask me to do something like that. He *cares* about me."

For a second, Günter's calm composure cracked, his jaw clenching, eyes flinching. "He's using you. You're under a spell, and he's *using* you."

"These conspiracy theory excuses for hating him are pathetic," sneered Jim. "You've been trying to come up with reasons to keep me away from him since the start, and I'm sick of it. It's like you're acting jealous, and you've no bloody right to be. What, just because we're both gay you think you have some sort of claim on me? Never mind the fact you hadn't even told me you were gay before you started freaking out about Dorian talking to me!"

Günter just glared at him, breathing deep and heavy through his nose, shoulders tense. Finally he said, dark and low, "Sure. It's because I'm jealous. Let's go with that."

"What's that supposed to—" But Jim couldn't finish, because Günter had closed the distance between them in a blink, then proceeded to smother Jim's words with his lips. As far as kisses went, it wasn't the absolute best. A bit awkward, actually. Yet, there was a fierceness and a fire, which rocked Jim to the core and made something shift painfully within his chest. It felt like something was trying to claw its way to the surface, digging through muscle and shredding veins in its wake.

Jim's fingers gripped at Günter's shirt, trying to keep him there even as Jim pushed him away with a pained cry. His whole body was shaking, and Günter was reaching out to steady him, eyes so damn concerned. "Stop," rasped Jim. "This isn't right."

"Why?" Günter's voice was soft, cautious, and his hands hovered just beneath Jim's arms in case he needed to support him again. For some reason, Jim was still gripping onto Günter, couldn't get his hands to let go.

Why, Jim's mind repeated. He thought of the black folder with the glossy images and the grandfather expecting Günter to fulfill his duty. He thought about Günter explaining to Lucy that he kept his preferences a secret. There had been many times in the past when Jim had been warned away from dating closeted men, hearing relationship horror stories from others.

Would Günter really be like that, though? His immediate

family knew, so it wasn't like he was living a total lie. Still, there was something pecking at Jim, telling him it would be a Bad Idea to date Günter. Which didn't really make sense, because he'd been rather gone on the bloke from the moment they'd met.

Right. He fancied Günter. He fancied him quite a lot, to be precise. It should be easy for him to fall into another kiss, pull Günter close, and just let it happen. It should, but it wasn't. Jim was being presented with exactly what he wanted on a silver platter, and his mind wasn't letting him take it.

Was it because he was already in a relationship? Desperate, Jim tried to conjure up an image of Dorian, tried to remember a tender moment or even the flicker of affection they surely felt for each other. His mind only supplied him with blinding white fog and a shrill, piercing sound that stabbed through him like a physical spike. He felt sick.

"I know you like me." Those words out of Günter's mouth had the fog clearing from Jim's vision, but didn't make him feel any less queasy.

Finally releasing Günter's shirt, Jim stumbled back and closed his eyes. "I have to go," he somehow managed to get out, despite feeling like he would vomit if he even opened his mouth.

"I can drive you," Günter offered, still speaking so gently, as if worried any loud noises would shatter Jim into a thousand pieces. Jim was certain that if he opened his eyes, he'd find Günter looking back at him with nothing but friendly concern.

"No. I. I can't. I don't." Holding his hands up, Jim tried to make a waving motion that he hoped Günter would understand. "I need to not be around you right now."

Before Günter could say another word of protest, Jim fled.

He wasn't entirely proud of himself, running away like that, but he couldn't think of what else to do. Everything hurt and each step was like trying to walk with weights tied to his ankles. Luckily Günter lived in a nice area, so Jim didn't have to worry about not paying attention to his surroundings as he practically stumbled down the sidewalk.

His phone chirped to alert him to a text, and Jim pulled it out half dreading to see what Günter would have sent. Alice's name shone up at him instead, and Jim let out a huff as if he'd been kicked in the chest. *Just confirming that I'll pick you up tomorrow,* it read. Krysti's service. Jim really didn't want to go, but knew he'd appear heartless and cold if he avoided it. No one would know that it was just because he knew she wasn't dead, and he hated the very thought of watching her family mourn her while he was powerless to tell them the truth.

Typing a quick text back to confirm their plans, Jim wondered just how much more he could take before he broke. Everything just felt as if it was piling up on top of him until he was bent beneath the weight and smothered in its bulk. Maybe he should have gone the way of having his memories wiped while he still had the chance. Hell, maybe he would still be able to revisit that option.

While he had his phone out, he went ahead and pulled up the Uber app and arranged a ride. His driver was about ten minutes out, and there was a little cafe next to him, so Jim decided to pop in for a cuppa.

The barista took one look at him and her full red lips went from a friendly smile to a concerned frown. "Chamomile," she said with a definitive nod after her dark brown eyes gave him a full look-over. "Have a seat, and I'll bring it over." Without even ringing him up or taking his money, she just turned around and started preparing his tea.

Bemused, Jim shuffled over to the high bar set up in the window. From there he figured he'd be able to spot his taxi. No sooner had he settled onto the high stool than the barista was setting a large paper cup beside him. The tea bag's string dangled down the side like a tail, the tag at the end sporting a logo that looked organic and posh. "How much?" he asked, leaning forward in his seat to retrieve his wallet.

"Don't you worry about it," the barista insisted, warm and quiet. She looked Latina, likely in her forties, with her glossy black hair pulled up into a messy bun. Her dark blue apron had the name of the shop, *Both Worlds*, within the image of a sun morphing into a moon. Her name tag identified her as Yaretzi.

"You the owner?" he asked, then internally cringed at his own bluntness. He was truly off his game recently, with how utterly drained he felt.

"I am," she nodded, eyes gleaming as she smiled. Then her face sobered a bit and she leaned in closer, dropping her voice to something barely above a whisper. "There's something clinging to you. A dark magic." Tapping the cup, Yaretzi continued, "You'll need something more than this to get rid of it, but I don't know what, sorry."

"Pardon?" Jim studied her more closely, trying to determine if she was one of those New Age nutters, or if she was something a little more related to his part-time job.

Yaretzi's gaze ran all along Jim's body, but he had the feeling she was looking at something else. "I've never seen this," she confessed quietly.

Just then a black car pulled up outside, the driver leaning forward to look around at the sidewalk, and Jim's phone dinged in his pocket. "I have to go," he said, voice apologetic as he slid off of the stool and picked up his cup. "Thanks for this." Jim held up the tea and tried to give her a smile, but her eyes were so sad and concerned that he couldn't hold it.

"Take care," she commanded gently, nodding to him as he left.

Once in the car and en route to his house, Jim sipped his scalding tea and considered her words. He thought about what Günter had been trying to say, and how trying to focus on Dorian had physically hurt. Willing his hands not to tremble, Jim shot Dorian a text telling him not to come over that night because he was sick and had a big paper to write.

Chapter 17
Gossip

"That's awesome," agreed Eva, smiling as she held the phone to her ear. "I'm glad you're having fun."

"Totally," Krysti all but squealed down the line. "I can't believe they're just, like, letting me have access to their super huge library of priceless books. Like, I have to wear these special gloves when I handle some of them, because they're *so old*. And sometimes they're in a different language or, like, super old English, but Mick can totally translate them. I knew he was some kind of mega genius or whatever, but I had no idea he was a polyglot! At least not to this extent. Do you think it's because he's not human?"

Eva bit her lip to hold back a laugh. "I don't know. I mean, I think that has less to do with why I'm trilingual than just being raised by parents from two different countries."

"True," Krysti allowed, and Eva could hear her shifting around, probably getting more comfortable wherever she was sitting. "But maybe it's more that his supernatural ability is something to do with his mental faculties? Maybe he'll never be able to do the fire thing like Lucy or whatever, but he's able to learn more and faster than any human? After all, there are supernaturals who are known specifically for being abnormally smart."

Making a little sound of agreement in the back of her throat, Eva nodded even if Krysti couldn't see. "I guess that makes sense. Like how tengu are naturally gifted at pretty much any kind of combat."

Snerking out a little giggle, Krysti chided, "Way to toot your own horn, there."

The smirk that came to Eva's lips was dangerously close to a warm smile. It was incredible to hear Krysti doing so well and acting like her typical bubbly self. "I'm just saying you could be right. Have you presented your hypothesis to him?"

"No, not yet. I probably will at some point, though. It's just, how do you bring that up in conversation? 'Hi, how are you? By the way, I think you might be wrong about your supernatural genes being dormant, and I suspect you're some sort of Norse god of knowledge?' Yeah, no. That's a little awkward."

"Wait, isn't Odin the Norse god of knowledge, though?" Eva's brow crinkled as she thought back to the stories. "And there was something about him making a trade to learn all of the languages...he was hanged or tore out his eye or something."

There was a slight pause, and then Krysti made a little hum. "Yeah, you're right. Weird. Maybe Mick is just meant to be the knowledge god of a new generation? That happens in pantheons, right?"

"You really should stop using the word 'god' unless you want to completely inflate his ego," Eva pointed out with a chuckle. "It's not like people still believe in any of that."

"But they will again someday, right? That's the point of Fenris, isn't it? To show humans the truth, to remind them of everything they forgot." It was strange to hear Krysti say it so matter-of-factly, no more wobble or uncertainty in her tone.

"Yeah," breathed Eva, gaze flicking to Uktena who sat in the bench seat across from her and glared out of the giant windows at the planes coming and going. She cleared her throat and said more steadily, "Yeah, you're right."

A woman's voice came over the loud speaker, announcing

that they were about to begin boarding. "I gotta go, Krysti, sorry."

"It's okay! Be safe, alright? Call me again when you can. Miss you!"

Rising to her feet, Eva felt herself grin. "Miss you, too. Talk to you soon."

As soon as she ended the call, Uktena asked, "Better news than earlier?"

The reminder of Mick's call, his update on what was happening with Jim, turned Eva's bright mood dark and sour. She was furious with herself for not being there to help Jim, and part of her felt guilty for having left without him. Despite Jim's protests, Eva should have tried harder to convince him to come. He wouldn't be in that mess if only he had left with her and Lucy.

"Krysti and Mick are doing their mutually favorite thing, it seems—research." She tried to drum back up the happy feelings from moments ago.

Uktena just nodded absently, glance shifting from the line they were stepping up to and the planes outside. "That's nice."

"First time flying?" Eva had noticed his anxiety increasing the closer they got to the airport, but she hadn't wanted to say anything to offend him. By that point, though, it was getting a little worrying.

"Unfortunately no," Uktena ground out as they slowly shuffled forward. "I just hate flying. Not my realm."

Ah. Eva nodded knowingly. "And it's the realm of your enemies."

Eye twitching, Uktena hissed at her, "Let's not talk about that right now, please and thank you."

"It's okay," Eva assured, only a little mockery in her tone,

"I'll protect you."

"You joke, but that is literally the only reason I agreed to the Chairman's order to get on one of these monstrosities."

Wow, so that was...huh. Part of Eva felt rather honored to be seen as someone Uktena could trust like that, but the rest of Eva also started to worry if there was a legitimate threat to them by taking a plane. "What are you worried will happen?" she asked.

Fidgeting with his ticket, he went back to glancing out at the sky. "Nothing, so long as things stay clear."

His words reminded her of the way he'd been right before the thunderstorm, and she figured there must be a connection between storms and the bird folk who hated his kind. "I have the window seat, right?" Eva pointed out, tapping her ticket against her palm. "I'll watch the skies for you."

Shooting her a quick, grateful glance, Uktena nodded.

***

Eva tried not to laugh when they landed in LA and Uktena somehow managed to slither his way to the front of the line so he could get off the plane first. She took her time, didn't cut in front of anyone, and smirked when she finally made it to the gate and found him pacing.

"Come on," he urged, obviously trying to keep his voice authoritative despite the lingering anxiety. "We need to meet up with our contact here." They had left all of their weapons back in Montana, in the care of another agent who would be responsible for returning them to Fenris headquarters. Yet another agent would be meeting up with them there at the airport, passing over the keys to a new ride that would be stocked full of everything they could possibly need.

Resisting the urge to roll her eyes, Eva motioned for him to go ahead and lead the way. As they walked, she noticed he started to lose some of his tension, but his strides remained wide and fast, as if he wanted to put the entire experience behind him as quickly as possible.

Just as they were about to reach the exit, a man bumped into Uktena, hastily apologized, then continued on his way. It barely slowed them down, and they were quickly out the door and heading to a parking garage. "Don't we need to find our contact?" asked Eva, striding hard and fast to keep up and pitching her voice low.

"Already did," Uktena mumbled under his breath, then withdrew a set of keys from his pocket.

Impressive. Eva's eyebrows rose as she tried to replay the instance when the guy had bumped into Uktena, and couldn't recall seeing his sleight of hand. "But do you know what it looks like and where it is?"

Mouth twitching in a tiny, proud little smile, he flicked his thumb on the keychain so she could see a little card dangling off of it that had some writing on it. He quickly read the card, then looked around to fully get his bearings. "This way," Uktena nodded, and they set off again.

Their temporary vehicle turned out to be a battered old Jeep, but at least it was a hardtop. It was painted white and had beach-related stickers all over it. There was even what appeared to be a rack for holding surfboards. "Isn't this a bit conspicuous?" she asked as they slipped inside.

"Not at all," Uktena assured, turning the old thing on with a worrying rattle. "People are more likely to be suspicious of a black SUV than something like this. Though, we'll have to change our appearances, too, so we can better blend in."

Wrinkling her nose at that, Eva asked, "Change our appearances how?"

He cast her a glance while navigating his way out of the garage. They drew close to the pay gates, and he pulled down the visor to retrieve the ticket. "Don't suppose you know how to alter your look through shifting, like your mom?"

Chagrined, Eva glared at the dash. "No."

With a little hum, he let the conversation drop for a moment while he fed the ticket into the machine and paid. Only once they were pulling out onto the highway did he continue. "We'll work on that at some point. The magic for it should be close enough to my own that I can give you some pointers. For now, though, we'll just have to settle with getting you a wig and sunglasses."

"Why do I have to wear a disguise? I've never been to California."

"You're a fugitive, essentially. The Gehealdan no doubt has bulletins out on you all over the country, if not the world. Any Gehealdan operative could recognize you."

Dread bubbled in her gut, and Eva sagged back in her seat. But this was the life she had chosen, she reminded herself. For Krysti's sake, if nothing else. Deception shouldn't be difficult for a tengu to manage. Besides, she was an actor, so she was used to dressing up as other people and taking on different personas. Everything would be fine.

*

"No, not blond. Too cliché and obvious." Uktena pressed at her upper back, redirecting Eva away from the blond wigs.

"Fine," she huffed, "then what do you suggest?"

"This." They stopped in front of a long, flowing strawberry blond wig.

"Still has blond in it." Her tone was flat, unimpressed. In all honesty, though, she was actually a little excited about creating a new character to perform. They had already stopped at a clothing store on the way, and she had traded in her jeans and faded RENT shirt for blue leggings beneath a long, loose, sheer cream vest layered over a pale green tank. Then, of course, to complete the airy, beachy look, were floral flip-flops.

Rolling his eyes, Uktena motioned for the lady at the counter to come over. "Yes, but it'll make you more of a redhead than a blond. I think it will work perfectly with your greenish eyes, and make you seem less Asian." At her glare, he went on to explain with forced patience, "They will be looking for a girl who is half Japanese, so you want to look as different from that as possible. This will make people think you're probably at least part Irish. Trust me."

As the associate approached, Uktena flashed her a charming smile. "My cousin would like to try this one on."

"Of course," the woman complied, taking down the wig and heading towards the back where it looked like a mini salon. "You will need to pay for a wig cap," she reminded over her shoulder.

"No problem," he assured cheerily as they followed.

Eva leaned closer to Uktena, brows low over narrowed eyes as she whispered harshly, "*Cousin?*"

He leaned in and muttered into her ear, "You give people way too much credit." Then he was straightening up as they approached the salon chairs.

Giving Uktena one last curious glance, Eva took a seat in one. The associate immediately began winding Eva's long braid around the back of her head, then slipped the wig cap on and tucked up Eva's bangs.

"You having this braid makes things so much easier," the associate praised, smiling brightly. Then she took the wig off of the foam head and set it on Eva's. After a few adjustments, she was stepping back looking thoroughly pleased. "Oh, that looks so cute on you," she gushed before spinning the chair so Eva could look in the mirror.

As much as she hated to admit it, Eva did think the wig looked pretty good. Somehow it seemed to make her hazel eyes look more green than brown. Over her shoulder, Uktena was smiling rather smugly and informing the associate that they'd take it and Eva would wear it out.

At the register, he threw in a pair of stylish, dark sunglasses, but declined the additional wig cap the associate suggested. "What about you?" Eva asked, once they had left the shop and were heading to the Jeep.

Uktena just smiled, and said nothing until they were loaded up. "I don't need a wig." His features began melting and shifting until he had a pointier nose, greener eyes, and shaggy surfer hair that was sort of auburn and shot through with highlights from the sun. Even his clothing changed, his henley warping into a short-sleeved button-up shirt with a dark blue wave theme, his jeans becoming khaki shorts. He definitely looked like he could be redheaded-Eva's cousin, or even her brother.

"And you can teach me that?" she asked quietly, scrutinizing every minor change to his features. Were those freckles?

He shrugged and started the Jeep. "I can try. You have more than your mother's blood in you, so you might not even have this kind of magic. But, we'll work on it at some point."

"We've tried," admitted Eva with a sigh, fiddling with her new sunglasses, tearing off their tag and picking at the sticker that advertised UV protection. "Günter and I can do a lot of shifting that's similar to what Mom does, like how we can shift only parts of our bodies at a time or even blend the wolf with the tengu. But, we can't do the other stuff she does, like how she can change her face to look older."

"Well, it's two entirely different kinds of shifters you have in you," he explained as he navigated the streets of LA. They seemed to be heading up to a hillier area, the houses getting larger and spaced farther apart. "Your father has two natures, which he shifts fully between, and your mother technically only has one and is capable of more diverse shifting, but it's not complete like his is."

"Yeah, they've explained that before. I just don't *get* it, really."

Uktena seemed to think on that for a moment. "Maybe because you have three natures. You have human, tengu, and wolf. It's a rare thing to have more than two natures." After glancing askance at her, he added, "And your natures aren't always distinct and separate from each other, which is even stranger."

"Okay, but I still don't really get what that means, I guess? I'm just...me. Aren't I all of those things, all the time? Just being me? I'm still me when I'm in any of the forms."

"Well, yes. I'm not saying you have different personalities.

Just...different essences? Maybe that's a better word for it? The semantics are tricky, especially since different people have developed different words, but pretty much it comes down to there being two different kinds of shifting: complete and illusory. Complete shifters fully become what they shift into. For your father, that means he fully becomes a wolf. If you use your tengu eyes to see the truth while he is a wolf, he will still look like a wolf to you. If you look at him again while he is human, he will look human. Yet, if you look at your mother when she's a human, she will look like a tengu. If you look at her while she is a hawk, she will still look like a tengu. Her shifting is illusory, in that even though she physically does alter her body's form, her nature does not change."

Thinking about that, Eva remembered feeling Tahchat's human hand on her face even while seeing a coyote in front of her. If her natures were a little mixed, though, what exactly did that mean for her?

Eva opened her mouth to ask more about that, because it was a different perspective from what she'd been told by her parents, but her mouth clicked shut when she spotted flashing lights ahead. They slowed down as a group of cars and people came into view, and Uktena pulled over.

"Too late," he muttered angrily, shifting the Jeep into park. He flashed her a sharp grin, eyebrows raised. "You ready to play your part?"

Grinning back, Eva slipped on her sunglasses. "Lead the way, bro." She fashioned her voice a little after Krysti's, but with a somehow even perkier lilt.

With a little snicker, Uktena slid out of the Jeep and started sauntering towards the crowd. Eva saw that he also sported flip-flops, and she shook her head in amusement as she moved to follow him. She made sure to keep her steps light and bouncy as she scurried up to the people. "Ohmygod! What happened?" she gasped, pressing close to a guy on the edge of the crowd in a pink polo shirt with a popped collar. Raising onto her tiptoes, Eva jumped a little in an effort to see around people. All she could make out were cop cars in front of a huge house.

"Carina Montgomery was found murdered," the guy answered, seeming all too excited to dish out the juicy gossip.

"Bro, did you hear," cried Eva, twisting to grab Uktena's arm and pull him close. "That actress from those chick flicks was just *murdered*!"

"They don't know if it was murder or not," corrected an older woman ahead of them, turning to give them a chiding look.

The man beside Eva rolled his eyes with something almost a sneer. "Because a bullet through the front of the skull is really indicative of suicide."

"I heard it was an overdose," added a middle-aged woman with perfectly coiffed hair and heels with her expensive jeans.

"No way," a young trophy wife stage whispered, "I heard she died tripping down the stairs and broke her neck."

"Well you know what I heard?" interjected a handsome young man with spiky brown hair, perfect teeth peeking out from behind a slanted smile. It was more than obvious that he thought he had a tasty bit of gossip to add, and found the subject darkly amusing. "You know all those kids that went missing lately? I heard that Carina was 'collecting' them." He lifted his eyebrows in a pointed look. "And one of their parents figured it out and took justice into their own hands."

"No way," breathed Eva, letting her mouth go slack in shock. She leaned in closer to him, looking ever the part of someone getting morbidly fascinated by the whole sordid tale. "You're telling me she was some sort of pedophile or something?"

"Worse than that," said the guy, and everyone around them was paying full attention, devouring every detail. Slowly he leaned in even closer to Eva, and it was then that she picked up the scents of gunpowder, garlic, and mistletoe. Of course, Eva kept her face locked in intrigued excitement and didn't even flinch at the realization that she'd stumbled upon a Gehealdan operative. "I heard she tortured and killed them," the guy revealed, nodding gravely even as a smile played at the corner of his lips.

All around them erupted gasps and "My god"s and "Poor dear"s. "That's sick," Eva cried out, appalled, giving the agent the kind of strong reaction he obviously wanted. Then she was grabbing at Uktena's arm again and pulling him away, exclaiming, "*So* gross, I just can't even."

Uktena patted her hand and led her away as if they were going to return to their Jeep. As soon as they were both certain that the crowd had dismissed them, Uktena switched their direction to duck around one of the neighboring houses.

"So now we scope out the area, see if there are any witnesses who have a *different* perspective." His altered eyes were darting around the area, and he tipped his head back a bit to take in deep breaths through his mouth, a scenting move very familiar to Eva with her werewolf kin.

"That man was Gehealdan," she whispered.

He only nodded, then began gently guiding her a certain direction. "I could smell it, too." Then, a few paces later, he darted her a quick, proud smile. "You did well."

Eva grinned back, letting the modest praise bolster her. It had been more than a little unsettling to encounter someone from Gehealdan so soon, and she was glad that Uktena had insisted upon a disguise. Adrenaline was pumping through her veins in a way she hadn't felt since that time she and her friends had fumblingly attempted to kill a strigoi.

It turned out that Uktena was leading them to the pool behind one of the nearby houses, where they found a tall man with bleach blond hair and a deep tan skimming the leaves out of the water. "Uktena?" called Uktena in greeting, which was a little strange to hear.

"Maxa'xâk," corrected the blond man, but he smiled wide to show off gleaming white teeth. "But you can call me Chad. Dude, though, you're Uktena? What brings you out here, bro?" He stopped skimming the pool long enough to approach them and offer up his hand for a fistbump.

Reciprocating the gesture, Uktena gave a careless shrug. "Just enjoying the choice weather. But I'm not the only one far from home. What brought you to sunny SoCal?"

Chad's grin widened and he motioned grandly around him, one hand still holding the pole of the net. "Why does anyone move out to LA, bro? The call of the Silver Screen."

Maintaining her bubbly persona, Eva brightened and bounced a little on the balls of her feet. "That's so exciting! I'm an actor, too, ya know?"

"Right on," enthused Chad, nodding happily. "Maybe someday we'll be costars, brah!"

"Totes!"

With a humoring chuckle, Uktena slid back into the conversation to ask, "So do you know what happened to that one actress down the street? There's, like, a crazy huge crowd."

"Oh, dude," breathed Chad, blue eyes widening, "she totally got snuffed out by the G-men."

"No way," Eva whispered, leaning in with furrowed brow. "What did she *do*?"

"Well that's the thing," exclaimed Chad, waving the pole a little but still being careful to keep his volume low, "she didn't actually *do* anything. Like, they're totally blaming her for all the kiddies disappearing in the area, yeah? Because she's a shark and all. But the thing is, if the G-men had actually done their job they would have figured out there's a kappa running around."

Genuinely shocked, Eva drew back a little. "Kappa? Wait, seriously?"

Chad nodded vigorously. "Little Japanese dude with the bowl head? Yeah, soon as he showed up is when the first kid vanished. Kept seeing him right before each disappearance. Doesn't take a genius to put two and two together, brah."

*

"Understood," Uktena said into the phone, tone clipped as he watched the road. Then he clicked it off and dropped it into his lap before shifting to get more comfortable in the seat. "Don't pout," he reprimanded Eva absently, not even glancing at her.

"We shouldn't just leave a kappa on the loose," she said for what had to be about the tenth time since they had returned to the Jeep. They were thirty miles out of LA and she still felt wrong about leaving without dealing with the kappa. It felt like an annoying itch beneath her skin and an almost painful tingle along her nerves that had her knee bouncing and her fingers digging into her arms where they were crossed over her chest. Both of their disguises were long since discarded, but Eva would gladly pull the wig back on if she could turn around and deal with the existing threat.

"Fenris has been notified, and an agent will probably be sent out immediately to work on relocating him." His voice was pitched to placate, all exaggerated patience.

So bothered by his tone, it actually took Eva a moment to fully process his words. "What do you mean relocate?"

Uktena did glance at her then, releasing a sigh through his nose. "I've told you before, if you want to go around executing people, you should have stayed with the Gehealdan. In Fenris, we try not to discriminate or kill folk just because they are being true to their natures. Aside from establishing settlements where refugees can live safely, we also work at relocating some folk to places where they can be themselves away from the risk of frequent human interference. The kappa, for example, will likely be relocated to a more secluded water source, where he may only pose a risk to the random human every few years."

"But how is that an acceptable risk?" Eva practically growled.

"You need to get over your prejudice," he snapped, all patience gone. "Werewolves are known for killing and eating humans, too. There is *nothing* about you that puts you above a kappa."

Shame flooded Eva, washing away her previous tension. Turning away to watch the world blur by, she whispered, "Sorry."

"No," sighed Uktena, and he sounded a little tired. "*I'm* sorry. I'm angry, and it's not right for me to take it out on you."

"Angry about what?" When she looked back at him, she saw him tighten his jaw and clench the wheel so hard the leather wrapping creaked.

"It's just," he started, but then seemed to get so frustrated he had to pause for a moment. "He used the name given to us by the Lenape, but you saw what he chose to look like."

Eva screwed up her face in confusion. "Who, Chad? What was wrong with how he looked?"

"He was *white*," hissed Uktena.

"I thought your folk don't have a human nature? No true human form? So you can look like any kind of human you want, right?"

Two miles went by before Uktena replied, voice quiet and dark. "It's disrespectful."

"*You* looked white for your disguise."

"That was temporary, and born of necessity."

"So maybe his is, too," Eva tried to reason. "Maybe he only looks like that to try to get acting jobs because he knows Hollywood is still gross and racist, and when he goes home he looks Lenape."

Uktena seemed to reluctantly allow her that point, bobbing his head back and forth before giving a tight shrug. "Perhaps."

"But, like, why is it disrespectful, anyway? Again, I thought you didn't have any human in you."

Lips pursing, Uktena took a moment before explaining. "It's honestly probably very similar to why your mother tends to look Japanese, and why her offspring bear the features of Japanese humans. Sometimes spirit folk form a very strong connection with the humans that develop alongside them. In some cases there is even some mixing of DNA, some cross-species breeding, to the point where there's no telling if a spirit folk has any human genetics or not."

"Spirit folk?"

"What you call 'supernaturals.' That's a term most indigenous spirit folk won't use, because it implies we *aren't* natural, when nothing could be further from the truth. Our term doesn't mean spirit as in ghost, but as in essence. It also often refers to the spiritual aspect we serve in Native American belief systems."

Nodding, Eva thought she understood. It reminded her of the term *kami*, and how it often translated to "venerated spirit," even though it didn't necessarily refer to a ghost-like being. "Okay, but, so you feel a particularly strong connection to the Cherokee humans?" she asked, directing them back on topic.

"Mostly I feel a kinship with them and all of the humans who first lived on this continent. Like them, my home was invaded by others from foreign lands. My folk were forced out or killed, much like many other indigenous spirit folk, to make room for these newcomers. Then, to top it all off, the foreigners decided that their rules would be applied to everyone here, regardless of our participation status with the Treaties. When once the many folk who lived here used to coexist with the humans, we were suddenly being forced to stay hidden or risk death. So, no offense, but foreigners are associated with death and oppression, both of my kind and of the humans who named me."

That...was a lot to think about. The child of immigrants, Eva had been raised to view America as a land of opportunity for everyone, no matter where they came from. People moved there to find a better life or to explore new possibilities. She hadn't really stopped to consider what that meant for those who had already been there. Even when it came to supernaturals, she was so used to being surrounded by folk of foreign origins in America that she never really thought about the indigenous folk.

"So that's why you joined Fenris," she eventually guessed, something like guilt keeping her voice quiet. "Because the spirit folk of this continent should be free to coexist with humans, just like before."

"That's a big reason for my loyalty to the cause, yes. There is no place for those foreign laws here."

Chapter 18
Insubordination

Günter sat there in his Toyota staring at the familiar, rundown house in the woods. Absently he wondered why it was that only the strigoi had the Saturday restriction, and not its genetic cousin the striga. Maybe someday he'd get the chance to really examine them both on a cellular level or even get a peek into their DNA. It was, after all, the true goal of his medical training, no matter what little white lies he offered up to his parents.

On the porch, the cats that typically lazed about started to gather in a line, all of them staring straight at Günter. There was a thump-thump on the roof of his SUV, and then a fluffy grey cat was walking down his windshield. Once on the hood, it slowly turned and blinked at Günter with bright green eyes that seemed to be judging him quite harshly. He supposed all of this meant that he should stop his dallying and just get on with it.

Trying not to let all the feline stares bother him, he got out and approached the house. The cats moved just enough to allow him to walk up the steps onto the porch, but they turned as he went and continued to watch him.

He didn't even have to knock before Branka was swinging the door open and greeting him with a dull glare. "Finally decided to come talk, I see. No more sitting like a creep in your car. Well, come in, come in." She waved rather unenthusiastically into her house, but still moved aside to give him room all the same.

"Sorry to just drop in like this," he apologized, ducking his head a bit. The rudeness of his unannounced visit was one of the reasons he had found it difficult to just walk up to the house. Well, that and the lingering suspicion that she worked for Fenris. As angry as he was at the moment with his superiors within Gehealdan, he still firmly believed in the organization and everything it did for supernaturals.

Branka seemed to soften a bit, even going so far as to offer him a faint smile. "No trouble at all, dear. What brings you out this way? Nightmares like young Lucy? Need to do well on a test? Communicate with the dead? Maybe just a peek at what your future may hold?" She motioned towards the couch. "Sit."

Shaking his head to both decline the invitation and as a sweeping answer to her barrage of questions, he took a steadying breath. "I need your help." If it came out a little like a plea, that was fine. Günter felt he was rapidly moving beyond the threshold of his pride.

She studied him closely then, all traces of a smile gone. What did she see, he wondered. Did striga have a special sight, like how the whole world seemed to change if Günter shifted his eyes to wolf or tengu? "Well, I certainly owe you a boon," she murmured before giving a little nod. "Speak your request, and I'll see if it's something I can do."

"Jim," Günter started, striving to keep his jaw from clenching and jamming up his words.

"Ah, so you have finally noticed?" Her eyes seemed to twinkle a bit, a teasing smile on her face.

Confused and impatient, Günter shook his head. "What? No, never mind, look...one of the Lamiae has put Jim under a thrall, and I need your help to free him."

Face paling, Branka looked away. "You are certain it is one of the Lamiae?" she asked, eyes focusing on anything other than

Günter's face, where only moments before he thought he'd burst into flames from the intensity of her scrutiny.

"Yes. I'm certain."

Her eyes squeezed closed then and she shook her head in regret. "I am sorry." It was spoken with absolute sincerity, and Günter felt the words rip into his gut. When she opened her eyes again, she finally looked back at him. Somehow she looked almost as pained as he felt. "In the time before the Treaties, those under their thrall would be dead within the hour. No one ever had the opportunity to break the spell, or even realize it was in place before it was entirely too late. I have never, in all my years, ever found record of anyone breaking the thrall of Lamia."

No. No, that was unacceptable. "There has to be *something* that can be done," he insisted, seething and desperate.

Looking a little lost, Branka could only shrug. "Death, I'd say. Either that of the thrall or the Lamiae. It is the only thing that may work, and even that is merely a guess. Who is to know if the thrall does not simply waste away in longing even if the Lamiae should die?"

"That's not.... I won't let that happen!" Günter could feel the tug of his body wanting to shift. Part of him longed to fly or run, hunt down the one hurting Jim, and *destroy*.

"What do you want of me?" asked Branka, tapping at her scarf-adorned chest with her palm and obviously agitated. Whether Branka was getting upset over Günter's attitude or her own failure in the matter, he couldn't tell. "I may be the witch in the woods, but this is no fairy tale. It cannot all be solved with True Love's Kiss. In the old tales, the human did not always win, you know."

"This isn't some cautionary tale for little kids," spat Günter, and he started to pace. "This time the human isn't alone, and there's a monster on *his* side."

Branka drew up short, eyes going round before they looked unfathomably sad. "Oh, child, you are no monster."

Unable to tolerate wasting another moment there when he could be elsewhere helping Jim, Günter huffed and dodged around her to get to the door. "I'll collect my boon another time," he said in parting before slamming the door.

***

"I'm going to kill him." Günter tried to close the office door behind him, but Phil grabbed it as he raced to follow him inside.

At his desk, Czar paused in mending a book spine to look over the rim of his glasses at Günter. "Kill whom?"

"Dorian. I'm going to kill him. Execute him. Whichever. It needs to be done." Günter seriously hoped that Phil had already had that promised talk with Czar, because this wasn't something he wanted to waste time arguing over.

Czar removed his glasses and leaned back in his seat. "He'll be executed, yes," agreed the old man. His false eye glistened more than his real one in the light from the tree-like table lamp. "Phil an' I discussed matters, figured you had yerself some good points there. Carmen and Montenegro were gonna be assigned tha task on Mond'y."

"No," barked Günter, and some small, still-rational part in the back of his mind quaked to be talking in such a way to a superior. "*I'm* doing it, and I'm doing it *today*." He tried to ignore that little part of himself, and squared his shoulders in the demonstration of absolute conviction. There was no way in hell he was allowing Dorian to spend another two days holding Jim under a thrall. The very thought was disgusting.

Slowly Czar leaned forward, arms folding over the desk. "You don't give the orders here, boy."

"Well maybe you shouldn't, either!" Absolute silence fell over the office after his shout stopped resonating.

Behind Günter, Phil was the first to disturb the tension with a pointed clearing of his throat. "Stand down," he whispered to Günter in warning.

"No, screw this." In just a few brisk steps, Günter cleared the remaining distance to the desk, where he slammed his hands down and leaned in towards Czar. "I'm loyal to the Gehealdan and their cause. You know damn well I am, because you've been spying on me. Hell, I'm not even upset about that. I'm more than willing to put myself in life-threatening situations for you. I would *die* for this organization. But I cannot just sit back and watch one of our team suffer like this. So I'm going to walk out of this office, head out to my car, and then track Dorian down and tear out his goddamn throat. You want to punish me for that, fine. Just wait until I've done it, and I won't even mind if you decide to execute me." Günter mustered every scrap of his bravery together to have the strength to look Czar right in the eye as he said it all. Inside, he was trembling, and he knew there was a real possibility he could be severely punished for stepping so far out of line. Still, he'd meant every word, including the line about accepting his own execution.

Face a blank mask, Czar stared right back into Günter's eyes. There was something fundamentally chilling about Czar's gaze, and not because one eye was made of glass and surrounded by a nest of scars. They were the eyes of someone who had been alive for far too long and had seen far too many horrifying things. For a flicker of a moment, Günter questioned Czar's humanity. The man never did smell quite right.

"You do what you feel you must," Czar said after he evidently found something in Günter's expression that helped him reach a verdict. "Ain't no need to punish an executioner fer doin' his job."

Just as Günter felt himself start to relax a little, Czar added, "Though might I suggest waitin' until night? Get the kid at home, make it look like an accident. Bring Carmen with you; she's good at dealin' with the higher-profile nons who pose as humans."

Günter didn't like giving the bastard even just a few more hours of life, but he knew Czar had a point. If Günter didn't want to compromise the very basis of secrecy on which the Gehealdan stood, he couldn't do anything that would risk exposure. "Fine," he nodded with a little reluctance. "Tonight, then."

A tiny, almost pleased smile came to Czar's scarred lips. "Tonight."

Chapter 19
Hunger

"We'll be back in a couple of days."

Lucy smiled at Eva's words and pressed the phone a little closer to her ear as if that would get her closer to her friend. "Good, I'm glad. It's been nerve-wracking thinking about you out there traveling all over, running into murderous fish people."

Laughing, Eva assured, "That was only one time. Uktena has been pretty adamant about not engaging with anyone else. Strictly information retrieval."

"Right, I know," said Lucy. "But one instance of you getting brutally attacked is still one instance too many."

"*Brutally* attacked." Eva snickered, her tone dismissive. "Whatever, I'm fine. I told you I didn't end up with even a scratch."

"You also told me you had *been* scratched—bitten, actually—but you just healed. Which means you got *hurt*. Which is not cool, Eva. Not cool."

"Yeah? How's your *hand* doing?"

Flexing her still-bandaged hand, Lucy felt the faint tug of the stitches and new scars. "Touché."

"In any case," said Eva, and Lucy could hear the smirk in her voice, "we shouldn't be encountering any trouble on our way back. Though," and her tone turned a little teasing, "I saw the news say there's a thunderstorm crossing where we'll be tomorrow..."

"Oh, shut up," Uktena could be heard yelling faintly in the background, which caused Eva to erupt into cackles. Obviously Lucy was missing some sort of inside joke there.

"Well, just be careful. And I know you'll probably have to be debriefed or whatever, but come see me and Krysti as soon as you're able once you're back. We miss you."

"Aw," Eva mock-cooed, "I miss you, too."

Lucy was about to snark something back when there was the distinctive chime of someone ringing her bell. "Wup, someone's here!"

"Go. I'll see you soon."

"Okay, love you, bye!" She hung up on Eva's amused laughter, and headed to the door. A quick look at her phone's screen told her she wasn't late for her session with Ren, so at least it wasn't him coming to find out where she was.

After pressing the button to open the door, Lucy was pleasantly surprised to find her father and Sigyn. Then his dour expression fully registered, and concern flooded her as she quickly stepped aside to let them in. "What's wrong?"

Váli stormed inside in large strides, talking as he moved. "He insists you're ready to leave the building."

Trailing behind him and looking infinitely patient with her son, Sigyn added gently, "He is a wise man, and I trust his judgment."

Instead of dignifying her statement with a response, Váli just shot his mother a dark look before turning to Lucy and attempting to school his features into something less angry. "Dr. Sartre has informed me that he will not be making the trip here for your session today, and insists you go visit him at his new office near Penn State."

That threw Lucy for a loop, and she blinked as she tried to keep up. "Wait, when did he move?"

"A few days ago," Sigyn explained with a soft smile. "He's been coming here to keep up with everyone's sessions, but traveling back and forth takes time away from obtaining new clients and thus fresh sustenance." She gave her son a pointed look even as her lips continued to smile pleasantly. "It makes sense that he would want to have us come to him, now. A man must eat."

Even though he snarled a little, Váli didn't seem to have a good rebuttal. After taking a deep breath, he again smoothed out his features when he turned to address Lucy. "I'll have a very capable guard accompany you, so you should be perfectly safe."

It was only then that Sigyn's smile vanished, and a line of concern formed between her brows. "I do wish you'd send some of your verúlfr with her, instead."

"I've told you, Mother, they are otherwise engaged," he all but snapped at her, before closing his eyes in contrition. "Sorry. I'm just frustrated from him springing this on me last minute."

Sigyn placed her hand on Váli's arm. "It was so you could not have the chance to really object," she explained in a soothing voice.

"I know," Váli ground out. "Which doesn't make it any better."

"So when do we need to leave, in order to get there in time for the session?" asked Lucy, hoping to maybe distract her dad from his sour mood.

"Now, actually." He stepped away from Sigyn and fiddled a bit with his cuffs as he visibly worked on composing himself. "I'll head down to the lobby now to make certain your escort is there with the car. Come down as soon as you're ready." On his way out, he paused long enough to give Lucy a kiss on her cheek and a smile of genuine affection. Then he was gone, and Lucy once again found herself left behind with Sigyn.

Her grandmother smiled at her, but her spring-bright eyes seemed a little troubled. "Be careful," urged Sigyn, stepping up to take Lucy's hands in her own. She had soft, warm hands with long, elegant fingers. "I have had a bad feeling all day, since I woke. Loki would accompany you himself, but business has called him away until tomorrow. I think Váli is so agitated because he is also unable to go with you."

Lucy's heart did a little skip-jump in alarm. "Why? Is it really that dangerous out there?"

"Not usually, no. This is a very secluded area, and so far there has been no indication of the Gehealdan suspecting we're here. Dr. Sartre is only an hour or so away, and it should be a very uneventful trip there and back." She gave Lucy's hands a little squeeze, then moved to fetch a hoodie draped over the arm of the couch. It was black with a repeating skull-and-crossbones pattern. Looking a little amused by the print, Sigyn brought it over to Lucy and held it up for her to put it on.

Doing as her grandmother bid, Lucy turned to slip her arms through the hoodie. "But then why is Dad so agitated over not being able to take me?"

Instead of answering, Sigyn smoothed the hoodie along Lucy's back, and came around to make certain the front was neat and straight. Then, her eyes lifted to meet Lucy's, and her face was a tranquil mask. "Your father is very protective of those whom he loves." She smiled again, but Lucy felt it still did not reach her eyes. "Just be strong, whatever happens. You have warrior blood within your veins, the blood of mighty beings once revered as gods."

None of this really helped ease Lucy's nerves. "Can't we just call and cancel?" she asked, voice a little desperate as Sigyn walked her to the door.

"The thing about fate," confided Sigyn, pausing to grab Lucy's black coat hanging by the door before they left, "is that it cannot be outrun. It will find you in your home just as easily as it will find you on the battlefield. We can either choose to let it sneak up on us, or we can meet it head-on, shoulders squared." She handed Lucy the coat as they approached the elevator, and Lucy clutched it to her chest.

"You're talking like I'm going to die or something," Lucy laughed nervously, begging Sigyn with her eyes to tell her how ridiculous the very idea was.

"Oh, no, dear," Sigyn exclaimed, just as the elevator before them gave a ding and its doors swung open. "Nothing that bad, I'm sure."

Lucy felt her body relaxing a little, even as her mind continued to whirl in confusion. Stepping onto the elevator, she asked, "So then what is it?"

All Sigyn offered in reply was a shake of her head as the doors between them slid closed.

*

"This is Hadwin," her father introduced, motioning towards the tall, tan man beside him. "He will be driving you and ensuring your safety." Váli's posture and voice both seemed rather stiff, and Lucy figured he was just trying to keep himself calm and composed, especially in front of Hadwin. After all, it wouldn't do to have one of the leaders of Fenris pitching a fit where anyone and everyone could see.

"Nice to meet you, Hadwin." Despite her lingering worry, Lucy smiled as brightly as she could and nodded her head at the man.

Váli then stepped up to Lucy and pulled her into a tight hug, kissing her on the side of the head. "Have a good session with Dr. Sartre." As he pulled away, his gaze seemed to flit all about Lucy's face, and he gave her hair a few gentle pets. "Be safe."

"Nothing to worry about, sir," Hadwin assured, twirling the keychain on his finger. His accent reminded Lucy of mafia people in movies, so she figured he must be from somewhere like New York. Though she wondered what sort of folk he was, because there was no way her father would be sending her with a human.

With a little nod, Váli fully stepped back to allow Lucy to leave. "Love you," he told her quietly as she passed.

Heart bursting with warmth, Lucy grinned and returned the sentiment. Then she was pulling her coat on and following Hadwin out the door.

Hadwin led her to an inconspicuous grey sedan. "Back or shotgun?" he asked with a casual friendliness.

"Shotgun, I think. It'll feel weird riding in the back. Like I'm someone fancy enough to have a chauffeur."

"Aren't you?" he laughed, opening the door and sliding in. When she was also seated, he continued, "Considering your lineage and all, you're above a queen."

Lucy scrunched up her face and shook her head vehemently. "No way."

Tossing his head back with another hearty laugh, Hadwin started up the car and headed down the long drive away from the Fenris building. "*Way*. Humans used to claim their kings were little gods on earth, but that's nothing compared to the real thing, I say."

Still, it was a weird thing to think about. Lucy looked down at her hands in her lap, running the fingers of her right hand lightly along the bandages on her left. Shouldn't gods heal faster? Shouldn't gods be able to control their powers so they don't accidentally blow up car engines? As gods went, Lucy still felt she was a pretty sorry excuse for one. Maybe things would change after she learned more control, but part of her was skeptical that she'd be anything more than a human with spontaneous combustion abilities.

As if sensing her dark mood and hoping to lift her spirits, Hadwin started in on a series of stories about his comically horrible relationships. Twenty minutes later, he was in the middle of telling her about a nymph who claimed to leave him for the Jersey Devil—"It's not even *real*! Like, how am I supposed to take that?"—when a man in a bathrobe wandered out in front of them.

Just as it had been for most of the trip, they were on a wooded back road. Any houses were tucked away down long, gravel driveways, marked only by rusting mailboxes that stood as lopsided banners. It was possible the man could live around there, but it definitely looked like he had been walking for a while. His bathrobe was dirty and tattered a bit, and his bare feet were covered in mud and leaves. He was a middle-aged white man with a receding hairline and a bit of a gut.

Even as Hadwin screeched the car to a stop, the guy didn't even seem to notice them. Lucy felt a weird chill up her spine as she watched him just sort of shuffle around, eyes not really focusing on anything. "God, it's like we just stepped into a zombie movie," she whispered, pressing back into her seat.

"The hell," exclaimed Hadwin in exasperation before

honking his horn. When that still had no effect on the man, Hadwin huffed and rolled down his window to shout at him. "Buddy! Hey, man! You lost? You need some help? Hey, you want me to call someone for you? Hey, buddy, you hear me?"

Without warning, a shot rang out and Lucy turned to watch Hadwin's body go limp. "No," she breathed, reaching out a shaking hand to touch him. He didn't stir. This couldn't be happening. Yeah, her grandmother had warned her something bad might happen, but this—*why*?

Suddenly her door was opened and someone was grabbing her hair while also reaching around her to unbuckle the seat belt. Screaming, she tried to break free, but nothing she did worked. All of her training in the Gehealdan seemed to vanish from her mind in her blind panic. It hurt like hell when her shoulders slammed into the ground, her legs still partially in the car, booted feet jerking.

"Go to this spot," mumbled the man who continued to drag her. It was a younger man than the guy in the bathrobe, with wild, unkempt blond hair and grey eyes that didn't seem to focus on anything. "Go to this spot," he repeated again under his breath, chapped lips barely moving. Despite the chill of oncoming winter, he was only in boxers and a dirty T-shirt. One hand still in her hair, he wrapped the other around her throat and kept pulling at her until she was fully out of the car and almost entirely in the shallow ditch on the side of the road.

Footsteps preceded another man, this one short and at least fully dressed in jeans and flannel. A gun glinted from his hand, and Lucy felt the screams clog up in her throat when she realized he was the one who had killed Hadwin. Behind him was the man in the bathrobe, shuffling along as he followed.

Just what the hell was going on? Who *were* these people? Why were they *doing* this? There was no way they were Gehealdan.

"Go to this spot," the man with the gun said, voice weirdly hollow. He slowly moved closer, and Lucy screeched as she reached up to try to claw and punch at the man still holding her.

Then something clicked in her very core, and where her hands touched the man, his skin bubbled and broke. Lucy dug her nails in to the blistering flesh and pulled. The man released her and jerked away screaming, causing hot blood to spray across her face.

Finally free, Lucy pulled herself to her feet and staggered away from Boxers Guy. Gunman raised his weapon with the jerky motions of a marionette. "Go to this spot," he said, as if that made any sense at all.

Lucy absently licked her lips, a sharp metallic tang erupting on her tongue, and for a moment she was hyper-aware of everything around her. The sweet scent of pine, the musty decay of leaves on the forest floor, the brisk bite of early snow on the air. She could smell the stench of burning flesh behind her, the gunpowder clinging to the man in front of her, and a lingering stink of piss on the guy in the bathrobe. Somehow she knew the nearest car was a few miles off, hearing the faint hum of its engine. Most of the wildlife had been frightened away by the earlier gunshot, but there were some birds slowly flittering back. Crows mostly, likely drawn by the blood.

Then, just as quickly, everything seemed to narrow down into a pinpoint focus. Hungry. She was so *hungry*. All around her was the scent of prey, of warm, ripe flesh.

As she lunged at Gunman, it felt like something sharp grazed her in the side just above her hip, but it wasn't enough to slow her down. Besides, the man's hand caught fire like a struck match, and there was the sound of something like popcorn, then he was dropping the useless gun to the ground. Nothing more to worry about. Nothing more to stop her. God, she was *so* hungry.

Within moments, all of her senses were awash with *red*.

*

"Lucy. Look at me. Lucy, I need you to focus on me. Come on, look into my eyes." The voice sounded far off, or as if coming to her through several layers of thick walls.

Slowly, like waking from a dream, her senses began to return. There was warm pressure on her cheeks, her knees felt a little achy, and there was something sticky on her hands. Blinking, her eyes tried to come into focus, filtering and sorting light into shapes. A pair of black eyes were right in front of hers, and she'd recognize them anywhere.

"Ren?" It came out scratchy and thick, like she had a cold.

An encouraging smile, transforming a sickly face into something almost handsome. "That's right, Lucy. It's Ren. Can you just keep focusing on me? We're going to stand up now, okay? But I need you to just keep looking at my face and don't look anywhere else. Can you do that for me?"

Relief flooded Lucy. They had made it to Ren's office, after all. She must have just dozed off and had a nightmare. Returning Ren's smile, she nodded and let him tuck his hands up under her arms to help her to her feet.

It was when her boot slipped on something wet that it began to fully sink in that she wasn't in the car or his office. They were outside, on the side of the road, right where she and Hadwin had—oh god.

"No," she sobbed, lifting her hands to clutch at Ren's shirt. She stared in horror at the tacky red blood that smudged and stained the white fabric. "Help," she whimpered. "They have a gun. They killed Hadwin."

Making soft shh-ing sounds, Ren pulled her close and tucked her face against his shoulder. "It's fine now. No one is going to hurt you. Just either keep your eyes closed or look only at me as we move to my car, alright? Or, if you want, we can walk like this, or I can even carry you?"

"Why can't I look?" she asked, terror spiking. "What's wrong? Why can't I look!"

His hands soothed up and down her back and his arms continued to hold her safe and close. "You don't need to see any of this, Lucy," he whispered, sad and honest.

"Any of *what*?" It was then that she registered the smells of burnt skin and shit and the unmistakable scent of blood. Her stomach churned and she tried to push away from Ren. "I need to throw up," she warned.

"Okay, okay, let's get you over here..." He hurriedly shuffled them for a bit, their feet occasionally slipping on things Lucy didn't want to see. When they finally got to an area he deemed safe, he turned her and urged her to lean forward. He even pulled her hair back for her as she was incapable of doing anything other than bracing her hands on her knees and hurling.

Lucy made the mistake of opening her eyes at one point, seeing chunks of what looked like raw meat in her vomit, which turned her stomach even more. She didn't open her eyes again after that, keeping them squeezed tightly shut. Even once she was done and Ren was wiping what felt like a handkerchief across her mouth. Even when he was directing her to his car. All she did was sit there, silent tears streaking down already sticky cheeks, and tried to ignore how her clothes felt stiff and damp.

She didn't open her eyes again until the car came to a stop, and Ren said softly, "We're back at Fenris."

Slowly opening her eyes, she looked up at the glass and steel building as if it was the best thing she'd ever seen. Then she saw Sigyn standing at the series of doors at the entrance, and Lucy cried in relief.

Váli then burst out of the building, black hair flying and pale eyes wild. He was at the car in seconds, opening the door and practically collapsing on Lucy. "I should have been with you," he groaned into her hair. "I'm so sorry."

"I'll move back into the Fenris building," she heard Ren say, resigned and tired. "For now."

Instead of answering, Váli just carefully helped Lucy out of the car and up the steps to where Sigyn waited.

"Let's get you all cleaned up," Sigyn said in greeting, her usual sweet smile in place.

Ren's footsteps followed them, and Lucy felt her father stiffen where he remained pressed against her side. "Let him come," Sigyn commanded softly to her son. "It's best he stay close."

"She's not Donnie," grumbled Váli. "She doesn't need Sartre to keep her monsters at bay."

"But she does," corrected Sigyn, before turning to lead them inside.

Chapter 20
Easier

"You should talk to him," Alice quietly urged with a nudge to Jim's side.

He followed her line of sight to Kyle a few feet ahead of them in the black-clad crowd leaving the service. "Don't see why." For once the git didn't have an entire salon's worth of gel in his hair, and he was even dressed in a half-decent suit.

Frowning, Alice shook her head sadly. "Don't be like that. He told me what you said."

"All of it true." Jim would dare her to deny it. None of them really liked Kyle, had all said as much one time or another.

When she fell silent, Jim thought Alice had decided to just let it go. They made it all the way to her car before she spoke again, leaning against her door instead of getting inside. "It's just," she started, choked and halting, "we're all we have left. We should stick together."

The sad thing was, Jim knew she was wrong, would be even if Eva's and Krysti's deaths were real. Eva, Krysti, Lucy...they had been the glue of their little group. Lucy brought with her Alice and Kyle, Krysti was who had originally connected Eva and Lucy, and Eva brought Jim. As sweet as Alice was, Jim didn't know how well they'd get along just the two of them, and he knew for damn sure he had no interest in being friends with Kyle.

Turning his back to the car, he leaned against it and tilted his face to the sky. Such a bright, cheery day for such a sad occasion. Though he supposed Krysti would want a sunny day for her funeral.

"I once did a series of paintings representing the greater

arcana in tarot. Or, well, I *started* to do a series. Only got a few in, but still." Jim took a breath and then continued, "Anyway, I had to research each of the meanings, yeah? Card thirteen is death. That's what it's called, what it shows, but it *means* change. Often it just represents the person going through some type of complete transformation, or a transitional period in their life. I used to wonder why that was assigned to death, of all things, which I had always perceived as an ending. Now, though, I think I might get it. Death changes things. You can never go back to how your life used to be once you've been affected by death."

"But that doesn't mean we can't be friends anymore." Alice's voice was so small, and it prompted Jim to push away from the door and hurry over to her side. She clung to him as soon as he wrapped his arms around her, and he just let her cry it out on his shoulder. "I don't want to be alone," she confessed through sobs.

"You won't be," was the promise he offered up, even though he didn't know exactly *what* he was promising. Did he mean he'd always be there for her? Because he couldn't honestly promise that. Maybe he just meant that she would make new friends, move on, find happiness again someday. That sounded right.

They stayed like that for a long time, even as all of the other cars cleared out of the parking lot. Only when her crying died down and she had full control over herself did she pull back and move to get into the car. Jim followed her lead, and she took him home in silence. He didn't know what she was thinking, and didn't dare to ask and risk another breakdown.

When she dropped him off, he reached over and squeezed her hand, offering her a quick smile. Meager thanks and comfort rolled into one, but he didn't know what more he could give her in that moment. "Maybe Lucy will get back in touch soon." That was a gift wrapped in poison, he knew, but at least it could provide her some temporary comfort until so much time passed that the words ate away at her.

"Maybe," she agreed with a nod and shaky smile. Her dark eyes were still glistening as she waved at him in parting before he closed the door.

***

A few hours later, and Jim was chiseling away on Günter's neglected statue while Yes played loudly through the speakers of the little stereo he kept on one of the work tables. He was sweating and his muscles were already starting to ache, but it felt good to be working on something. Even though Dorian came over nearly every night, it never really felt like Jim was getting anywhere on his piece. The sketches seemed incomplete, and there hadn't even been a clay version made. Not only that, but Jim hadn't even touched Günter's statue again since Dorian started modeling.

Günter's words tried to worm their way into Jim's thoughts, and he drove them away with every strike of the mallet to the chisel. For now, he was just roughing out the basic shape, not even to the stage where he needed to worry about fine details. Though, really, just a little more pitching away here and there, and he could switch off to a toothed chisel and maybe start on at least the wings.

So thoroughly absorbed was he in his task, he didn't even notice the door slam open or even realize anyone was there until a pale hand grabbed his shoulder and pulled. When spun around, he was confronted with Dorian, eyes flashing in anger. "They did it again," seethed Dorian, his words almost lost in Yes' blaring guitar riffs. Then, huffing, he released Jim to storm over and turn off the radio. "They did it *again*," he repeated.

"Did what again?" asked Jim, watching his boyfr—watching Dorian in confusion. "What's wrong?"

"What's *wrong*?" snarled Dorian, prowling slowly back to Jim. "They falsely executed yet another of my siblings. I'm sick of it. Sick of waiting patiently, collecting what scraps you're able to scrounge up for me, while my family struggles to find a way to stop the murder. No more waiting." He curled his hands possessively around Jim's hips. "It's time we get proactive. Time to send them a message."

Everything tried to blur a bit, but Jim blinked it all back to focus. "What are you going on about? Send whom a message?"

"Do you have a gun?" Dorian asked instead of answering, voice nearly a purr, all dark and dripping with seduction. One of his hands came up to run playfully teasing fingers along Jim's chest, fiddling a bit with his buttons. "I bet a big, strong Gehealdan member like yourself has lots of guns, right?"

Snorting, Jim leaned back as much as Dorian's grip would allow, and raised his hands a bit to show off his mallet and chisel. "These are all I've got, I'm afraid. I'm pants at shooting, so there's no way Czar would let me pack heat. More likely to shoot my cock off than hit the target, he said." Pausing, Jim thought back to that moment, head tilting. "Almost verbatim, actually."

That didn't seem to be the answer Dorian wanted to hear, and he scowled before smoothing his features back to something alluring. "But you have access to guns, right? You can walk right in there, go to the armory or whatever they have, and take whatever you want."

"If I want Carmen to shoot me, yeah." Jim squinted at Dorian. "What you need guns for, anyway?"

"Not me," corrected Dorian, leaning in as his gaze drifted to Jim's lips. "You." They were kissing before Jim could question that, and then he forgot what his question even was. All of the ache in his muscles melted away, and his mind cleared itself of any troubles.

"You're going to teach them," Dorian whispered against Jim's lips. "Show those assholes they can't just slaughter us without repercussions. You're going to—" Breaking off with a frown, Dorian leaned back and turned his head. Jim tried to follow, tried to get their lips together again, but Dorian just gently pushed him aside.

"Something stinks," muttered Dorian, eyes darting around the studio. As they moved, they seemed to darken, until black swallowed up even most of the whites. "Smells like fear." He began circling around the place, walking the perimeter, tilting his head and leaning in closer to something now and again. On about the fourth circuit, he stopped in front of the large cupboard. "How long have you been there?" he asked the cupboard, voice musing, which Jim found very odd, indeed. Not only could the cupboard not answer, but it had always been there from the start.

Opening the doors, Dorian took deep sniffs. Then he was reaching out and grabbing at nothing, before pulling what looked like a little man out of thin air. It wasn't even a foot tall, legs stubby and arms a tad too long. Jim got a look at beady eyes and a nose that took up most of the tiny man's face, before Dorian was—

Dorian was opening his mouth impossibly wide, displaying two rows of sharp, jagged teeth. Then he was shoving the tiny man headfirst into that gaping maw. At first the tiny man struggled, but then Dorian clamped his jaws down on him, piercing into the little thing so deeply it nearly cut him in two. When the struggling stopped, Dorian opened his mouth wide again and tilted his head back, shoving the small, mutilated man deep until he entirely vanished down his gullet.

Fear paralyzed Jim, and his eyes darted to the door. But then Dorian was turning back to him, smiling with a human mouth and beautiful, gleaming eyes. Blood was smeared and dripping from his perfect lips. "Now we're truly alone," crooned Dorian, sounding pleased. Dorian seemed to notice Jim's discomfort, because his smile faded and he tutted as he slowly approached. "Don't be alarmed. I'm just protecting you." Without missing a step, he wiped at his mouth with his sleeve until the blood was all gone.

"Protecting me?" From what? A wee little man who probably couldn't scare a cat?

"They were spying on you," explained Dorian with a solemn nod. "Who knows how long that little pest has been lurking around you, taking all your secrets back to *them*." His lips curled on that word, as if it tasted foul. Jim didn't think it could taste any worse than a raw little person.

When Dorian was close again, Jim could smell blood and salt. Nimble fingers began to unbutton Jim's shirt, and for some reason he couldn't move to stop it. "I'll always protect you," confided Dorian, expression warm and sly. "Won't you protect me?"

"From what?"

"The people who are killing my family. If they have their way, they'll probably kill me, too."

Dropping his tools, Jim clutched at Dorian. "They can't. I won't let them hurt you."

With a pleased moan, Dorian rewarded him with a sweet kiss. Jim wanted more, *needed* more. "So good to me." A cool hand slipped beneath Jim's parted shirt and stroked along his heated skin. "You'll go kill the bad people who want to hurt me, won't you? You'll protect me."

"Of course," gasped Jim, trying to pull Dorian closer, leaning in for a kiss that Dorian obliged to give him.

"Hey, you ready to go?" Günter's voice called casually, and Jim looked over Dorian's shoulder just in time to see his friend turn to walk through the still-opened door, only to stop short. All at once, Günter's handsome features twisted into something bestial and furious. He growled low before emitting an ear-splitting screech.

Jerking around to face Günter, Dorian shoved Jim between them as a shield. "Remember," he whispered hotly into Jim's ear, "you said you'd protect me."

"Get out of the way," Günter ordered Jim, waving him aside with a taloned hand. "I'm supposed to wait until tonight, but screw it. Let's do this now, shark!"

There were the sounds of scrambling behind him, and then Jim's hand was grabbed and Dorian was wrapping Jim's fingers around the grip of a point chisel. "Protect me," he repeated, then pushed Jim towards Günter. "Stop him."

Like a clod, Jim just stood there, confused and disoriented. Nothing was making sense in his mind. There was the urge to protect Dorian, to save him from any harm, but how could he fight Günter? *Why* would he fight Günter?

Taking advantage of Jim's hesitance, Günter darted around him and advanced on Dorian. "Jim!" cried Dorian, desperate and afraid as he stumbled away and tried to keep Günter at bay by pulling chairs into his path. "Protect me!"

Jim turned, watching the pathetic chase scene as they tore up his studio.

"There's something clinging to you. A dark magic."

"Jim! Stop him!"

"He's using you. You're under a spell, and he's using you."

"Jim! He's going to kill me! *Protect me!*"

He remembered so many instances of finding himself standing there in his studio, confused, chunks of time lost. Tears on his cheeks he lied to himself about. A piercing sound splitting through his brain if he tried to focus on the foggy moments.

Dorian had run out of studio and chairs, and Günter was on him, pinning him down with one hand and raising the other as if to strike. Shoes squeaking on the smooth floor, Jim ran to them. With his free hand he grabbed Günter's raised arm, then pulled him back with all of his might. Miraculously, Günter moved, tripping away from them and staring at Jim with wide, betrayed eyes. For a long moment, Jim stared into those eyes, then he raised his chisel.

"Yes," urged Dorian, sitting up and smile growing wide, teeth elongating. "Kill him!"

Still, Günter made no move to defend himself. Even his features melted back to human, amber eyes glistening. He offered Jim no words, just a minute shake of his head.

"What are you waiting for?" yelled Dorian.

Swinging the chisel down, Jim twisted just right to lodge it deep within Dorian's skull.

There was no more yelling after that. All was silent except for Jim's breathing, suddenly coming in labored pants.

Gripping Dorian's shoulder with one hand, Jim began pulling

the chisel back out. As if desperately trying to keep the chisel where it was, the wet, squishy flesh of Dorian's brain seemed to be sucking the metal in as Jim pulled. So, he gave Dorian what he wanted. He plugged him through at another point in his skull. Then another. Finally he let the limp body fall to the floor, but Jim wasn't done. Not nearly done.

Collapsing to his knees, Jim plunged the chisel into Dorian over and over again. The wet sounds echoed through the studio, accompanied by Jim's angry grunts. He didn't know how long he sat there stabbing the corpse, but he kept going until it was unrecognizable as a person. A fitting look, for something so wretched. So *disgusting*.

When Günter finally dragged Jim away and pried the chisel from his hands, Jim was crying. Deep, wracking sobs unlike anything he could recall since childhood. "It's done," soothed Günter, wrapping Jim tightly into his arms and rocking him gently. "He's dead. It's done."

Günter called Czar and told him what had happened, while Jim stared blankly at the pulpy mess that was once Dorian's face. As soon as Günter was done, he went right back to holding Jim. He turned them around where they sat on the floor, so Jim couldn't see Dorian anymore. They even scooted far enough away so that the pooling blood wouldn't reach them.

"You were right," said Jim, and his voice sounded dull and unfamiliar to his own ears. "You were right from the start." Blood had already gotten on his sneakers, though, and he stared in fixation at the dark blotches where his feet were sprawled out before him.

"Shh," Günter hushed, never pausing in his gentle rocking. "It doesn't matter now. It's done."

But it did matter, didn't it? What Dorian had done to him...Jim couldn't just shake that off. Still, it was hard to really think about, and felt like some abstract concept. In some way, it didn't even feel like it had happened to him, but to someone else and he was merely hearing it secondhand.

An indeterminable amount of time passed, and then Phil and Pulchrum seemed to suddenly appear. Phil let out a low whistle, and Pulchrum made some joke about how he always did like sushi. None of it felt real, and Jim wasn't sure how to really react. Some part of him felt a little ashamed to be sitting there in front of them, tucked up in Günter's arms like a babe. The rest of him honestly couldn't be arsed to care, because Günter was comfortable and made him feel safe.

Phil squatted down in front of them, for once his perpetual smile gone. The color of his eyes was similar to Dorian's, and Jim wanted him to go away. "We need to get you out of here for a little bit," said Phil, in a voice like speaking to a frightened animal. "Günter will take you back to the shop, get you all nice and clean. Pulchrum and I will fix up your studio, make it look like nothing happened. Alright?"

But they couldn't actually erase it all, just the evidence. Nothing could go back and change everything, give Jim those stolen moments back or cleanse him of what he'd done.

"Come on," Günter urged gently, helping Jim to his feet. He seemed so calm, and Jim envied him that. Maybe it was because killing had become old hat to Günter, after all those Saturday nights spent in graveyards, elbow-deep in one strigoi's chest after another. Jim wondered if it got easier. If there was ever a next time, would Jim's hand be steadier? Would he feel so hollowed out afterwards?

He felt Phil and Pulchrum's eyes on him as Günter walked him out of the studio. Thank god his parents were always so absorbed in their own work that they wouldn't notice if Jim hosted a rave in his studio, let alone murder someone and then have strange men come and clean it all up.

Günter held his hand all the way to the car, and Jim wondered how he could stand to with all of the blood. "You didn't do anything wrong," assured Günter, though the words didn't fully sink in for Jim. They felt scratchy and ill-fitting. Killing was wrong, wasn't it? Jim's hand still hurt from the pressure and vibrations of the chisel as it broke through bone or bounced right off.

A moment replayed in Jim's mind, of back at their first execution, watching Lucy chop away at the corpse. He'd feared her in that moment, feared the sort of violent nature that could lend her the strength to do that, even if the body she mutilated was already dead. There had been a steely conviction in her eyes, though. A determination.

Later, however, as the pieces burned, she had cried and he had held her. Jim thought he maybe understood her a little better, now. He had done a horrible thing, but it was necessary.

Calm slowly began to seep through his cracks. If given the chance, he'd do it again. In a way it was good that all Pulchrum and Phil could erase was the evidence, because the deed was something Jim didn't actually regret.

After that night, Lucy had never cried about chopping the bodies again, and Jim thought he was starting to understand that, too.

*

They entered through the security door in the back, and Czar was there holding the heavy steel open. Stopping just within the threshold, Jim turned to lock eyes with Czar and said, "He ate a little man he found inside my cupboard."

Czar frowned, troubled, but then nodded in thanks for the information. "You alright, son?"

Thinking hard about it for a moment, Jim decided he wasn't quite yet, but he probably would be. So, he shrugged, then turned to follow Günter into the back hall. Günter led him down the stark corridor until they reached a door marked with a creepy baby-like thing peeking at them from behind a tree. *Tiyanak*, a voice supplied in Jim's head, a product of days spent walking that hall and attempting to memorize each supernatural depicted. Even though it was a room Jim had never had the chance to enter, he didn't care enough to pay attention to Günter's fingers as he punched in the code for the lock.

Inside was a small locker room, complete with benches and a short row of shower stalls. Jim figured Günter, Carmen, and Montenegro used it after executions, if needed, instead of going to Günter's apartment like he and the others had done.

"I'll get you some clean clothes," Günter offered, awkwardly hanging back in the doorway.

"Stay," Jim asked of him instead, the thought of being left entirely alone with his thoughts far too daunting. Once he got a confirming nod from Günter, Jim made his way towards one of the stalls. Usually he wasn't shy about stripping down in front of anyone else, had done it for years in school for gym, but right then he needed a barrier.

Curtain closed, Jim reached up to unbutton his shirt only to find it fully open, blood splattered across his bared chest. The trace memory of Dorian expertly undoing his buttons had him torn between gagging and laughing. Instead, he fought back both, closed his eyes, and shrugged off his shirt. As he tossed it over the curtain, Jim said, "He claimed they were innocent."

On the other side of the curtain, Jim could hear Günter stepping closer and the whisper of fabric as he picked up Jim's shirt. "Do you believe him?"

He thought about that as he unbuttoned his fly, musings momentarily disturbed by the flash of relief that at least he had only ruined one of his work jeans. "I know he was upset." Toeing off his shoes, he then slid his jeans and boxer briefs down. "But if they were really innocent, why not just take it up with the Gehealdan? Why do what he did?" He pulled off his socks, piled everything together, and then nudged it under the curtain with his foot.

"Maybe they tried going to the Gehealdan," reasoned Günter. And wasn't that just Günter to a T? So bloody *reasonable*. "Or maybe, like you said, they couldn't go to the Gehealdan because they weren't really as innocent as they claimed. Who knows; maybe they never were as innocent as everyone thought, and were just better at covering it up until recently."

Last was his headband, which was thankfully just a rolled-up handkerchief instead of one of his vintage scarves. He didn't toss it over, however, instead holding on to it to use as a washcloth. The water pressure was blessedly strong, and it took only seconds for the heat to kick in. Standing under the spray, Jim tilted his head down and watched the water run red around his feet.

"I'm sorry I didn't believe you." He'd been unable to speak the words in much more than a whisper, and for a moment he worried Günter wouldn't be able to hear it over the sound of the shower.

"Don't be." But of course he heard it, because Günter could hear better than any human. "It was part of his magic."

Rubbing the sopping kerchief across his chest, willing the water to finally run clear, Jim allowed himself to remember Günter's kiss. It felt like a missed opportunity, but one that would have been a lie. He saw now that it was just a ploy to get Jim to snap out of it.

"I know you like me."

Jim tried not to be mad, knew it wasn't a case of a friend exploiting him, but of trying every method possible to save him. At least he knew Günter cared enough about him to fight for his freedom. That was something.

Grabbing the half-used bottle of shampoo sitting in the corner of the stall, he draped the kerchief over his shoulder so he could drizzle some into his palm. "Thanks for trying, at least." He scrubbed the shampoo into the roots of his dreadlocks, then carefully sponged the soap in along their short lengths. Just because he was showering in a crisis didn't mean he had to get careless and undo his hair's progress.

"Anytime." Judging by the volume and tone of Günter's voice, he was directly outside of the curtain. "I'll always be there if you need me."

Smirking through a mirthless laugh, Jim turned and tilted his head back to carefully rinse his hair. "You shouldn't make promises you can't keep. We both know you'll be gone all summer."

There was no response, and Jim sighed through his disappointment as he grabbed back up the shampoo and used it to soap up his kerchief so he could get proper clean.

"You can come with me," was the hesitant, almost shy offer that came eventually.

Jim finished scrubbing and then rinsing off while he considered it. "If Czar will allow us both to leave." He shut off the water, and then stood there feeling lost.

A fluffy towel was draped across the curtain rod. "I'll convince him. Tell him it's a matter of honoring a promise, and I'm a man of my word."

The towel was surprisingly soft as Jim ran it against his skin. For some reason he had just expected something utilitarian and almost rough. "Does it get easier?" His hands began to shake, and he tried to convince himself it was just the chill of standing wet and naked.

There was a pause, the sound of Günter shifting beyond the curtain. "Does what?"

"Killing?"

Releasing a long breath, Günter took some time before he replied. "I don't know how to answer that."

"Fair enough."

Epilogue

"I thought you were neutral." Loki stood at the long, curving wall of windows that ran the length of his office, and stared out over the surrounding forest. What had been ablaze with color weeks ago was now mostly a sea of grey skeleton trees dotted with tufts of evergreens.

Behind him, Sartre was sprawled in one of the guest chairs. "I am," said the vârcolac with a careless shrug. "But I don't see what that has to do with your son being an idiot."

Chuckling at his daring cheek, Loki shook his head. "Make a habit out of insulting your employers?"

"Only when they deserve it. It's been three days, and he still won't let me work with her." The leather of the seat creaked as Sartre shifted. "Your wife agrees with me."

"My wife," Loki responded slowly, letting just a hint of warning bleed through, "is just under the impression you're a fix-all solution. You keep away Donovan's shadows, and now supposedly you ground Lucy. If I didn't know any better, I'd worry Sigyn's simply taken a shine to you."

"I ground Lucy because I'm familiar and because we've been working together on control. It's a conditioned response by now, practically. Need I remind you that *you're* the one who arranged to have me tutor her in that."

It began to snow, and Loki watched the little flakes twirl their way past his window. Soon they would turn the grey forest dazzling white, and everything would look like home. "We both know you can't stay here. You need to eat."

"I'll be fine."

"You should really know better than to try to lie to me."

Sartre sighed and the leather creaked again. "Fine. You're right. Then I'll move back to where I had established a new practice. Maybe I can just drive out here every weekend and work with her then. Check up on the others."

"Your help isn't really necessary. Váli was able to learn how to control it, as were the entirety of the species he created. I have full faith that Lucy will be able to manage it, too."

Snorting, Sartre rose from his seat. "I get it. I'm not needed anymore because I'm too much of a pacifist."

With a smirk, Loki turned away from the window and started towards his desk. "Glad we've settled that, then. Though it would still be quite welcome if you could make those weekend visits to check in on the others."

Sartre chuckled and shook his head. "Sure." With that, he saw himself out.

As soon as he left, there was a buzz from the phone on Loki's desk. "Sir, Agent Uktena is back and waiting to see you."

He quickly pressed the button to respond, "Send him in."

Uktena walked in looking more than a little amused. "I hear you've had some trouble while I was gone."

"A few surprises, yes, but nothing we can't manage." He waved to the guest chairs before taking a seat in his own. "I hope you weren't waiting long."

"Not at all. Though I spotted a rather important guest arriving right on my tail, so I'll make this brief." Going along with his words, Uktena elected to stand.

Loki's eyebrows rose. "I wasn't aware anyone of import was scheduled to arrive today."

That brought a wide smile to Uktena's lips and a playful gleam to his eye. "Oh, then you'll be pleasantly surprised."

Already feeling his spirits brighten, Loki motioned for Uktena to get on with it. "Very well, then give me your report."

"You'll be pleased to know that all went well, with only minor casualties."

"Casualties?" Well, that certainly worked to put a damper back on his mood.

"The näcken in Montana didn't seem to realize who we were and attacked."

"Ah yes, I had heard about young Eva's tussle. All three were killed?"

"Yes, but fully devoured. There should be no signs left, nothing to implicate us."

Loki nodded, calculating. "Good. And everything else went as planned, you say?"

"I'd say yes, if what I've heard from Agent Belobog is any indication, not to mention your unexpected guest." Uktena nodded back towards the door.

"And your assistant? What are her thoughts at the conclusion of your little 'investigation?'"

With a low laugh, Uktena shook his head. "She is entirely convinced we're an innocent third party doing the Lamiae a favor. Which, word certainly must have traveled fast, because the credibility she adds was no doubt what prompted your guest to make an appearance."

Ah, it was always a beautiful thing to watch a plan come to perfect fruition. "I told you she would be a valuable addition. You should consider making her a full agent."

"Perhaps I will." There was the hint of pride in Uktena's words. Then he was smirking and stepping backwards towards the door. "I'll submit a more detailed report later. I'm sure you're eager to move to better things."

"Thank you," smiled Loki, rising from his chair. "As ever, your service is much appreciated."

Chuckling softly, Uktena turned to make his exit. "Want me to send her in?"

"If you would, please."

Uktena ducked his head in a low nod, then left. Only a moment later, the door was sliding open again to reveal a beautiful woman. She wore a long, deep blue gown made of a fabric that flowed across her body like water, tantalizingly hinting at her curves. Over her head was a large, silky scarf worn like a hood and trimmed in beautifully detailed embellishments and gleaming gold disks. Across her mouth was a matching veil, leaving only her dark, piercing eyes visible.

Bowing low, Loki greeted, "To what do I owe the honor of your visit, Your Royal Highness? And please, no need to mask yourself here. The whole point of Fenris is to come out of hiding."

"They murdered my children," explained the woman, voice as deep and captivating as her gaze. She hesitated for a moment, then lifted a hand to draw down her veil. Beneath her perfect nose was a wide, gaping mouth filled with rows of intimidatingly sharp teeth. "So I've come to accept your invitation."

The story continues in book three of
The Hollow Sun series:
Paper Lanterns

Acknowledgments

Here we are again, and once more I've so many wonderful people to thank. My mom for always encouraging me (even if she often wonders where the dark things come from). Tommy, as always, has been my support and soundboard. I'd also like to thank Ollie, Kayla, Sanjana, Elsa, Alena, Michelle, and so many others. Thanks to Lea for lending Eva her name. She'll try to make good use of it. Last but not least, thank you to everyone who read the first book and let me know you actually enjoyed it. Your words give me life.

DL Wainright

is married with two cats, and loves folklore, horror stories, and long walks on the beach at night.

For ways to contact or follow DL on social media, go to www.thehollowsun.com.

Made in the USA
Monee, IL
24 May 2025